Shooting the Moon
Brenda Novak

D0042482

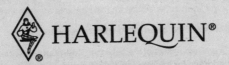

HARLEQUIN®

TORONTO • NEW YORK • LONDON
AMSTERDAM • PARIS • SYDNEY • HAMBURG
STOCKHOLM • ATHENS • TOKYO • MILAN • MADRID
PRAGUE • WARSAW • BUDAPEST • AUCKLAND

ISBN 0-373-71058-5

SHOOTING THE MOON

Visit us at www.eHarlequin.com

Printed in U.S.A.

To my oldest daughter, Ashley,
for already exhibiting the self-possession and integrity
I so admire. Your presence in my life nourishes my soul
in a way I could never explain. If you forget everything
I've ever taught you, remember this: My love is everlasting.

"You got my sister pregnant, remember? I know what kind of man you are."

He laughed, the sound rumbling from deep in his chest. If Lauren had been anyone else, someone who didn't know who or what he was, she would have smiled automatically. He had that kind of charisma. She hated him, yet he appealed to her on a very basic level.

"Last I checked, it took two to make a baby," he said. "But you must be like your father. He never saw things that way, either."

"My father was trying to look out for his daughter. He was trying to get Audra out of the mess *you* got her into."

"I didn't need his help. I was willing to take care of my own messes."

"Which is why you took the money my dad offered you to get out of town and did exactly that, right?"

Harley's eyes narrowed and all traces of the smile he wielded so effectively disappeared. Lauren pressed her advantage. "Who do you think has loved Brandon and cared for him all these years, practically raised him?"

"Regardless of who's raised him, his mother's dead," he said. "And I'm here now. I've come to collect what's mine."

Dear Reader,

As a writer, I'm often asked about "favorites." What story is my favorite? Which characters? Which setting? Well, *Shooting the Moon* definitely has a place on my list of favorites. It's one of those stories that flowed easily from my heart and came naturally to my pen. I'm not sure if it was the characters and their intriguing blend of strengths and weaknesses, or the conflict, which was very poignant and real for me. But as Harley and Lauren revealed themselves to my imagination, I grew to respect and like them more and more. I hope you'll have the same experience.

I love to hear from readers. You can contact me at P.O. Box 3781, Citrus Heights, CA 995611. Or simply log on to my Web site at www.brendanovak.com to leave me an e-mail, check out my book signings or learn about my upcoming releases.

May we all, in the end, achieve the ultimate or "shoot the moon."

Brenda Novak

Books by Brenda Novak

HARLEQUIN SUPERROMANCE
899—EXPECTATIONS
939—SNOW BABY
955—BABY BUSINESS
987—DEAR MAGGIE
1021—WE SAW MOMMY KISSING SANTA CLAUS

CHAPTER ONE

NOT HIM! NOT NOW!

A wave of nausea hit Lauren Worthington as she gaped at the man on her front doorstep. She'd known this day would come. Over the past few years her parents had grown complacent, had insisted Matt ''Harley'' Nelson was out of their lives for good, but deep down Lauren had always known better. His leaving them alone indefinitely would be too simple, too easy. And from what she knew of Harley, he was not a simple man. Neither did he do anything the easy way. It had been ten years since she'd seen him, but she remembered that much.

''What do you want?'' she asked, lowering her voice and closing the door between them until only a crack remained. The last thing she needed was for her nephew Brandon, who was watching television in the other room, to see Harley, or for their conversation to somehow catch the boy's interest.

''What do you think I want?'' he asked, hands on hips, one leg cocked as though he was perfectly comfortable knocking on their door after all these years.

Why had she answered the bell without first checking the peephole? Lauren berated herself. But the answer was clear. She lived in Hillside Estates, a gated, upscale community of homes not far from Portland, Oregon, worth half a million dollars or more. They had security. They had cameras. They had little or no crime. Besides, it was barely ten o'clock on a Saturday morning. Who worried about peepholes on a Saturday morning?

Lauren had felt perfectly safe opening her house without a second thought, but now she feared what her mistake would cost her—and Brandon. She could only see a slice of Harley Nelson through the crack she'd left in the door, but it was enough to know that her sister's ex-boyfriend hadn't changed much. About six feet tall, he was still thin but muscular, still handsome as the devil, still wearing black leather, and still riding the kind of motorcycle that had given him his nickname. Lauren knew because a beautiful new Harley was parked in the driveway behind him.

"Audra isn't home," she said, bluffing. She needed him to leave so she could figure out what to do about his sudden reappearance. Her parents would know how to handle this—her father could solve anything—but he and her mother were in Europe for another four weeks, and without them, Lauren was completely on her own. Somehow she had to regain her equilibrium. Think. Get Harley to go so she could...what? Hide Brandon until she came up with a smarter plan?

Unfortunately Harley didn't seem too eager to give her the chance to do that. He stayed right where he was and didn't look as though he was going anywhere, at least anytime soon.

"Considering the fact that Audra died in an alcohol-related car accident nearly six months ago, I'd be pretty surprised if she was here," he said.

He knew. Oh no, he knew about poor Audra. What was she going to do?

"I-I'm sorry. I have to go. I'm expected at—I'm expected." She tried to close the door the rest of the way, but his booted foot whipped out and wedged in the opening before she could latch it.

Lauren inched the door open again but still blocked the entrance with her body.

"I'm getting the impression you're not very excited to see me. Are you trying to hurt my feelings?" he asked, giving her a glimpse of his send-the-girls-wild smile, the one she'd drooled over in high school.

Fortunately it didn't do anything for her now. Lauren was too worried about the confidence in Harley's face and bearing. The longer she talked to him, the more she noticed that in some ways he *had* changed. The reckless teenager she'd known had transformed himself into a calm, self-assured adult. Which frightened Lauren more than anything, because it made him so much more of a threat.

"I'll call the police if I have to," she warned.

"If that's what you're planning to do, you'd better go and do it," he said. "Because I'm not leaving until I get what I came for."

Lauren could scarcely swallow for the fear clutching her throat. *Please don't let it be what I think it is.* "And what is that?" she managed.

He must have heard the panic in her voice because he hesitated for a moment and studied her, his eyes unreadable. "You must be Audra's baby sister."

Lauren was surprised he remembered Audra had a baby sister. She'd seen him around school lots of times, but he'd never spared her a second glance.

"The name's Lauren," she informed him. "I'm sure you never knew that."

"Why, did I call you something different?"

He hadn't bothered to call her anything. He was too starstruck by her sister, once they became an item, and too busy flirting with all the other popular girls before that. Someone like Lauren, an honor student, a *bookworm*, held no attraction for him. She used to admire Harley from a distance, but after he'd gotten her sister in trouble, she'd been glad he'd passed over her. Not that she'd expected anything else. Most guys had preferred her blond bomb-shell of a sister. Audra had been beautiful, popular, fun-loving. Lauren was plain, quiet, studious.

"We didn't know each other," she said, "which is why you'll have to excuse me. I don't feel comfortable having a strange man at the door."

"We knew each other," he said. "We just didn't know each other well. I wasn't allowed to come to the house, remember? And I've been called a lot of things, Lauren, but strange generally isn't one of them."

"That's because there are so many more applicable ep-ithets to choose from," she said, unable to resist.

Lauren expected her remark to make him angry, but he simply raised an eyebrow, then gave her that crooked smile of his. "Epithet?" he repeated. "Evidently all those hours you spent in the library did your vocabulary some good, though I doubt it did anything for your social life." He looked her up and down. "And I'll bet your excite-ment factor hasn't notched up any. Not with you going around spouting things like *applicable epithets.*"

"Maybe *you* should've spent a few more hours in the library. It might've done you some good."

"You spent enough time there for both of us. Besides, you were always too busy hiding behind your glasses and reading a thick textbook to know what was going on around you, so how would you know what's applicable to me and what isn't, especially after ten years?"

"Some things don't change," she said. "And some things are more apparent than others."

"Especially to the gifted Lauren Worthington, huh?"

He said her name in an uppity, nasal tone Lauren didn't appreciate, but being from the wealthy Southwest side, she'd heard it before. Casting a quick glance behind her to make sure Brandon was still absorbed in his TV pro-gram, she lowered her voice even further. "You got my sister pregnant, remember? I know what kind of man you are.''

He laughed, the sound rumbling from deep in his chest. If Lauren had been anyone else, someone who didn't know who or what he was, she would have smiled automatically, despite the animosity between them. He had that kind of charisma. She hated him, yet he appealed to her on a very basic level.

"Last I checked, it took two to make a baby," he said. "But you must be like your father. He never saw things that way, either."

"My father was trying to look out for his daughter. He was trying to get Audra out of the mess *you* got her into."

"I didn't need his help. I was willing to take care of my own messes."

"Which is why you took the money my dad offered you to get out of town and did exactly that, right?"

This time Lauren's barb hit a tender spot. She could tell by the way Harley's eyes narrowed and all traces of the smile he wielded so effectively disappeared. "Stick to your books, Lauren. You don't know anything about what happened," he said. "But then someone as tightly wound as you wouldn't. The closest you've probably come to love is the definition of it in some encyclopedia."

Lauren felt her back stiffen. Just because he'd never found her attractive didn't mean she hadn't had other boyfriends. Those relationships had never evolved into marriage, but she'd gotten intimate and fairly serious with a couple of different men. Her inability to make a commitment didn't mean she wasn't *capable* of love.

Or did it? Was that the part that hurt most? Had he hit a little too close to home?

Regardless, Lauren's love life—or lack thereof—wasn't the point here. Brandon was all that mattered. She'd built her life around him, and she wasn't about to lose him now.

"Who do you think has loved Brandon and cared for him all these years, practically raised him?" Certainly not her sister, who was never quite the same after her affair with Harley.

"Regardless of who's raised him, his mother's dead," he said, "and I'm here now. I've come to collect what's mine."

Lauren's hand tightened on the door until her knuckles stood out. "You gave up your rights to Brandon when my father paid you to leave," she said, her words a harsh whisper. "You agreed."

He shrugged, only the tenseness of his body belying his seeming indifference to her words. "So I've had a change of heart. Sue me."

"If we have to, we will. My father's not going to take this lying down."

"I don't care how he takes it, but he'd better get used to the idea."

"There's no way he's going to let you come waltzing into Brandon's life at this late date and whisk him away from everything and everyone he's ever known. What kind of father would do that, anyway?"

For the first time, Lauren thought she read a hint of doubt in Harley's expression and knew, in order to avoid a custody battle, she had to play on it. It was what her father would have done.

"Think about it," she said. "He has a good life. We've given him everything, much more than *you* could've provided. You were eighteen years old and penniless, for Pete's sake, a product of the inner city, raised in a broken home by an alcoholic mother. It would be pure selfishness to take Brandon away from here—now or in the future."

She certainly hadn't tempered her words, but neither had she scored much of a victory if the muscle that flexed in his cheek served as any indication.

"He'll have what he needs. I can take care of him now."

"So what?" she responded. "He already has everything. He doesn't need *you*." Lauren felt a flicker of guilt for driving her point so ruthlessly, but she was desperate—desperate to keep Brandon, desperate to protect what she'd established over the past ten years. She might have failed her sister, but she wouldn't fail her sister's child. Which meant she couldn't feel sorry for Harley Nelson. He hadn't felt anything when he'd broken Audra's heart, taken their father's money and left town ten years ago, had he?

Turning, he seemed to gaze out over the lawn, a plush, green carpet that sloped down toward the street beneath a warm spring sun. She watched him look across at the neighbor's, then examine the porch and shutters, even the red brick of the house. What was he thinking?

"I want to see him," he said at last.

"I don't think that's a good idea. I don't want to confuse him."

"Then tell him I'm a friend of yours or something."

Lauren bit her lip, praying for inspiration. Would she be a fool to allow this? Her head said yes, but her heart had a difficult time with no. He was Brandon's father, after all....

"Will you go back wherever you came from if I do?" she asked.

"Maybe."

"Maybe?"

"I'm not making any promises, Lauren, except this one. I'm not leaving town until I see him, so you may as well let me in now."

Lauren didn't know what to say. Letting Harley see the beautiful boy he and Audra had created might make him that much more determined to wrench him from his home.

But could she deny Brandon the chance to meet his father? How important would that be to him later?

"I'll think about it," she said.

He hesitated but finally pulled a pen and a business card from his jacket and circled a number. "Fine. You do that, then call me on my cell."

"Aunt Lauren, it's over! Can I go to Scott's house?" Brandon sang out, and Lauren knew she had only a second or two before her nephew came to find her.

"Okay," she said quickly, speaking to Harley, but he didn't move. Evidently he'd heard Brandon, too. Before he had a chance to respond, however, Lauren closed the door with a resounding bang, and this time he didn't try to stop her. Pressing her back against the heavy wooden panel, she squeezed her eyes shut and took a deep breath.

"What's wrong?" Tall for his age and possessing the same dark hair, olive skin and green eyes as his father, Brandon loped out from the kitchen, carrying a donut in each hand.

Lauren couldn't answer. She waited, silently counting the seconds until she heard the roar of Harley's motorcycle.

"Nothing," she said, her knees going weak in relief.

"Who was at the door?" he asked, watching her curiously.

"Just a friend. You don't know him," she added, and at least that part was the truth.

FOR THE FIRST TIME in years, Harley rode his motorcycle without a helmet. He wanted to let the air whip through his hair, hear it roar in his ears, feel it sting his face. He didn't care if it was dangerous. He didn't care if it was illegal. Somehow the physical sensations were sustaining. They helped him deal with the emotions clashing inside him, emotions poignant enough to make his eyes water without the help of the wind.

He'd heard his son's voice. He was sure of it. The look on Lauren Worthington's face had confirmed that it was Brandon. And that moment had...what? Shaken him. Left him weak, breathless. Scared him.

But it had done something else, too. Brandon's voice had reached inside him and filled him with a craving so simple and powerful it nearly overwhelmed him.

He wanted his son. He wanted him so badly it hurt.

Slowing for a traffic light, he briefly closed his eyes, trying to shut out the memory of his visit to the Worthingtons. For years he'd told himself to forget the past. It was better that way, right? Better for the baby. Better for Audra. Better for everyone. The Worthingtons owned a string of video stores, had always been as rich as Midas. What could he possibly give his son that they couldn't? That was the question Lauren had flung at him today, the one that had chased him away in the beginning, and it was the one that still burned, uppermost, in his mind.

Otherwise he'd have Brandon with him right now.

The light turned green. Harley gave the bike some gas and shot out in front of traffic. Turning at the next light, he wound down out of the hills to the city, where he wove through the busy streets to the low-rent district.

He could give his son the love of a father, couldn't he? That was more than Harley had grown up with. But when he'd looked into Lauren's stricken face, enough doubt crept in to make him wonder, all over again, if he was doing the right thing.

The Springfield Apartments came up on his left, and he pulled into the lot, parked and cut the engine. According to the letter he'd received, Tank Thompson lived here now. In Apartment 208.

Harley scaled the stairs leading to the second story of the garden-style apartments, taking them two at a time. He was angry and confused, but the frustrating thing was that he didn't know what, if anything, he should do.

Maybe it had been a mistake to come back. What made him think he could atone for his past sins after ten years?

He knocked at 208, and rap music poured out of Tank's apartment as a small, curly-headed girl, only about three years old, opened the door.

"Hi, there," he said. "I'm Harley Nelson. Is Tank around?"

"Daddy, it's for you!" the little girl called over her shoulder.

Daddy? In his letter, Tank hadn't mentioned having a child of his own. He hadn't mentioned much at all. He'd just sent Audra's obituary clipping, nearly five months after the fact, along with a brief, handwritten note saying: *Thought you'd be interested. Long time no see. You still kickin'? Tank*

But then Tank had never been one for written correspondence. Neither was Harley, for that matter.

The little girl disappeared for several minutes and returned tugging a bleary-eyed, hungover-looking Tank to the door. He was about fifty pounds heavier than when Harley had seen him last, shortly after graduation, but Harley would've known his friend anywhere.

Yawning, Tank scratched his head and blinked twice. "Well if it isn't the jackass who buried my truck in the river during high school," he said, breaking into a smile.

Harley laughed. "You were the one who wanted to see if I could ford it. How the hell was I supposed to know the damn river was so deep?"

"You were drunk enough to try crossing the Columbia."

"And you were drunk enough to let me use your truck to do it."

Tank shook his head. "It's a wonder we survived those years. How've you been, man?"

"Good." Harley nodded to the little girl who was

standing next to Tank, watching them. "You have a daughter now?"

"Yeah." Tank winked at her, and she smiled shyly. "Too bad I don't have her mama anymore. We separated a year ago. Divorce was final just last month."

"That's tough."

"You're tellin' me. Now I gotta live in this dump while she and her new boyfriend enjoy the three-bedroom, two-bath townhouse I'm paying for." He ruffled his daughter's hair. "Worse, I only get Lucy here on weekends."

"She's a beauty," Harley said.

"Yeah, takes after her mama. Can you come in? Stay a while?"

Harley thought of the hours ahead of him. He had a few other friends he wanted to visit, but nothing more important until Lauren Worthington called. *If* she called…

"Sure, I can stay," he said, stepping inside and taking a seat on a rust-colored couch reminiscent of the sixties. Except for the large-screen television that took up one whole corner of the room, the other furnishings looked no better.

"Things haven't changed much since high school, huh?" Harley said, eyeing the beer cans and cigarette butts that littered the coffee table.

"Ah, don't let the mess fool you. I've cleaned up my act a lot since then. Last night we had my buddy's bachelor party here is all. We hired a stripper, played some poker and drank more than we should've."

"What did you do with Lucy?"

"The lady next door took her. She sits for me now and then."

"Who's getting married?"

"Guy named Dan. You don't know him." He put a hand to his head and squinted. "I'm almost sorry I do."

"What are you doing for work these days?"

"Concrete, same as always." Tank slumped into an

easy chair across from the couch. "When my dad retired, I took over the business, and lately we've been branching off into landscaping. My brothers work for me."

"All of them?"

"All except the oldest. Damien's too good for concrete. He's an attorney here in Portland. What about you?"

"I own a Harley Davidson dealership out in California where I live."

Tank raised his eyebrows. "You always said you'd have one someday. But how'd a poor boy like you manage something like that?"

"The stock market's been good to me."

"The stock market?" Tank sat up straighter—then, putting a hand to his head, he checked the movement. Shifting more gingerly, he said, "Boy, have you changed. What brings you back this way?"

"The article you sent."

He grimaced. "Yeah, well, I found your address on the Internet and almost wrote you a long time ago. It was too bad what happened to Audra, but the way she was living, something was bound to happen sooner or later, you know?"

Harley leaned forward, placing his elbows on his knees. "What do you mean? How was she living?"

Tank sent his daughter off to play in her room, then moved closer to Harley. "She wasn't the same girl we knew in high school," he said. "She got into crack pretty heavily, went downhill from there."

Crack? Audra? Harley couldn't imagine her stern, overbearing father allowing Audra to get involved with drugs, at least not to the point of addiction. But then he remembered how much she liked to party in high school—and how much she'd always resented her father. Maybe she'd done it to fight back, to establish her freedom. Wasn't that what had drawn her to him, someone her father had designated as off limits?

"I didn't know," he said.

"I figured you didn't, but I wasn't sure you'd want to know. I mean, what could you do about it?"

He could have come and taken his son. That was why he'd come here now, wasn't it?

"So who's been caring for Brandon? The sister?"

Tank smiled wistfully. "Little Lauren. Talk about opposites. You couldn't find two sisters less alike."

Harley had to agree with him there. "She's pretty serious."

"She's a straight arrow, man. All responsibility."

"I bet it was hard on her to watch what was happening to Audra."

"I guess," Tank said. "She keeps a stiff upper lip, like her parents. Doesn't say much."

"So Lauren still lives with them?"

"Yeah, why not? There's space enough in that house for an army."

"Didn't she go to school?"

"Graduated from Lewis and Clark in only three years. Since then she's worked for her father in the corporate office or done community stuff."

"She never married?" Harley asked.

"No. Damien used to date her. That's how I know about Audra. But he just couldn't get her to respond to him."

Harley didn't have a hard time believing that, not after hearing Lauren say, "He doesn't need you." The woman didn't hesitate to go for the throat. He doubted *she* needed anybody, either. "She's a lot more attractive than she used to be," he said.

"Yeah, well, the braces are gone, and she's not so scrawny anymore. I think she's a knockout."

Harley didn't like her well enough to concede anything stated that strongly, so he said nothing.

"Damien was crazy about her for a while," Tank continued, "but he could never make any headway with her. Just getting her to kiss him was like breaching Fort Knox."

"What happened between them? Did Damien finally break it off?"

"No, I think he would've kept on trying as long as she let him. She broke it up, saying she just didn't feel anything more than friendship for him. But you know?" Tank glanced down the hall, where they could hear his daughter talking in a high voice, playing house. "I think she's still a virgin. I'd bet money on it."

At twenty-seven? "Wasn't she just a year younger than us in high school?"

"Yeah."

"Most women have some experience by twenty-seven."

"Not Lauren. After what happened to Audra, her father's been even more protective. And already she was a daddy's girl. Anyway, Damien never got anywhere with her."

"Did he ever see Brandon?"

"All the time. Audra started with the drugs when Brandon was still a baby, and Lauren stepped in so her parents wouldn't have to. They have legal guardianship, but he's like her child now. She takes him everywhere with her, volunteers in his classroom at school, drives him to karate lessons, takes him and his friends to the mall, you name it. She's very devoted."

Devoted enough to want to keep Harley out of the picture so she could have Brandon to herself? She'd called his desire to take his son selfish, but what about her desire to keep him?

"Does he seem happy?" he asked.

"Oh, yeah. She's doing a good job, if that's what you're worried about."

Harley wasn't particularly worried about that. He would

have expected nothing less from an HA—high achiever—like Lauren. She'd been in every honors class their school offered and, if he remembered right, Audra had once laughingly told him that her sister won every short story contest she entered. Not that he understood why anyone would enter a short story contest, especially a teenager. But people like Lauren did that sort of thing. They usually set up exhibits at the science fair, too. "What's her father doing these days?"

"He's still a bastard. Damien hates him, but he left for Europe last I heard. He and Lauren's mother spend a couple of months there every spring."

Interesting information. It was only mid-May; there were still a few weeks of spring left. Was that why Lauren hadn't called her father down on him this morning? "You think he's still in Europe?"

Tank shrugged. "Don't know. Damien doesn't call Lauren very much anymore. He's trying to get over her. Why? Are you going to take Brandon home with you?"

"That's the million-dollar question," Harley said. But he knew if he tried to get custody of his son, the Worthingtons weren't giving up without a fight.

CHAPTER TWO

LAUREN SAT in a plastic chair at the small, glass-fronted karate school where Brandon took lessons, enveloped in the unpleasant smell of mildew, perspiration and discarded tennis shoes. She stared at the card Harley Nelson had given her that morning. Judging from the logo embossed in fancy script below his name—"Burlingame Harley Davidson"—he was a motorcycle salesman.

How fitting, she thought, picturing him in his leather jacket, jeans and boots. It was probably the only kind of work he could get. He didn't have a degree. He'd barely graduated from high school. And his occupation would certainly explain the expensive bike she'd seen in her driveway. Harley probably blew every dime he made on his two-wheeled transportation and couldn't afford a car.

"Too bad you *didn't* spend more time in the library," she muttered, feeling vindicated for his less-than-flattering comments that morning. "I guess an education is a little more important than an excitement factor, huh?"

"Did you say something, Lauren?" Kara, Brandon's classmate's mother, had been sitting next to her for the past thirty minutes, looking for an opportunity to start a conversation. She was a nice woman, even if she did love the sound of her own voice, but Lauren wasn't in the mood to listen to her today. Quickly averting her eyes, she mumbled something about talking to herself and retreated back into her own thoughts.

Should she let Harley meet Brandon or not? She'd

asked herself that a hundred times over the past six hours, but she couldn't come up with a good answer. Bottom line, she ran risks either way. If she let Harley see Brandon, it could snowball into something big and ugly and difficult. If she refused, it could snowball into something big and ugly and difficult.

She sighed, and saw Kara in her peripheral vision trying to catch her eye, but Lauren didn't look up. She had to call Harley, had to say something, she decided, running her thumb over the embossing on his card. Otherwise he'd show up on her doorstep again and next time might not end so well.

If only she could get hold of her parents, learn their opinion. She'd left a message at their hotel in London, but she hadn't heard from them and guessed they were on a side trip to Bath or the Cotswolds or someplace else. Which meant it could be another day or two before they knew she was trying to reach them.

She doubted Harley would wait that long. It was her impression that patience wasn't one of his strong suits.

A round of *keeyiis* drew Lauren's attention back to the karate class. Brandon stood in the front row facing the mirror. He smiled when he caught Lauren watching him, and Lauren's heart twisted at the thought of seeing him drive off on the back of Harley's motorcycle. She'd die first. He was such a wonderful boy—bright, healthy, talented.

Harley didn't deserve him, she told herself, but even as the thought passed through her mind, she wondered if her damning judgment wasn't a bit too harsh. He'd been eighteen when he'd gotten Audra pregnant. He'd made some pretty poor choices back then, but he wasn't the first teenager to do so. What if he'd changed? Matured? Didn't she owe it to Brandon to at least find out? He asked her so many questions about his father.

Slipping her phone out of her purse, she dialed the number for Harley's cell, which he'd circled on his card.

When he answered, she thought she heard rap music in the background, as well as other voices. Where was he spending his time? At a pool hall?

"It's Lauren Worthington," she said without preamble. "Hi."

She'd expected him to start pressing her immediately, but he didn't. He waited for her to speak, only she didn't know how to get things started.

Finally, he broke the silence. "So what have you decided?"

"I haven't. Not yet," she admitted. "I was hoping I could talk to you first."

"When?"

Lauren took a deep breath. Was she crazy to be doing this? "Tonight?"

"Okay. At your place?"

"No, somewhere neutral."

"A restaurant?"

"That's fine."

"You name the place."

"There's a sushi bar not far from the theaters downtown. Tokyo House. Do you know it?"

"I think so. What time?"

Lauren checked her watch. It was nearly five now, and she still needed to make dinner for Brandon and arrange for a baby-sitter. "Seven?"

"I'll be there."

"Good," she said, but in truth she hoped he wouldn't come. It would make things infinitely easier for her if he just disappeared. But how realistic was that?

"Anything else?" he asked.

"No. See you at seven." She hit the end button and finally glanced up to see Kara watching her eagerly.

"Are you thinking about buying a Harley Davidson?"

she asked, gazing at the business card. "My husband owned one once. It was a beautiful bike. A little scary, though. He used to take me on weekend trips, when the weather was warm enough. Wind gets pretty cold, you know. That's why it makes sense for a biker to wear leather. So I went out and bought us complete matching outfits, in red. And we joined a club. It was a lot of fun, really." A far-off look came over her face. "I wonder if I can still fit into those pants. I haven't tried them on for ages. Oh well, I guess I'll have to dig them out of storage and see, huh?"

Lauren tried to break in long enough to say that she had no intention of ever owning a Harley, that motorcycles frightened her immensely, but Kara didn't seem to be looking for an answer. She was telling Lauren about a vacation she and her husband once enjoyed where they almost took the Harley but decided, at the last minute, to take the Mercedes instead, which turned out to be a good choice because it was one of the hottest summers on record, and they were going to the Grand Canyon, and just think about all that dust and heat out on a bike....

Lauren yawned discreetly behind her hand and tried to follow the story well enough to nod or exclaim in all the right places, but her mind kept drifting back to Brandon and Harley and whether or not tonight would tell her what she wanted to know.

LAUREN HAD CALLED, which was more than Harley had expected her to do. He wouldn't have given up regardless, but her cooperation made things a little easier. Maybe they could reach an agreement. Maybe he could get her to see reason. Lauren wasn't the boy's mother, after all. As much as she'd done for him—and Harley was grateful— she was still only his aunt, and she had her own life to live. She was young, for crying out loud. And attractive.

She needed to get out, meet someone, have children of her own.

And let Brandon go with his father. After ten years, Harley felt it was his turn.

If only he could convince her of that.

"Tank, I'm out of here," he called from the living room. His friend was in the kitchen getting some juice for Lucy. They'd ordered a pizza and spent the afternoon watching a golf classic on television while reminiscing about the past, but Harley had to get going if he didn't want to be late for Lauren Worthington.

"Hey, you comin' back?" Tank asked, poking his head around the corner. "You can stay here, you know. It's just me and Lucy tonight, and just me most other times. I got an extra room and everything."

Harley didn't know exactly what his plans were. He'd checked into the Holiday Inn last night, but he'd brought only a few changes of clothing and had no idea how long he'd end up being in town. It all depended on what happened with Lauren tonight.

"My stuff's at the hotel. I'll probably just—"

"Don't stay at a hotel. Come back here," Tank interrupted.

Lucy slipped around the corner to smile at him, and Harley smiled back, thinking he'd probably enjoy the company. "All right," he said. "You got an extra key? I don't know how late I'll be."

"I'll put one under the mat."

"Sounds good. Later."

Harley jogged down the steps and straddled the seat of his bike before realizing he didn't have his helmet. Lucy had been playing with it earlier. He considered going back to the apartment to see what she'd done with it but decided not to waste the few minutes that would take. He didn't want to miss Lauren, give her any excuse to deny him the chance to see Brandon. Besides, he'd already ridden without a helmet once today. Another fifteen minutes wasn't going to matter.

Not bothering to zip his jacket, he raised the kickstand and cruised out of the lot. He could have gone to the hotel, shaved, cleaned up, changed clothes, but to a certain extent, he refused to meet Lauren's expectations of a stand-up guy, refused to conform to the clean-cut, preppy type she most likely admired. Which, if he really thought about it, probably had something to do with the reason he'd chosen to drive his motorcycle to Portland. But he didn't want to think about it, because then he'd have to face the other realities of his past, too.

The restaurant was coming up on his right. Though the lot was nearly filled to capacity, Harley easily spotted Lauren Worthington standing next to a pearl-colored, upper-model Lexus parked close to the entrance. Long dark hair pulled back, she wore a black tank sweater, black pants that narrowed and hit just above the ankle, and black-leather shoes with a slight heel. She looked slender, elegant—and rich.

The gangly young girl who'd worn braces and glasses thick enough to magnify her eyes had certainly grown up. But Harley wasn't sure he approved. Now Lauren looked like the kind of woman who frequented a tennis club, carried a Louis Vuitton handbag and hurried away from her cappuccino so she wouldn't miss her manicure appointment. In short, she'd turned into her mother.

She waved to let him know she was there. He snapped on his signal, but before he could drive into the lot, the flashing lights of a police car came up from behind.

Shit, not me, he thought, and pulled to the side of the road, hoping the cruiser would continue past him.

When it parked behind him, he knew his luck had run out. Damn! Five minutes more and he would've been safely ensconced in a booth with Lauren, deciding his son's future. Instead, she was standing on the curb, watching him get stopped by the police, and it wasn't hard to make out the look of "just as I'd expect" on her face.

Forget it. It's just a traffic ticket. Even the great Worthingtons must get a traffic ticket now and then.

A policeman approached wearing the usual khaki-colored uniform and an Officer Denny name tag. He was carrying a gun and pepper spray on his belt, but he had a boyish face that made him look as if he could still be in high school. "Hello, sir," he said, his expression a study in earnestness. "Are you aware that we have helmet laws in this state?"

In this state? Evidently Officer Denny had already noted Harley's California plate, and being an out-of-state resident never helped when dealing with local law enforcement. Harley knew at that moment that he probably wasn't going to get off with a warning. He just hoped Denny would finish with him before Lauren got it in her head to leave. "Most states have helmet laws now," he replied.

"Then you know you should be wearing one."

"I'm aware of that, yes."

"Do you own a helmet, sir?"

Did it matter? He didn't have it with him, so what was the point? "Yeah."

"Where is it now?"

Harley didn't know exactly where his helmet was. He didn't care. He just wanted to talk to Lauren. "It's at my friend's house." Shifting, he lowered his voice. "Listen, Officer, I don't mean to be rude, but could we skip the lecture and cut right to the chase? I realize I'm guilty of a traffic violation. I'll pay the fine. But I'm in a big hurry. Is there any chance you could just write me up and be on your way?"

"A helmet could save your life," Denny continued, obviously reluctant to let Harley interrupt him before he'd finished his spiel.

"I know. It's there to protect me from myself. Isn't it grand that others care so much about my safety? Too bad their concern is going to cost me a hundred bucks, but those are the breaks. Can I have my ticket now?"

Denny's brows knitted as though Harley's briskness had offended him. "Maybe you should just relax and let me see your license and registration," he said, his voice taking on a sulky tone.

Harley showed him the registration he kept in his saddlebags. Then he fished his license out of his wallet and waited while Denny carried it back to his cruiser.

It'll all be over in a minute, he told himself, then waved to Lauren to let her know he was coming. But when Officer Denny returned, he wasn't writing on any clipboard. He was fingering his holstered gun and wearing a worried expression.

"Looks like I'm going to have to place you under arrest," he said.

LAUREN COULDN'T BELIEVE IT. Harley was being taken away right before her eyes. He hadn't been in town a day, and he was already in trouble with the police! What had he done? Robbed a liquor store? Run down a pedestrian? Sold drugs to local school kids?

Was that how Audra had gotten started on crack?

The thought that Harley might be responsible for ruining her sister in more ways than one caused the smoldering resentment Lauren felt toward him to deepen. What had she been thinking, setting up a meeting with him in the first place? Her father had always said he was no good—nothing but a two-bit punk—and obviously Harley hadn't changed. Witnessing his arrest was proof positive.

She watched the officer shepherd Harley toward his car, noted Harley's angry strides, his jerky movements, the intensity on his face when he spoke, and wished she could hear what was being said. But she didn't want to get that close. She'd already learned everything she needed to know, hadn't she? It was best to keep her distance—a decision she deemed wise when the officer tried to cuff him and Harley suddenly whirled as though he might throw a punch.

"Don't do it, it'll only make things worse," she muttered, clenching one hand around her car keys. Harley couldn't hear her, of course. It wouldn't have mattered, anyway. He wasn't the type to take advice from her or anyone else.

Besides, she *wanted* him to be arrested, didn't she? It would buy her some time.

The officer's hand went to his gun as though he was threatening to use it, and Lauren held her breath. "Just cooperate," she said, and finally Harley allowed the cuffs and was put in the backseat.

The officer leaned against the hood of the car, periodically talking into his radio until a tow truck came to impound Harley's bike. Then he got behind the wheel and drove away, and the last thing Lauren saw was Harley staring back at her through the window, jaw clenched, eyes bright with fury and the red-and-blue lights of the patrol car still swirling above him.

What kind of fool was she? Lauren asked herself when they were gone at last. She'd been afraid she was judging Harley too harshly—the boy who'd gotten her sister pregnant and run out on her! As if there could be a judgment too harsh for someone like that!

Her father was right. She was justified in keeping Harley as far away from Brandon as possible.

Feeling almost giddy with relief, Lauren took her cell phone from her purse and called her best friend, Kimberly. Everything was going to be okay. Anyone with a record wouldn't stand a chance against her father and his lawyers.

"Lauren, where are you?" Kim asked as soon as she'd

said hello. "I just called your house and the baby-sitter said you'd left on a dinner date. What happened? I thought we were going dancing tonight."

Oh, jeez. Lauren had been so worried about Harley and Brandon, she'd completely forgotten about their plans to go dancing. And Kimberly really counted on getting out. After college she'd married a guy who'd been more interested in ogling the models in *Victoria Secret* catalogues than in giving Kimberly any attention. They'd remained childless, divorced six years later, and Kimberly had returned to Portland three months ago. She was living with her parents and looking for an accounting job, but she wanted desperately to get married again. "I'm sorry, Kim. I feel terrible. I should've remembered to call, but something pretty monumental came up."

"What? Have you met someone new?"

"Even more monumental than that. Remember Harley?"

"Brandon's father?"

"Yeah. He's back in town. He showed up on my doorstep this morning."

There was a long pause, then, "You're kidding me."

"No. He was supposed to meet me for dinner tonight so we could talk, but he got himself arrested just as he was turning in to the restaurant. Unbelievable, isn't it?"

"What did he do?"

"I don't know."

"You didn't *ask?*"

"What difference does it make? He's not a good person. That's all I need to know."

"We already knew he wasn't a good person. A good person doesn't get a girl pregnant and run out on her. But aren't you a little curious about what he did wrong *this* time?"

Now that the first blush of anger had subsided, Lauren realized she was more than a little curious. Yet she hadn't

felt compelled to get involved. She still wanted to go on
with her life as if Harley had never dropped back into it.

"No," she lied. "I think I should just take it as a sign
to stay away. Besides, if I need to know, I can always
find out. Chief Wilson is a good friend of my dad's."

"Great! Tell me as soon as you call him."

Lauren frowned and finally made her way back to her
car, opened the door and sank into her seat behind the
wheel. "Why are you assuming I'm going to call him? I
said I *could* call him."

"Have you forgotten who you're talking to here?
We've been best friends since first grade. There's no way
someone like you is capable of letting something like this
go."

Lauren opened her mouth to argue, then closed it again
when Kimberly added, "Besides, *I'm* dying to know. Do
you want me to call down there for you?"

"No, I'll do it," she said, giving in to the inevitable.
Kimberly was right. No way was she going to be able to
ignore this. Especially because she had no guarantee that
Harley wouldn't be back on her doorstep tomorrow morning.

"So, why were you and Harley getting together, anyway?" Kimberly asked. "Does he know about Audra?"

"Yeah. I'm not sure how he heard, but he knows."

"Does he want a relationship with Brandon?"

"I think so. He wants to see him, at any rate."

"What are you going to do?"

"Keep Brandon as far away as possible. I may need
you to take him for a few days. Can you do that?"

"Sure. Anything. You know he likes it here."

Lauren bit her bottom lip and ran her hand over the
smooth finish of the steering wheel, hating the thought of
disrupting her nephew's life. But she had to do something
until her parents returned, until she at least heard from

them, right? What if Harley got out of jail and kidnapped Brandon? They might never be able to find him again.

That possibility terrified Lauren, and she massaged her temples in worry. "He loves your dog," she said, hoping to bolster her confidence that she was doing the right thing.

"My *dog?* What am I, chopped liver?" Kimberly demanded.

Lauren laughed for the first time since she'd seen Harley coming toward the restaurant on that damned motorcycle. "No, of course not. I was just thinking aloud, about all the benefits of having him stay with you."

"He'll be fine, Lauren. You know I'll take good care of him."

"I know."

"Where are you now?"

Lauren twisted in her seat to glance up at the Tokyo House sign that lit the entire front of the building. She hadn't eaten since breakfast, and she loved the food at this place, but dinner was the last thing on her mind. "Downtown."

"When are you bringing Brandon over?"

"I don't know. It depends on how long Harley's in jail, if he's even going to jail. The fact that they cuffed him makes me think he might be there for a few days, but maybe they just took him in for questioning or something."

"Chief Wilson will be able to tell you."

"Right."

"And don't worry. You can bring Brandon over no matter how late it is. My parents won't mind."

"Thanks a lot."

"You bet. Lauren?"

"Yeah?"

"How does he look? Harley, I mean."

Lauren sighed and stared through the window at the spot where the police had hauled him away. "Better than ever," she admitted.

CHAPTER THREE

THE PAST TWENTY-FOUR HOURS hadn't been easy. Harley had been booked and jailed for the heinous crime of having an old, unpaid speeding ticket. He'd spent most of Saturday night in a concrete holding cell behind a very thick door, waiting for a judge to set his bail, which ended up at a thousand dollars because he was a resident of another state and considered a flight risk. Then Tank had picked him up and he'd spent much of the day trying to get his bike out of impound, which had involved more effort than he ever would have imagined and cost him another two hundred dollars.

On top of everything else, his court date wasn't for two weeks. Either he had to stay in town and wait for it, but that probably wouldn't work because he didn't dare leave his business in the hands of his manager for so long. Or he had to come back here, which would be expensive and time-consuming.

"That's not a good face," Tank said, eyeing him above a hamburger the size of a football. He'd taken Lucy home an hour earlier so it was just the two of them.

Harley glowered at him from the couch. Tank had offered him dinner, but he wasn't exactly in the mood to eat. He was tired and miserable, and still angry about the way his weekend had turned out. Most maddening of all was the fact that the speeding ticket that started the whole thing was over ten years old. Had Officer Denny not been so zealous, had he not called in for a more extensive search than the computer initially offered, the ticket probably wouldn't have shown up, not after so many years. Harley couldn't even remember getting pulled over at the end of his senior year. But back then he'd had bigger concerns. His mother had just kicked him out of the house because her new boyfriend didn't like him. Audra had just told him about the baby. And Mr. Worthington was pressuring him to take two thousand dollars and leave town. Though he was too proud to keep it, he'd finally accepted the money and given it to his mother for the food and clothes she'd grudgingly provided over the years. Then he'd split without a clue as to where he was going or how he'd survive.

Who would've worried about paying for a speeding ticket in the middle of all that?

"You gonna be okay?" Tank asked.

Harley shrugged. "I'll live."

"It's over now. Forget it."

If Lauren hadn't been standing outside the restaurant when he'd been arrested, Harley thought he could forget it, or at least put the incident in some perspective. But every time he closed his eyes he saw the look of affirmation on her face when that greenhorn Denny cuffed him, and it made him long to hit something. He'd only been in town for the weekend, but already he was short on patience and long on grievances. One of them was Lauren's superior attitude. He didn't want his son raised by a woman who considered a broken nail a major catastrophe. He wanted Brandon to be part of the real world, to deal with real people and grow up to be a real man, not some petted, spoiled boy living in luxury without knowing a hard day's work. Lauren had asked what Harley could give him. Well, he sure as hell knew enough about the real world to give him that.

"Who're you calling?" Tank asked, watching Harley

punch the numbers on his cell phone with more force than necessary.

"Lauren Worthington."

"Right now? Do you think that's a good idea? I mean, last night didn't go so well. Maybe you should give her a day or two to—"

"To what?" Harley demanded. "Forget about it?"

"I don't know. Maybe. You said she saw the whole thing, and she comes from a pretty protected world. It probably freaked her out."

"So what? There are worse crimes than an unpaid speeding ticket. One of them is never getting to see your son. Besides, you're talking about a girl who was first in her class. She's not going to forget about anything."

"Maybe *you* will," Tank said around a mouthful of burger.

Harley's stomach growled, making him regret skipping dinner, but he didn't want to waste any time eating. He wanted to finally settle the score where Brandon was concerned—if Lauren would only answer her phone. "She's just like her folks," he said between rings. "Her mind's made up about me and nothing I do is going to change it. If anything, last night only confirmed what she wanted to believe in the first place."

"Lauren's a nice girl," Tank said, defending her.

Harley lifted a hand to indicate he needed a moment of silence. Lauren's voice mail had finally picked up. He hesitated, wondering whether or not to leave a message, then decided he'd keep trying to reach her instead. It wasn't as though he could count on her to call him back.

"You have her home number?" he asked, hanging up.

Tank shoved some chips into his mouth. "What did you call?"

"The number she phoned me from yesterday was stored on my cell."

"The home's unlisted," he said, "but Damien would have it."

"Would he give it to us?"

"Sure, why not?" Tank swallowed the last of his food and grinned. "He might be a stuffy lawyer, but he's still my brother."

Leaning far enough forward to set his plate on the coffee table, he grabbed the cordless phone. After a short conversation during which Tank repeatedly said things like, "I just want to talk to her, okay?" and "What does it matter? She's not your girlfriend anymore," he handed Harley a number written on a gum wrapper.

"Thanks," Harley said.

"What are friends for?"

Harley cocked an eyebrow at him. "For nearly getting one drowned in the river, if I remember— Hello?"

Lauren had answered.

"It's me," he said.

There was a long pause, then, "How did you get this number?"

"I'm familiar with some good, old-fashioned torture techniques. After a few minutes with me your friends and neighbors were more than willing to talk."

"I can relate to the desperation they must've felt to escape from you. What do you want?"

"I want to talk, just like we were going to do last night."

"Before you robbed a liquor store or whatever you did that got you arrested?"

Robbed a liquor store? This woman had a very vivid imagination. "I'm sorry to disappoint you, but it wasn't anything that dramatic." He was tempted to explain just how undramatic it was, but his pride wouldn't allow it. He wasn't about to grovel at Lauren Worthington's feet, hoping for her approval.

"I understand," she said. "When something happens

a lot it becomes common, everyday. The *excitement factor* goes down, is that it?''

He remembered saying something to her about the excitement factor in her life and realized she was throwing his words back at him, but he wasn't in the mood to play games. ''As far as I'm concerned, our business together is a completely unrelated issue.''

''I'm afraid I disagree. Your background and character are an important part of the issue, but then, *I* have a nine-year-old boy to consider.''

''You have *my* nine-year-old boy.''

Silence.

''Meet me,'' he said, softening his voice in hopes that he could still gain her cooperation. Before he decided anything, he wanted to see Brandon, talk to him. Was that so much to ask?

''No.''

He held back a frustrated sigh. ''Then I'll come over there.''

''It won't do you any good. You won't be able to get in. We have security.''

''The kind of security I passed with a wave and a smile when I came to the house yesterday?''

''They're more diligent at night,'' she said. ''They won't let you through the gate this time.''

Especially after she called and told them not to. ''Then I'll hop the fence.''

''You'll be arrested. Again. And this time they'd probably keep you. Stalking a woman is a lot more serious than an unpaid speeding ticket.''

So she'd been playing him. She already knew why he was arrested. ''I thought I robbed a liquor store. I'm such a bad guy it's hard to keep up with all my offenses, huh?''

''You're probably working your way up.''

''Yeah, I've heard most armed robberies start with unpaid speeding tickets. It's a definite sign of trouble.''

"I've already seen enough signs to know you're trouble, Harley," she said, but her voice didn't hold the same bitterness it had when he'd spoken to her at the door. She'd also used his name for the first time. Somehow that encouraged him, made him feel as though she was finally starting to see him as a person instead of the devil incarnate.

"You don't know anything about me," he pointed out. "Not really. The only thing you have is your father's word."

"And my sister's experience. Taken together, that's a pretty strong argument."

"Haven't you ever fallen in love, Lauren?" he asked, dropping the sarcasm and defensiveness and stripping it down to a simple, sincere question.

She didn't answer, and for a fleeting moment he found himself wishing she would. *Hadn't* she ever fallen in love? Didn't she know what it was like to feel so passionately about someone that you simply couldn't keep your hands to yourself? That you wouldn't—couldn't— heed an outside threat to stay away because it was like being asked to stop breathing? If not, she'd never understand, and he'd be wasting his time if he tried to explain it to her. Love wasn't something that made logical sense.

"Come on," he said. "I'm only asking for a few minutes. How can you tell a man who's never seen his son that you won't even entertain the idea?"

"You should have thought about seeing Brandon ten years ago."

"I *did* think about it, dammit." He felt his irritation with Lauren grow and wished Tank wasn't in the room. What, did Lauren think leaving Portland had been easy for him? That he'd been able to turn his back on his child without a second thought? He hadn't had a serious relationship since Audra. Hadn't even wanted one. It was as though that part of him, the capacity to love, had stayed behind. "I offered to marry Audra, but your father wouldn't hear of it," he admitted.

A slight pause. "You ran out on my sister. For money. I hardly call that a marriage proposal," she said, now sounding tentative, wary.

"She wanted two things that couldn't exist together—me and her father's support. Your father put conditions on his support, and you know what she chose."

"So you ran."

She was still looking for easy answers, still wanting to place the blame neatly on his back and walk away—with his son.

"No, I asked her to leave with me. But she wouldn't turn her back on Daddy and his wallet." Harley shoved a hand through his hair. He hated dredging up the past, resurrecting old, better-forgotten feelings, but he'd known what this trip would cost before he came. If it was penitence and remorse Lauren wanted to hear, he had plenty of that to spare.

"Listen, she clung to safety and security, and I guess I can't blame her," he went on. "I had nothing to give her." Except his heart, he added silently. But that hadn't been nearly enough for the spoiled Audra.

"You're lying," Lauren said, but the pitch of her voice had changed and at last Harley sensed some uncertainty. "She loved you."

After ten years, he'd begun to doubt that Audra's feelings had ever rivaled his own. When Brandon was only a few weeks old, she'd dropped by his mother's house, without the baby, and given Beverly the birth details. But then his mother's lover had left her and she'd immediately packed up and moved to California to be close to Harley. And neither of them had heard from Audra since.

"She might have loved me a little, but she loved her lifestyle more," he said.

Silence again.

"I know she's gone now, and I'm sorry for that, Lauren," he continued, "but if you could be big-minded enough to remember how she really was instead of seeing her as some kind of saint, I think you'd realize that I'm on the level."

Nothing. Had he made her angry? Or was she capable of being as fair as he was asking her to be? "Lauren?"

"Meet me at Thai Basil," she said at last.

"That's another restaurant?"

"Yeah, at the corner of Twelfth and Yamhill. I'll be there in twenty minutes."

"I'll be waiting," he said.

"I just hope it won't be in a car with red and blue lights."

HARLEY WAS ALREADY at the restaurant when Lauren arrived. She recognized his sleek black motorcycle as soon as she got out of her car—only this time there was a shiny burgundy-colored helmet sitting on the seat.

Nervously smoothing the denim skirt she'd chosen to wear, along with a white cotton blouse and a pair of high-heeled sandals, she took a deep breath. She'd thought that adding a few inches to her height might lend her some courage, but she was still only five foot six and mere inches weren't enough to compensate for the fear rushing through her veins.

She eyed the restaurant as though it was something dark and threatening. What if everything Harley had told her on the phone about Audra and her father was a lie intended to manipulate her?

In that case, she was letting him make a fool of her. She'd certainly regret it and would definitely pay for it later.

But what if he was telling the truth?

This morning Chief Wilson had said that Harley had been picked up for an unpaid speeding ticket, posted bond and been released, which hardly made him a dangerous criminal. She'd taken Brandon to Kimberly's, just to be safe, but the fact that Harley hadn't done anything seriously wrong—and that he hadn't touted the reason for his arrest when he'd spoken to her on the phone, despite her baiting—lent him some credibility. Problem was, if Harley had actually tried to do right by Audra and she'd refused him because of her father's intervention, maybe Harley *wasn't* such a bad guy. And if he wasn't such a bad guy, then Lauren couldn't conscionably—

Whoa, slow down, she cautioned herself, pinching the bridge of her nose as if she could physically clear the thoughts from her mind. *Not such a bad guy is a pretty far cry from decent human being.*

Either way, she couldn't really walk away without hearing him out, could she?

Hesitating, she glanced between her car and the restaurant. Once she entered Thai Basil, there'd be no turning back. Once she walked in, she'd cross that invisible line between Harley and her family, and in doing so betray her sister's memory *and* her father's wishes.

If only her father was here to finish what had been started eleven years ago. She'd taken care of Brandon for most of his life, even when he was a baby and she was still in her senior year of high school. But she didn't know the gritty details of what had happened between Audra and Harley. She and her sister had never been close. Audra hadn't confided in her. Their father had run interference and concealed as many of the facts as he could— because he was so terribly disappointed in Audra and embarrassed that a daughter of his would involve herself with someone like Harley, and do the other things she did.

But now her father was half a world away, and Lauren's conscience was dictating that she at least hear what Brandon's father had to say. For Brandon, if not for Harley.

Throwing back her shoulders, she took a firm hold on her purse and went inside, where the inviting aroma of lemongrass, basil and curry wafted around her and Oriental music played softly in the background.

Even before her eyes could adjust to the dim lighting, Harley was beside her, telling the hostess they were together. He gently clasped her elbow, guiding her to a table in the far corner, then pulled out her chair and took his seat across from her. "Thanks for coming," he said.

He'd spoken only three words, and already Lauren wanted to bolt. Was it because he sounded so sincere, so relieved that she'd agreed to meet him? She didn't want to soften. She felt infinitely safer and more comfortable hiding behind what she'd believed to be true for so long. But it wasn't fair to remain purposely blind, deaf and dumb.

"Lauren?"

She'd ducked behind the menu almost the moment she sat down, but lowered it now to look up at him—and immediately wished she hadn't. He was wearing a simple cotton T-shirt beneath his black leather jacket, a pair of faded jeans and black boots. He wasn't exactly setting any new fashion trends, but what he lacked in cutting-edge style he compensated for with raw masculinity. His T-shirt pulled across his muscular chest. His jeans molded to his body like a second skin, not because they were tight but because they dipped and curved in all the right places. And he smelled…incredible. Lauren was accustomed to her dates smelling like the cosmetics department at Nordstrom where they no doubt bought their expensive colognes, but Harley's scent was less artificial, more like…leather and clean clothes, soap and warm skin.

"I shouldn't be here," she suddenly announced. She stood up to leave, but he caught her by the wrist.

"Don't be nervous," he said, his voice low. "We're only going to talk."

She stared down at his hand. His grip didn't hurt. It felt warm and reassuring, but he quickly let go as though he feared she'd take exception to his touch.

"It just isn't right," she said, feeling the pull of the exit and the bliss of ignorance beyond. "It seems like I'm...I don't know, consorting with the enemy."

He offered her a tentative smile. "Come on. We're just having dinner. We're not consorting. Besides, do I look dangerous to you?" His expression grew sheepish. "Yesterday's arrest aside, of course."

Lauren told herself not to return his smile, but the memory of his arrest, funnier in retrospect, combined with the knowledge that it had occurred simply because of a speeding ticket, got the better of her. "I can't believe you were dragged off right in front of me," she said with a small laugh. "You certainly have good timing."

His smile turned into a crooked grin. "Yeah, well it took some work to arrange it. Not everyone can manage to get arrested in front of the one person it's in their best interests to impress." The look of chagrin reappeared. "I'm never going *anywhere* without my helmet again."

"It doesn't seem like you to be cautious," she said, fidgeting with the back of the chair.

"No, it seems like you." He gazed up at her, now serious, and Lauren understood his meaning. He thought she was being too narrow minded—and maybe she was.

"I just want what's best for Brandon."

"And I'd die before I let anything hurt him."

Lauren told herself that of course he'd say something so reassuring. He was trying to win her confidence. But the sincerity in his voice convinced her. There was something about Harley Nelson that begged her to believe in him, if only a little. Why he affected her that way, she couldn't fathom, not after what had happened to Audra.

"I ordered some chardonnay," he said when the waitress appeared carrying a bottle of wine. "I thought you might like a glass.'' He nodded toward the chair. ''That is, if you're going to sit back down and eat with me.''

Lauren looked from Harley to the waitress. If she didn't leave now, she knew she might regret it for the rest of her life…but she couldn't make herself walk away from the hope in his eyes.

''I'll stay,'' she said. There wasn't anything wrong with spending an hour or so in Harley's company. If he was everything her father said, their time together wouldn't change the situation. And Quentin Worthington was rarely wrong.

Harley seemed to relax when she took her seat again. He smiled at her, but Lauren almost asked him to stop. That smile brought memories of silly schooldays, when she and Kimberly used to write notes to each other gushing about how handsome he was and speculating on whether or not they'd pass him in the halls after their next class. One time, at a school dance, Harley had crossed the floor, coming toward her, and Lauren was sure he meant to dance with her. Her breath caught, her stomach filled with butterflies. Then he'd extended his hand to the girl behind her.

Why had she remembered that? What could it possibly matter now?

''What's good here?'' Harley asked, studying the menu.

''I like the Pad Thai and the chicken-and-coconut-milk soup.''

''Should we get the Chicken Satay as an appetizer?''

''If you want. We're not on a date,'' she said, more sharply than she'd intended.

He scowled. ''What is it with you? Is having a little bit of fun going to betray everything you've ever known?''

''No. Meeting with you is.''

''Well, we're meeting already, so we might as well enjoy ourselves, provided you know how.''

"I know how to have fun," she replied, wishing she didn't sound so defensive. "It's just that I'm sitting across from the man who got my sister pregnant and has suddenly reappeared out of nowhere to threaten what I love most. What's fun about that?"

He stared at her for a long time, and again Lauren regretted sounding so harsh. What was it about Harley that knocked her off her balance? One minute she thought she was being too kind to him. The next she thought she was being too cruel. She couldn't seem to pick a lane.

"Tell me something," he said. "What would you do if you were me?"

Lauren didn't answer. She didn't want to look at things from his perspective, knew instinctively that it would only undermine her resolve.

"Lauren?"

"I don't know," she said impatiently. "I guess I wouldn't have left. I would've stayed around so I could know my son."

He cupped a hand to his ear. "What? I can't hear you for the silver spoon in your mouth."

"We're talking about character, not privilege or money," she retorted, curling her fingernails into her palms because she knew she wasn't being completely honest. She was well aware of his situation ten years ago—eighteen years old, penniless, the fatherless son of an alcoholic mother. With her own powerful father doing his best to shut him out, and Audra falling in line behind Quentin, what could Harley have done? Would anyone have stuck around in the face of all that?

"We're talking about a lack of options," he clarified.

The waitress approached to take their order. Lauren kept her eyes on her wine, slowly turning her glass by the stem while Harley ordered pad thai and soup for her, yellow curry chicken for himself and the chicken satay as an appetizer for them both.

When they were alone again, Lauren folded her hands in her lap and shot him a glance. "Maybe you didn't have a lot of options back then," she said, "but you were old enough to know what made a baby. Why didn't you use any birth control?"

His gaze never wavered. "I was so crazy about her that it might not have mattered, but for what it's worth, Audra told me she was on the pill."

It might not have mattered? How did one forget about something so important? "What about my father?" she asked. "You knew he didn't want you around Audra."

"And I was supposed to respect that? God, are you really so cold? I was in love with her!"

So his relationship with her sister had meant more than sex to him. Lauren had often wondered. But knowing that truth only made her feel worse. Or was it what he'd just said about her that stung? Damien Thompson had once called her an ice princess, but she wasn't cold. She'd just never been head over heels in love.

"If you'd stayed away from Audra, there wouldn't have been a problem," she said.

"You mean there wouldn't have been a Brandon," he replied, and he was right. How could she think such a thing? Brandon was the most wonderful child in the world. Dammit! Why was this so confusing?

"I'm sorry," she said, trying to regroup. "I realize you had a difficult childhood, and I hate the thought of you or anyone else suffering—"

"I'm not interested in your sympathy," he interrupted with a dark scowl. "I'm just asking you to understand that what happened back then isn't as black and white as you seem to believe. I'm not trying to ruin your life. I wasn't trying to ruin Audra's. I'm only here because I have a son I fathered ten years ago. I've never seen him, and I think it's time I changed all that, don't you?"

Every nerve in Lauren's body stretched taut. How much

of a change was Harley hoping for? He lived in California. He couldn't maintain any kind of close relationship with Brandon so far away. And Lauren couldn't let Brandon go anywhere with him. Even if she agreed, which she never would, her father wouldn't allow it. And Quentin Worthington had the resources to see his wishes through, while Harley was just a motorcycle salesman.

Noting the clear intelligence shining in Harley's green eyes, the aquiline nose, the full bottom lip and square, rugged chin, she saw much of this man in Brandon. Was that why she felt so attracted to Harley? Surely it wasn't the old schoolgirl crush, the one that had her staring after him in high school?

"What exactly are you asking?" she breathed.

"Let me see him."

"I can't."

"Lauren." He reached out and covered her cold hand with his warm one. "Please."

She closed her eyes. This was going to start something big. She knew it; she could feel it. And it terrified her. "When?" she managed.

"Tonight. After dinner."

"Not tonight."

His hand tightened on hers. "When?"

"Tomorrow," she said. At that moment, the waitress arrived with their food, but Lauren knew she wouldn't be able to eat a bite.

CHAPTER FOUR

WHAT A NIGHT! Lauren groaned as she trained one bleary eye on her alarm clock. It was five in the morning. She'd left the restaurant at eleven and tossed and turned until three. Then, when she finally fell asleep, she'd dreamed about Harley snatching Brandon from her. She could still see the triumphant grin he'd worn when he ripped the boy from her grasp, tossed him onto the back of his bike and roared away. It was a disturbing image that conflicted with the Harley she'd met for dinner last night, but at this hour, the sinister Harley seemed more real than not.

Shoving a hand through her tangled hair, she closed her eyes and tried to drift off again. *Don't think about it,* she told herself. She had another hour before she was scheduled to pick Brandon up from Kimberly's so she could get him ready for school, but she was too worried to relax. She'd promised to introduce Brandon to his father today. Would she be letting the wolf in the door?

The telephone rang, the noise startling and loud in the silent house.

She grabbed the receiver and cleared her throat before saying hello, then sagged in relief when she heard her father on the other end of the line. He'd gotten her messages. Thank heaven!

"Dad, I'm so glad to hear from you," she said. "I've been trying to reach you for two days. Where have you and Mom been?"

"We took the train to Paris for the weekend. Just got

back," he said. "What's wrong? The front desk here at the hotel said it was urgent. Is Brandon okay?"

Lauren sat up, cross-legged, and kneaded her forehead. She'd wanted to speak to her father ever since Harley had appeared, but now that she had Quentin on the phone, she was almost afraid to tell him what was going on. She knew he wasn't going to like the fact that Harley had popped back into their lives, and hated to admit that she wasn't maintaining a stronger defense against him. "Brandon's fine, Dad, don't worry. Everything's fine— for the most part." *At least right now.* "It's just that…well, Harley's back. He came here Saturday morning."

"What?"

Flinching from the blast of her father's voice, Lauren held the phone away from her ear. "It's true," she said when it was safe to move the handset closer.

"What do you mean he's back? Has he moved to town?"

"What's happened? What is it?" she heard her mother ask in the background.

"No. He lives in California," Lauren said. "He learned about Audra and came to see Brandon."

"Did you let him in?"

An ominous silence followed this question, one that made Lauren glad she could answer honestly when she said no. She didn't add, "not yet."

"Good for you, honey," he said. "Harley Nelson has no business with us. That boy's nothing but trouble."

That *boy?* Harley wasn't a boy any longer. He was a man now, and a man to be reckoned with, if her instincts could be trusted.

"Harley Nelson's back?" her mother cried.

"You tell him to go back to whatever rock he crawled out from under," her father said. "I won't let him say two words to Brandon."

The relief Lauren had experienced when she'd first heard her father's voice was quickly fading. "Audra's gone now, Dad," she said as he finally quieted her mother with a terse, "Just a minute, Marilee, I can't hear a thing she's saying with you squawking in my ear."

"What did you say?" he demanded, returning to the conversation.

"I said Audra's gone now."

"You think I don't know that?"

"Well, he *is* Brandon's father, his only living parent."

"I don't care if he's the man on the moon—Marilee, would you please shut up and let me talk?—Audra's dead because of him. Besides, we're all the family Brandon needs."

"We're all he's ever known," her mother put in.

"That might be true," Lauren said. "But what if Harley takes us to court? You realize he could win complete custody. We stand to lose Brandon altogether."

At last, a moment of silence. "What's he like now?" Quentin asked, his voice less emotional and more calculating.

Lauren pictured the tall, handsome spectacle that was Harley Nelson and tried not to feel so much as a flicker of admiration, but something fluttered in her stomach all the same. "He's taller and...a little broader," she said to avoid saying anything more flattering. She could have added that he was confident, almost cocky, and very real, very appealing—far different from any of the stuffed shirts she'd dated. But she didn't. "He still drives a motorcycle," she said so her description wouldn't sound quite so sketchy.

Fortunately her father didn't push her for any more details. "See?" he responded immediately. "He hasn't changed. Bad seeds rarely do. Probably doesn't have a pot to piss in. Don't worry, Lauren, there's nothing a man like that can do to us or Brandon."

So they had Harley outgunned as far as resources went. Did that justify denying him the opportunity to meet his own son? What about the moral side of the dilemma? And what about Brandon's wishes? If he were to find out his father was in town, surely he'd want to see him. "But if Harley sincerely regrets what he did, then it would only be right to—"

"Don't tell *me* what's right," her father snapped. "He couldn't regret what happened any more than I do. That son of a bitch cost me my little girl," he said, his voice growing hoarse with emotion.

Audra. Lauren felt the same sense of loss and regret she knew her father felt, but she had to ask herself how much of the situation ten years ago had been Audra's fault? And how much had been Harley's? Had she told him she was on the pill, as he claimed? If so, she certainly deserved a larger portion of the responsibility than the Worthingtons had ever allotted to her before. But the real question was whether or not Audra would've alienated her family and sunk into drug abuse without Harley starting her down the wrong road and abandoning her.

That was tough to say. Remembering the way her sister had behaved at school, flitting from one guy to the next, partying with the best of them and rebelling against any kind of authority, Lauren had difficulty placing *all* the blame in Harley's lap. "She was eighteen, Dad."

"So? What are you saying?"

That she was old enough to understand the consequences of her actions. Lauren had known better than to follow in Audra's footsteps, even at the tender age of seventeen. "She was almost an adult."

"How can you say that? Audra was just an innocent young girl when she met Harley."

"He was the same age."

"Maybe. But he was hardly innocent. And I tried to tell him to leave her alone. I told him what was going to happen. If only the little bastard had listened. Don't you remember me catching them in the front yard in the middle of the night, both of them nearly falling-down drunk? I told him to stay away from her then. I knew it was just a matter of time before he ruined her life, and I was right.''

Lauren heard her mother warning Quentin to watch his blood pressure, but he seemed to pay no more attention to that than anything else Marilee said.

"He's cost us enough already, Lauren. You know that,'' he muttered.

"What about Brandon? What about what *he* might want?''

"Lauren, Brandon's not even ten. He doesn't know what's best, and it wouldn't be fair to involve him.''

"Shouldn't we at least tell him that his father's in town? See if—''

"Why? What good would it do?'' he broke in. "If you bring Brandon into this, you'll only upset him.''

Lauren didn't say anything. She hated confrontations and avoided them whenever possible, especially with her father. But somehow it felt dishonest not to tell Brandon that his father had some interest in knowing him.

"Lauren?'' her father said when she didn't speak.

"I'm here.''

"I love Brandon, honey. You know how much.''

Lauren couldn't help responding to the softening in his voice. "I don't doubt that.''

"If Audra had listened to me in the first place, this wouldn't be happening. She'd still be with us. But she wouldn't listen, wouldn't let me do what I knew was best for her.''

Was Lauren making the same mistake? Was she undermining her father when she should be supporting him? The thought that she might be doing just that seemed to shed new light on everything.

"Okay," she finally said. "I won't mention Harley to Brandon, and I'll tell Harley to stay away. But what do I do if he won't take no for an answer? What if he won't leave us alone?"

"Then we'll get a restraining order against him until this can go to court. But don't worry. It won't get that far. The boy I remember from ten years ago wasn't the kind to stick around long enough to fight for anything. Do you think things are any different now?"

Yes! She thought things were significantly different. Harley wasn't a man who'd allow himself to be bullied or intimidated or denied. Not by Quentin Worthington or his fortune. How Lauren knew that, she couldn't exactly say. It had something to do with Harley's bearing and demeanor. At the same time, it was only a hunch and she could be wrong, so she hesitated to state her opinion too strongly.

"He's a little more determined than he used to be," she said.

"Then we'll be just as determined. He's not going to threaten my family's well-being a second time."

"Right. I understand."

"Where is he now?"

"I believe he's staying with an old friend of his." In fact, she knew he was. He'd said so last night. He'd even given her the number.

"Well, if he comes around again, you send him packing. If he won't leave, call the police."

"Okay," Lauren said, but her heart sank as she contemplated facing Harley and telling him she'd changed her mind. She felt sorry for him, for what he'd lost, even if it was largely due to his own poor judgment.

"I wish we were there to help you. Do you think your mom and I should come home?"

Deep down Lauren wished they would. She wanted Quentin to deal with the situation so she wouldn't have to. Let him sift the rights from the wrongs, make the tough decisions—and accept the responsibility.

What a cop-out, she thought, cringing at her cowardice. She was nearly thirty years old. It was time she took charge instead of expecting her parents to handle everything.

"Don't cut your trip short yet," she said. "Let's wait and see how things go. Maybe after I talk to him he'll just…go home." *Yeah, right!*

"Okay. But promise you'll call us after you talk to him."

"I will."

"I love you, honey."

"I love you, too, Dad."

"Here, your mother wants to say hello."

HARLEY SAT on the edge of a bed consisting of two mattresses and a cheap set of rails in Tank's spare room, waiting anxiously for the sun to rise. He was surrounded by boxes filled with who knew what—leftovers from Tank's marriage, probably, belongings that held too many memories to unpack—staring at empty walls and a dirty window with a broken blind. But he could've been sitting behind home plate at the World Series and it wouldn't have made any difference. He would still have been thinking of Brandon.

He was going to meet his son today. Harley had envisioned coming face to face with him hundreds, even thousands of times, but he'd never anticipated feeling so…apprehensive. It might've been different if Brandon was younger and less likely to be critical. Toddlers didn't care what a parent was like. They accepted whatever love they were offered. But a nine-year-old boy…

Harley stretched his neck, then squeezed the muscles in his left shoulder, wishing he could iron out a few of the knots. A nine-year-old boy would already know how to play ball and read and ride a bike. He'd have his own taste in clothes and his own opinions on what was cool and whether or not he might be interested in getting to know the man who'd fathered him.

What if Brandon didn't want to be bothered? What if he didn't want Harley to disturb his picture-perfect life with the Worthingtons?

He already has everything. He doesn't need you.

"You up, man?" Tank stood in the doorway, wearing nothing but a muscle shirt and a pair of boxers, his voice dispelling the echo of Lauren's words in Harley's head.

"Yeah," he replied, trying to stretch the kinks out of his neck again.

His friend yawned, then eyed the blankets that were still folded rather haphazardly behind Harley. "Didn't you go to bed?"

After his meeting with Lauren, Harley had stopped by the Holiday Inn to pack his things and check out. Then he'd let himself into Tank's apartment just after midnight, where he'd spent several hours on his laptop, seeing how sales were going at Burlingame Harley Davidson and answering e-mails sent to him by Joe Randall, his manager. He'd tried to sleep afterward but ended up pacing instead, and thinking about Brandon.

"I had too much on my mind. What are you doing up so early?"

"You kidding? I pour concrete for a living. I get up this early as a rule. Otherwise, I'm working late in the afternoon and it gets too damned hot. How'd it go with Lauren last night?"

"Good. Better than I expected." He certainly hadn't anticipated finding Audra's little sister, or any member of Audra's family, the least bit likeable. They lived in an expensive house, drove fancy cars, spent money as though it were water and had absolutely no idea what it was like to go without. Understanding and acceptance were concepts as unfamiliar to them as the idea of mowing their own lawn or painting their own house. But there was something about Lauren that made Harley wonder if she was really as bad as he'd assumed. She'd been decent last night. She'd allowed him to break through her icy reserve and reach what he hoped was her heart—provided she really had one.

"She gonna let you see Brandon?" Tank asked.

"Yeah, today as a matter of fact."

"You nervous?"

"No," Harley said, even though his heart raced at the prospect of what lay in store. God, he was scared. How did he introduce himself to his own child? Pick up in the middle of Brandon's life and make a meaningful contribution?

"I'm supposed to go over there for dinner," he explained. "Lauren suggested it might seem more natural if I came to the house and was treated like any other guest. She thinks it'll help maintain Brandon's emotional stability if we're friendly and supportive of each other."

Tank arched an eyebrow at him. "She's willing to be supportive of *you?*"

"Go figure," Harley said. "A sympathetic Worthington. It's a contradiction in terms, isn't it?"

"Does that mean she's gonna tell Brandon who you are?"

"Yep. Said she's always been honest with him and doesn't want to erode the trust she's established between them by lying to him now."

"Sounds like something she'd say. I told you she was a straight arrow."

"I prefer it this way, too. No games, no secrets."

A hint of a smile lit Tank's face. "Damien called while you were gone last night."

"Your brother? What for?"

"Just to badger me some more about why we wanted Lauren's number."

"Did you tell him?"

"No, I said I had a friend who was looking for a good lay." Tank's smile turned into a devilish grin. "He nearly had a coronary. I love to mess with that guy's head."

"He want her back?" Harley asked.

Tank scratched his belly. "Is the Pope Catholic?"

"Why? What's so appealing about her?"

"Didn't you look at her, man? She's gorgeous!"

"Her sister was even prettier, but there's plenty of pretty women out there who are less spoiled."

"You're assuming Lauren is just like Audra used to be," Tank said. "She's not."

"She can't be *that* different," Harley responded. "She's cut from the same cloth. She has the same asshole for a father, the same nervous Nellie for a mother, and she had the same snobbish upbringing. She still lives in the same damned fortress, for Pete's sake! So tell Damien to take it from me and stay the hell away from Lauren and anyone else even distantly related to her."

Tank anchored his fingers above the lintel and let it support most of his weight. "Yeah, well, I think she's pretty much made that decision for him. He's tried to get her back, and she won't budge. I just wish he'd quit moonin' over her. Watching him wallow in misery is so damned annoying, you know? What does he think, no one else has ever gone through a break-up?"

Harley gazed at the boxes cluttering the floor and knew Tank had done his share of hurting. "You seeing anyone now?" he asked.

"Damien set me up on a blind date with one of his paralegals a couple months ago. Woman by the name of Rhonda. He only did it because she was crazy about him and he wanted to distract her, but it worked. She doesn't call him anymore, and we catch a movie together every once in a while. What about you?''

"My business is my lover."

"Sex life's that good, huh?"

Harley shrugged. "I'm busy. When I get home at night, I'm exhausted, too tired to miss sex or anything else a woman has to offer."

Skepticism etched a disbelieving frown on Tank's face. "No way. I don't believe you've changed *that* much."

Harley couldn't help laughing. Tank was right, up to a point. He missed having a robust sex life, but he craved having someone who was emotionally significant to him far more. The older he got, the more convinced he became that life wasn't just about financial success or physical gratification. But he'd left his heart in Portland with an unborn baby when he moved to California ten years ago, and even though he'd had a few superficial relationships since then, no one had ever been able to fill the void. "Maybe your brother knows another female paralegal he can set me up with," he joked.

"I'll ask him," Tank promised. "Just be forewarned. If he sets you up with anyone like Rhonda, she'll be pudgy, pasty, too bold and emotionally starved."

"God, Tank, I thought you *liked* her!"

"I do. I'm desperate, so the relationship works for me. But that's hardly the kind of woman I see you with." He gave up hanging on the lintel and started down the hall, the floor creaking in protest. "Gotta run. The whole crew'll be waiting for me. Are you comin' back tonight?"

"Yeah. That okay?" Harley called after him.

"Sure. Stay as long as you like." The creaking stopped as Tank paused in the hall. "What are you gonna do before your dinner with Lauren and Brandon? You want to make a few extra bucks and come out on the job with me?''

"No, thanks. I'm going to get my hair cut and buy some new clothes."

"What's wrong with the haircut and clothes you got now?"

"Nothing. I just need to look…I don't know, more fatherly, I guess."

There was a pause and for a moment, Harley thought Tank had disappeared silently into his room. But then he spoke. "Can I give you a piece of advice, Harley?"

Advice? From *Tank?* "Shoot."

"Clothes and hair don't matter to kids, man. Just be yourself."

The floor started creaking again, a door closed and the shower went on.

Harley laced his fingers behind his head and rolled onto his back to stare at the ceiling. *Just be yourself.* Sounded easy. Made sense. But his "self" hadn't been good enough for Audra, and he was afraid he'd run into the same problem again, this time with Brandon. Especially if Quentin Worthington had poisoned his son against him.

He doesn't need you.

"Maybe not," Harley conceded, "but I need him."

CHAPTER FIVE

LAUREN GLANCED nervously at her wristwatch. It was already late afternoon and she still hadn't tried to contact Harley. She should have called him hours ago, first thing in the morning. Instead she'd procrastinated and was continuing to put off the inevitable by playing a game of Hearts with Brandon and his best friend, Scott, both of whom she'd just picked up from Mt. Marley Academy for Boys and Girls.

"What happened today at school, guys?" she asked, tossing a five of clubs on top of Brandon's ace of spades.

"You can't throw that," her nephew protested. "I led with a spade so you have to throw a spade."

"Only if I have one," she told him. "I'm out, so I can play any suit I want, remember?" She raised an eyebrow at him. "You're lucky I didn't give you any point cards. That ace is going to beat anything we throw, which means you're probably going to get stuck with the queen of spades. Unless you're holding it yourself, of course."

Brandon said nothing. He kept his attention on his cards, his brow wrinkling in concentration.

"I asked you two about school," she said as Scott laid down the dreaded queen of spades. She watched her nephew's face for any sign of displeasure that he'd just picked up another thirteen points, but saw none. Was he trying to shoot the moon? Gathering all point cards in the deck—every heart and the queen of spades—at the risk of missing one or more wasn't an easy thing to do, even with a good hand. If he succeeded, however, he'd set her and Scott back twenty-six points and win the game.

"School was okay, I guess," Brandon murmured, finally answering her question, but his eyes were still riveted to the fan of cards in his hand.

"What did you do at recess?" she asked.

Brandon led with the queen of hearts—almost a sure sign that he *was* trying to shoot the moon. But considering what Lauren held in her hand, he didn't have enough high cards to take the rest of the tricks. She considered playing the ace of hearts and letting him learn the hard way, then gave him something smaller to see if he could pull it off without an adult and veteran player working against him.

"Mallory and Sarah chase us every recess," Scott complained. "They won't leave us alone." He tossed Brandon a jack of hearts and a taunting smile. "You just took another heart, Brandon. You're gonna lose big! What do you have so far, twenty points?"

If Brandon had twenty points already, he only needed to collect another six to shoot the moon. Lauren suspected Scott didn't understand the game nearly as well as he said he did. Otherwise he would've realized that throwing such a high heart at this stage wasn't wise. "Those girls have liked you guys all year," she said, keeping the conversation on a neutral topic so she wouldn't give her nephew away.

Brandon chose to play an eight of clubs, which was probably a mistake. Lauren's last card of that suit was the ten, and all the face cards were out. She'd have to take the pile and any hearts Scott tossed into it, which meant Brandon wouldn't be able to capture all the points.

Sure enough, when his friend piled a heart on top of her ten, Brandon groaned. "Oh, man. I was so close. Look at this." He fanned out the cards he'd already taken. "I've got the queen of spades and nine of the thirteen hearts. I was only missing four."

"You did great, babe," Lauren told him. "It's tough to shoot the moon. You have to be holding a lot of good cards and play them just right."

"And if you don't make it, you're in major trouble," Scott pointed out.

Brandon scowled at him. "But if you *do* make it, you're the bomb. I would've won for sure."

"You'll have other chances," Lauren promised.

"Does that mean we can play another game?" he asked.

"Not now. Scott's mother is expecting him at home, you have to do your homework, and I have to start dinner."

"Aw, can't we go out for dinner tonight?"

"No, I've already defrosted a couple of steaks. I thought we could grill them outside on the patio." She'd also made homemade rolls, scalloped potatoes, a candied almond salad and Brandon's favorite dessert—cheesecake. Keeping herself busy with domestic tasks had helped her avoid thinking about Harley Nelson. But the time for his arrival was fast approaching and she couldn't put off dealing with the situation any longer.

"Why don't you go ahead and walk Scott across the street while I start the barbecue?" she said.

Taking her suggestion, Brandon followed his friend to the front of the house. As soon as Lauren heard the door slam, she took Harley's card from her pocket, wiped sweaty palms on her blue jeans and dialed his number.

I'm only doing what's best, she told herself. But if that was true, why did she feel so terrible about it?

Someone answered, but it wasn't Harley. It was a woman.

Lauren drew a bolstering breath. *He's no good. He probably goes from one relationship to another, breaking hearts along the way, and this is just the next person in line.* "Is Harley Nelson there?"

"I'm afraid not, but I'd sure like to reach him. This is Angela at Hudson & Taylor's. He was shopping here earlier. When he paid for his purchases, he left his cell phone on the counter."

Evidently she'd been wrong, in this instance, anyway. But that didn't make her feel any better. She couldn't reach him, and he was supposed to appear at her door in—she cast another nervous glance at her watch—an hour.

"Do you know his home number?" the woman asked.

"I have the number where he's staying," she said, grateful for whatever had prompted Harley to give it to her. "Hang on a second."

Taking the cordless phone, she went to her bedroom and found the slip of paper Harley had handed her just before she left the restaurant. She rattled off the number, then hung up and dialed it herself, far more eager to talk to Harley now that the possibility of being unable to reach him seemed all too likely.

"'Lo?"

"Harley?"

"No, it's Tank. Who's this?"

"Lauren Worthington. I don't know if you remember me, but I used to date your brother Damien."

"'Course I remember you. We went to high school together."

Part of the rowdy crowd, Tank had been popular, but Lauren had never really spoken to him until two years ago, when Damien had taken her to a family birthday party. "I'm looking for Harley Nelson," she said, fidgeting nervously. "It's important that I talk to him. Is he around?"

"Nope. Haven't seen him all day. But if he's late or somethin', don't give up on him. I know he wouldn't miss dinner at your place."

"That's just it," Lauren said. "He's planning to see

Brandon, but I...um...I forgot that Brandon won't be here. He's got..." Her mind raced as she tried to come up with an event important enough to justify canceling, but nothing presented itself. "...something he can't miss," she finished lamely.

Tank hesitated as though trying to decide whether or not to believe her, and she fought the temptation to prop up the lie with more senseless babble.

"That's too bad," he said. "I know Harley will be disappointed."

"Yeah...um...so will Brandon." *Except that he doesn't know what he's missing.* Closing her eyes, Lauren briefly remembered a conversation she'd had with Brandon just a few months ago.

I hope I'll be tall like my dad.

How do you know your dad was tall?

My mom used to talk about him.

What did she say?

That he was the cutest boy in school.

He was certainly handsome. She'd winked at him. *But you're going to be even better-looking.*

He'd smiled, but seemed to sink into a rather somber mood almost immediately after. *Grandfather doesn't think I look anything like my dad.*

Lauren had almost admitted that Quentin Worthington probably didn't see any resemblance between father and son because he didn't want to. But getting caught up in a conversation that would only disparage Harley wouldn't do Brandon any good. Her father had told him enough negative things about Harley already.

Grandfather didn't see as much of Harley as your mother and I did. Maybe he doesn't remember.

That's not it, Brandon had surprised her by saying. *I think he's afraid I'll turn out just like him.*

From the mouths of babes....

"I'll give him the message you called," Tank said.

Lauren massaged her temple. "Okay. And let him know he left his cell phone at Hudson & Taylor's, will you? A woman by the name of Angela has it."

"I'll tell him."

"Great. Thanks."

"Lauren?"

"Yeah?"

"Harley's…well, he's—ah, shit, never mind. It's none of my business. I'll let you go."

"What?" she prompted. Had Harley said something about her? About Brandon? About his plans?

Tank seemed to struggle with the words. "If it doesn't work out for Harley to see Brandon tonight, I hope you'll consider letting him come over another time. He's pretty excited about meeting his boy."

This, Lauren didn't want to hear. She couldn't think of Harley's feelings. She already had her own heart and her parents and Brandon to consider. Even Audra's memory seemed to be pulling at her. Lauren just couldn't tell which direction her sister would want her to go. After her relationship with Harley, Audra had grown very bitter and blamed their father for most of her mistakes. If she were alive, would she be in Harley's camp? If so, why hadn't she ever contacted him?

Ignoring the melancholy that threatened whenever she thought of Audra, Lauren said, "I'll keep that in mind," but she warned herself to forget about it instead.

"Who was that?" Brandon asked, toting his backpack into the kitchen as she hung up the phone.

Lauren whirled at the sound of his voice. She'd been so wrapped up in her conversation with Tank that she hadn't heard him come in. "No one you know, sweetie."

"Did Grandma and Grandpa call today?"

"I talked to them this morning."

"When are they coming home?"

"Not until the middle of June, remember?"

"Oh, yeah." Delving into his backpack, Brandon began to spread his books on the table. "I have tons of homework," he complained. "I don't know why Mrs. Cooper had to give us so much today. Fourth grade isn't supposed to be so hard."

"It's good for you," Lauren replied automatically. Brandon was enrolled in one of the best private schools in the state and usually had quite a bit of homework. But Lauren's thoughts weren't on his education. She was wondering what she'd do if Harley didn't go back to Tank's—if he didn't get her message. She certainly couldn't stay here and hope to turn him away at the door.

"Come on," she said suddenly. "Pack your stuff and bring it with you. We're going to Kimberly's."

"What?" Brandon paused in mid-motion. "I thought you were making dinner."

"We'll take it with us and finish it there."

He gave her a mystified look. "You're acting weird, Aunt Lauren, you know that?"

"Just because I want to go to Kimberly's? We go there all the time."

"But we don't carry our dinner over there."

"It'll be fun." Hopping off the stool at the desk, she hurried to the large walk-in pantry to get the picnic basket.

"Do I have to spend the night again?" he asked.

"Don't you like staying with Kimberly?" She found the picnic basket easily enough and hauled it out to the kitchen, where she started gathering their meal so they could leave as soon as possible.

"I guess," he said. "But I'd rather stay home. It's a school night, remember?"

"Isn't that my line?" She forced a smile, hoping he'd cooperate without her having to push. She hated to make him go to Kimberly's if he didn't want to, but he had to go *somewhere,* and Kimberly's place was safe. "We can make an exception every once in a while, you know," she added, getting the salad from the refrigerator.

Instead of packing up, he sank into his seat and started flipping his pencil against the table. *Tap, tap, tap, tap...*

"Then can I go to Scott's instead?"

"Not tonight."

Tap, tap, tap... "Why?"

"Because Kimberly's dog really likes it when you come to visit," she said, searching for the plastic lid that would seal the bowl containing the steaks and marinade.

"I have to go to Kimberly's because her dog likes me?" he asked with a grimace. *Tap, tap, tap, tap, tap...*

Too nervous to tolerate the noise, Lauren wanted to grab the pencil out of Brandon's hand. They needed to get out of the house quickly. What if Harley arrived early?

"Just get moving, okay?" she said, keeping her voice calm only with great effort. Brandon had some legitimate points—she *was* acting strange, spending the night on a weekday *did* break house rules, and they didn't generally pack up their dinner at the last minute and flee from home. But she couldn't explain her reasons, and she didn't have time to argue with him. She was the adult. He was the child. She needed him to obey, and fast.

Finding the lid, she covered the bowl and forced it inside the already crowded basket, then turned her attention to wrapping the rolls in plastic.

Tap...tap...tap... "But I don't see why Scott's house isn't just as good," he persisted, slouching lower in his seat. "I mean, it's across the street. You wouldn't even have to come get me for school."

"Just get your things, dammit!" she snapped.

The tapping stopped, and he jumped to his feet and began to fill his backpack, but she could tell from the expression on his face that he was surprised—and probably a little hurt. "What did I do?" he asked. "Why are you mad at me?"

Lauren gave up trying to close the overloaded basket. He didn't know she was only trying to do what was best for him, that she was worried and on edge. He was just being a kid. "I'm sorry, Brandon," she said, crossing the room and hugging him. "I'm just a little uptight right now and I need you to cooperate with me. Okay, honey?"

The confusion on his face didn't clear completely, but he nodded. "Okay."

"Everything will be fine," she promised, resting her chin on the top of his head. "I just...I just need you to stay with Kimberly for a few days while I take care of some things. Then our lives will be normal again." *God willing.*

"I miss Grandma and Grandpa," he said.

"They'll be home before you know it." She kissed his cheek and started to pull away, then stopped when he said something so softly she missed it.

"What, honey?"

"I said my mom won't. She's never coming home again."

It was almost the first time he'd mentioned his mother since the day she died. Lauren had tried to get him to open up and let the pain out, but he wouldn't. He'd stood dry-faced and resolute throughout the viewing and funeral, ignored anyone who wanted to remember her or sympathize, and had kept up that indifferent facade ever since. Still, Lauren knew that despite Audra's faults and shortcomings, Brandon had loved her with the kind of unconditional emotion so natural to children.

"It's not easy when someone you care about dies," she said.

"I *don't* care about her," he insisted, but there was a tremble to his lip that belied the harshness of his words. "She never wanted to be with me, anyway."

The knots of anxiety in Lauren's stomach grew painful. They had to go before Harley arrived. But this was the first chance she'd had to reach Brandon, to soothe him where his mother was concerned. If she brushed the opportunity away and hurried off, she was afraid he'd retreat behind the wall he'd built and never come out again.

"It's okay to be angry, Brandon," she said. "Your mother wasn't perfect. She made many mistakes. But I know she loved you."

"If she loved me, she wouldn't have done what she did."

"Look at me." Lauren tried to raise his chin so she could see his eyes, but he wouldn't allow it. He was staring at the hardwood floor, blinking swiftly to hold back tears—tears Lauren wished he'd let fall. *Go ahead, Brandon. Let the poison out so you can heal.*

"Your mother was just confused," she said.

"She didn't want me. She never did anything with me."

Lauren pulled him closer so he wouldn't have to worry about her seeing the tears swimming in his eyes, and rubbed a hand up and down his spine. "That's not completely true. I remember you going in to lie down with her at night sometimes. The two of you would talk about all kinds of things."

"That was only when she came out of rehab and was clean for a while. And it never lasted long."

Rehab. Clean. Most nine-year-olds didn't even know those terms—and Brandon was using them to describe his mother. It always saddened Lauren to hear him.

"I know," she admitted. There wasn't any point in trying to deny the fact that his mother had let him down. It would only make him feel guilty for what he was feeling when he had every right to be disappointed. He'd been cheated, and Audra's death was probably her ultimate betrayal.

"I can't explain why your mother did what she did," she said. "I know she was basically a good person, Brandon. She was just so unhappy. She couldn't find her way out of it, and nothing we did seemed to help. Maybe if I'd had more patience with her or tried harder to reach her as a friend...I don't know.''

"What happened to my mom isn't your fault," he said. "It's my dad's fault."

Lauren knew Brandon was only repeating what he'd picked up from his grandfather. But for the first time she considered what it meant to let Brandon believe what he did. Perhaps if she hadn't seen Harley again, if he'd remained nothing more than a memory, she might have let the statement pass. Heaven knew she'd spent the last ten years more or less believing the same thing. But now Harley was a real person, a flesh-and-blood man, and he seemed a lot less like the bad guy her father's words and her own imagination had painted him.

"No one is completely responsible for the decisions and actions of another, Brandon. We all meet people who influence us, but the decisions we make are our own. If we mess up our lives, it's our fault, no one else's.''

"But Grandpa said my dad broke my mother's heart."

"I'm not sure about that," she murmured, and then, even though family loyalty warred with what she now considered the underlying truth, she added, "Grandfather blames Harley because it's easier to blame him than your mother. He loves your mom; he doesn't love Harley. But your mother could have chosen a different path than the one she took. She had a lot more going for her than Harley did. She had a family who loved her. She had plenty of food, clothing and other necessities. She had the best counseling money could buy. I'm sure I could've done more to help her, but Grandpa tried everything. She just wouldn't grab on to the hands reaching out to her.''

"But Grandpa says my dad was no good, that things would be different if he hadn't—''

"Your father was very young when he made the

choices he did,'' Lauren interrupted, hearing a clock ticking somewhere inside her head. The steady rhythm seemed to vibrate through her, making her fingers and toes tingle, making her sweat. *Forty minutes until Harley was due to arrive. Forty minutes and counting…*

"He was eighteen, only nine years older than you,'' she went on. "And we don't really know what happened between him and your mom, so it's not fair for us to make such judgments, you know?'' She hesitated, wondering whether or not to delve deeper into the subject or start backing away. They had to leave, but the longer they talked, the more Lauren was tempted to tell Brandon that Harley was in town. Part of her believed that Harley would be good for his son. If he was consistent enough to give him the love and support he needed. If he'd share nicely and not try to pry him away from all he'd ever known. If her father and Harley could ever get along…

If, if, if. If only for a crystal ball.

"So you liked him, then?'' Brandon said, a trace of hope in his voice.

Lauren had admired Harley from afar—his looks, his confidence, his whole aura. But she hadn't been impressed with his actions. He'd partied too much. Skipped school. Left her sister pregnant. Regardless of the extenuating circumstances, those things were still true. And he wasn't exactly what she'd consider a high-achiever. "He's not— he *wasn't* so bad,'' she admitted, correcting her tense before Brandon could pick up on it. "Tell me something. Would you like to meet him? I mean, if it was possible?''

"Would I like to meet my own father? Of *course* I would. Do you think that could ever happen?''

She gazed down at Brandon's sweet, earnest face and almost blurted out the truth. But something made her hold her tongue. Probably the memory of her telephone conversation with Quentin. She couldn't hurt her father by rebelling the way Audra had once done. Twenty-seven years of love and mutual respect had established too strong a bond between them.

But even a bond like that couldn't stop Lauren from weighing the positives and the negatives. What did *she* feel was best? Did she believe Harley had a right to meet his son? If so, did she have enough faith in her own opinion to see it through?

"Maybe someday," she said. "Maybe someday soon."

CHAPTER SIX

HARLEY WASN'T USED TO dressing up. The people who bought his motorcycles viewed anyone wearing a suit and tie with a certain amount of distrust, which gave him the perfect excuse to embrace a more casual wardrobe. Once he'd put on the suit he was now wearing and stepped out of the dressing room, however, the sales consultant at Hudson & Taylor's had gushed over him and insisted he looked like a million bucks. But that was almost how much the damned thing cost, and she probably got a commission.

Taking a deep breath—or as deep as he could manage considering the unfamiliar restraint of his tie—he gave himself one last cursory glance in the rearview mirror of the car he'd rented today. His haircut was definitely on the short side. Taken together with the white shirt and conservative tie beneath his freshly shaved chin, he almost didn't recognize the man gazing dubiously back at him. At least he looked like someone a kid could be proud of, and that was definitely the goal. Brandon had been raised with the rich. Harley thought it best to blend in.

The car door creaked as he opened it. He set down one foot, clad in an Italian leather loafer—that pair of shoes had cost almost as much as the suit—then paused to gather his nerve. After ten years, he was going to see his son, talk to him, maybe laugh with him…even hug him. Harley could easily imagine clutching Brandon's small body to his chest. Closing his eyes, he could almost smell the faint scent of children's shampoo, could feel the dewy softness of a young cheek pressed to his neck. It made him hunger for those sensations like nothing he'd ever craved before. How could he love so much someone he'd never even met?

Swallowing the lump that had risen in his throat, Harley shifted so he could lean his head back on the seat and tried to blank his mind. He couldn't go into the Worthington home like this. He was too emotional. Dads didn't cry—especially dads who were still strangers. His son would label him a nerd for sure.

It took a few minutes, but thoughts of his court date and work and all the things he had to do when he returned home finally put him back in control. The tightness in his throat eased and he turned to retrieve the presents he'd stacked in the backseat—a huge stuffed snake for Brandon and flowers, a bottle of wine and a box of chocolates for Lauren—and got out of the car. He hadn't planned to buy Lauren anything, but once he'd started shopping, he couldn't stop thinking about her and how happy he was that she'd agreed to have him over tonight. His gratitude had translated into a preoccupation with her that had led him to find several items he wanted to buy—a blouse the color of her eyes, a bottle of perfume that smelled like heaven, a pair of gold earrings—all of which he'd ultimately put back. As modest as those gifts were, he was afraid she'd interpret them as a bribe instead of a token of gratitude. And he didn't think she'd prize anything from him, anyway, which was why he'd opted for the more traditional offerings of a dinner guest. She couldn't read anything negative into a bottle of wine.

The sun was just starting to set behind the Worthingtons' expansive house, and everything was quiet. Harley thought he might see Brandon playing outside, riding a skateboard or bicycling, but the only people about were a crew of gardeners, busy loading up their equipment down the street.

What a life. He shook his head, gazing at the neatly pruned bushes, the meticulously painted trellis over the gate to the backyard, and the abundance of decorative, aggregate walkways. Brandon's situation sure was different from what *he'd* experienced growing up. Harley's childhood had been filled with mud that oozed between his toes, frogs he caught in the mosquito-infested creek beyond the empty field next to his house and a second-hand, three-speed bike his mother had rescued from the dump, on which he'd had to make all his own repairs. He always had grease under his nails and on his well-worn jeans but, overall, he'd been happy in his younger years. He might not have been well-chaperoned or well-kept— his mother had been tired and old before her time and rarely left her spot in front of the television once she got home from work. But he'd always had a lot of friends. He'd played until dark every night, eaten dinner with whoever would invite him in, and generally run wild.

Those were the good times, he thought, smiling nostalgically as he made his way up the walk. Even his mother had had her better moments back then. She'd baked him birthday cakes, let him tear motorcycles apart and rebuild them in the carport. When he was a little older, she'd put up with a hell of a lot of loud music and loud cars. It wasn't until Phil came on the scene that things went downhill. And then they'd gone downhill pretty fast....

The memories faded along with his smile as Harley faced the front door. Stretching his neck, he adjusted his tie because it suddenly seemed too tight and hoped he wasn't sweating through his undershirt. He felt awkward and nervous, but if he wanted a relationship with Brandon, he had to start somewhere.

Now was the time. He was already ten years late.

Shoving the gifts under his left arm, he knocked and waited. Any moment the door would swing open and he'd see Lauren standing there. Serious, responsible Lauren. Elegant, intelligent Lauren. The ugly duckling who'd turned into a swan...

I think she's a knockout. When Tank had said those words, Harley hadn't agreed because he hadn't wanted to see what his friend saw. But after the hours he'd spent with Lauren last night, listening to her talk, watching the expressions on her face, he had to admit there was something special about her. Tank was right. She was attractive, of course. But there was more to Lauren Worthington, some quality Audra had never possessed....

"Where are they?" he muttered when no one came to the door. Adjusting his tie again, he knocked a second time, then checked his watch and tried to peer in through the living room window. He was right on time....

The tip of a white envelope tucked under the welcome mat finally caught his eye. Piling his gifts on the bench by the front door, he bent to retrieve it and found his name on the outside, written in a woman's flowing script.

He stared at the envelope for several long moments before daring to open it. Then he jammed a hand through what was left of his hair and broke the seal, wishing he didn't feel so damn vulnerable to what he might find inside.

Harley—
I feel so bad. I'm sorry to stand you up. I tried to reach you earlier, but couldn't. After spending the last twenty-four hours trying to decide what's best for Brandon, I'm convinced that disrupting his life right now wouldn't be a good thing. Please try to understand and help me do what's best for him. Go back to California and live your own life.

                                        Lauren

Son of a bitch…no Brandon. Harley winced as the disappointment hit. He should've known better than to get his hopes up. Lauren might have seemed different last night, but she was still a Worthington at heart, a chip off the old block.

He kicked the snake and toppled it on its side, shoved the candy and flowers out of the way and slumped onto the bench. "What's best for Brandon or what's best for you, Lauren?" he muttered. Wadding her note into a ball, he threw it at the prone snake, then propped his chin in one palm. Lauren seemed to think she could decide Brandon's future on her own. Her letter basically reiterated what she'd said at the door when he first arrived, the same thing Quentin Worthington had told him before he ever left—that Brandon was better off without a guy like him for a dad. On some level, Harley probably believed it, or he wouldn't have stayed away so long. But the yearning to know his son hadn't decreased over the past ten years. It was always there, underlying every thought, every emotion, every hope for the future, and he doubted that would change. He had a responsibility to his son and to himself, and if he was ever going to deliver, this was the time to make it happen.

Loosening his tie, he yanked it off, removed his jacket and rolled up his sleeves. The day was unseasonably warm, far too warm to be wearing a suit, but Harley wasn't going back to the apartment to change. Once he'd parked his car further from the house, he wasn't going anywhere. Lauren and Brandon had to come home some time, and when they did, he'd be waiting.

IT WAS NEARLY MIDNIGHT and a little chilly by the time Lauren pulled into her driveway. She'd spent the entire evening at Kimberly's, trying to keep smiling and acting normal for Brandon's sake, but she'd been miserable and was now eager for bed. She wanted to close her eyes and shut out the emotional turmoil of the last few days so she could get some much-needed rest. She also wanted to believe she'd done the right thing.

If only she could stop picturing Harley coming to the door to find no one home. If only she hadn't been such a coward and had tried to reach him first thing in the morning. If only he hadn't left his cell phone at the department store...

Don't worry about it. It's history now, she told herself. Harley's feelings and desires should have no bearing on her decision, anyway. She hadn't been involved in what happened ten years ago, and she hadn't asked him to drop into their lives again now. Looking out for Brandon was her only concern.

On that thought, she cut the engine and left her Lexus in the drive instead of parking it in the garage. She wanted to go in through the front to make sure Harley had found her note—and to see if he'd left her any kind of response.

The chirping of cicadas rose like a chorus around her as she stepped out of the car, and she could smell fresh-cut grass and the gardenias blooming alongside the house. Above, a blue velvet sky sported a round full moon that looked close enough to touch. What a beautiful night. So peaceful, so perfect. She should be coming home knowing that Brandon was safe in his bed, that her parents were having a wonderful time in Europe, and that she had nothing bigger to worry about than the fund-raising event she'd promised to chair in two weeks for the local women's shelter. Instead, her nephew was spending the night somewhere he didn't really want to be, and she couldn't think about anything besides Harley, Audra and her father and how unfair it was that she was caught— again—in a mess she'd done nothing to create. Her sister had always managed to find trouble, her father had always tried to save Audra from herself, and Lauren had always worked to minimize the damage caused by her sister's poor choices. Only she'd assumed, with Audra's death, that would all change.

Her heels clicked on the sidewalk as she approached the house, sounding loud and hollow. The lights in the yard were on a timer. They automatically came on at eight o'clock every evening, so it wasn't completely dark, but the front of the house was heavily shadowed until she drew close and a sensor detected her movement. Then the porch light came on and she nearly screamed. Someone was sprawled on the iron bench near the door!

"Where's Brandon?" It was Harley. Although his coat and tie had been discarded, he was wearing a suit, and he'd cut his hair so short Lauren probably wouldn't have recognized him if not for his voice. He looked...he looked like a businessman, a *successful* businessman, not a biker.

Evidently he'd taken their appointment tonight very seriously. And he'd decided to leave her more than a written response. "You scared me," she said, pressing a hand to her chest as if that would calm her fluttering heart. "What are you doing here?"

"You invited me to dinner, remember?"

A giant stuffed snake stared helplessly at her from where it lay, forked tongue dangling out of its mouth in a forever hiss. A bouquet of wild flowers had been tossed carelessly on the ground next to it, along with an almost empty box of chocolates, and Harley was holding an open bottle of wine. That he'd cleaned up so meticulously and come bearing gifts certainly didn't make her feel any better. Neither did the fact that he'd obviously had nothing besides a pound of chocolate for supper.

Why did she have to deal with this? He'd lived ten years without Brandon. Couldn't he just go away and leave her alone? "That was six hours ago," she said. "Didn't you find my note?"

He set the bottle on the ground but didn't sit up or stand as she expected. Folding his arms across his chest, he nodded toward a crumpled piece of paper lying off in the bushes. "You mean that?"

Lauren automatically moved to pick it up. "I tried to reach you by telephone earlier—"

"That's what it says, but I had my cell phone with me most of the day. You couldn't have tried very hard."

She'd just waited too long. But she couldn't admit that. It hinted too strongly at her conflicting emotions. "I'm sorry. I didn't mean for this to happen," she said. "I just...well, it took me a while to come to a...a firm decision."

"A firm decision." He tilted his head back and gazed down his nose at her and she couldn't help but appreciate how even and dark his skin looked against the crisp white of his shirt. "I think we're going to have to do something about that, Lauren, because I've come to a firm decision, too."

Oh, no. Here it is. "Let's not let things get out of control, Harley," she said quickly. "We have to think about Brandon."

"Problem is I don't think you're worried about Brandon. Not really. I think you're worried about yourself."

"That's nonsense!"

"Is it? You live in your ivory tower, untouchable by regular people, and spend your time doing...what? What does a woman like you do? Play tennis at the club? I think looking after Brandon helps you believe you have a life and you're afraid to lose that."

She had a life! What about the many hours she worked for her father? What about the volunteer service she rendered the community? Hours and hours had gone into planning the Independence Day parade, the walk-a-thon she'd sponsored to raise funds for breast cancer research, and her campaign to have a traffic signal put in at Oakmont and Pedler. She might still live with her parents at twenty-seven, have no love life, and dote on a boy who wasn't her own. But she spent her time in worthwhile endeavors.

"How dare you judge me like that!" she said.

Finally he stood and she could tell by the hard planes of his face and the flash in his green eyes that he was angry, far angrier than she'd first thought. "Are you joking? You and your family have made a national pastime out of judging me. You don't really know me—don't *want* to know me—yet I always come up short. According to the perfect Lauren Worthington I'm not good enough to be Brandon's father and play a part in his life. Well, who the hell gave *you* the right to make that call?"

He was pointing a finger at her, nearly jabbing it into her breastbone, but Lauren didn't back away. Brandon was Audra's son, too. And since Audra was gone, she was responsible for him. That meant she had to make some tough choices, and what she did about Harley was one of them.

If only what had once been clear-cut wasn't becoming so hopelessly muddled.

"We love Brandon, Harley. My parents and I are just doing our best to take care of him."

"And you're looking out for yourselves along the way. Well, enjoy it while you can because whether you believe it or not, I love Brandon, too. And I'm going to take him away from you if it's the last thing I do."

The resolution in Harley's voice terrified Lauren. She hated contention. She didn't want to fight, didn't want this to ruin everyone's lives. "If you really love him that's the one thing you *won't* do."

He stared down at her, tall, dark, intimidating. "You're giving me no choice," he said, then he grabbed his jacket, turned on his heel and stalked away.

What now? Lauren thought, watching Harley until he disappeared into the darkness. She had the sinking feeling she'd just awakened a sleeping giant. She should probably go in and call her father right away. But for some reason, she didn't want to talk to Quentin. Maybe it was because she'd bungled everything so badly and felt as though Harley's reaction was largely her fault. Or maybe it was because she knew reporting what he'd just said would be like touching a match to kerosene. Her father would cut short his trip and come charging to the rescue, and that could very easily make Harley more determined to fight.

With a heavy sigh, she let herself into the cool dark house, wishing for the good old days of just last week. Harley had said she didn't have a life, but he didn't know what he was talking about. Until he'd arrived on the scene, she'd been perfectly happy. She had her family or what was left of it, Kimberly, other friends. And she kept herself busy with work at home and at the office. Besides the usual day-to-day stuff, she organized charity events— no one could run a fund-raiser like she could. What was missing? Nothing. She was fine. Harley was the one who needed to grow up and get a real job.

Haven't you ever been in love? he'd asked, as if he knew so much about it. She didn't see a wife tagging along behind *him*. And she'd bet her last dollar he didn't have any other children—at least legitimate ones.

"You're no expert on love," she said aloud as she made her way through the empty house. "I don't need to listen to you." But she was upset and confused and wanted to listen to somebody. Or maybe she wanted someone to listen to her.

Slumping into the chair at the kitchen desk, she drummed her fingers on the oak top and stared at the phone. She probably had a custody suit on her hands, which wouldn't be very pleasant for anybody. But she'd win. Of course she'd win. She had a ten-year track record of providing her nephew with good care and a stable environment. And if the judge left the decision up to Brandon, he'd refuse to leave her. He'd tell everyone he was happy right where he was.

Wouldn't he?

CHAPTER SEVEN

"AREN'T YOU COMING to get Brandon?"

Lauren yawned and tried to scrub away the imprint of her arms on her cheek. She'd fallen asleep slumped over the kitchen desk and hadn't stirred until the phone wakened her just moments earlier. "Kimberly?"

"Yeah. Didn't your alarm go off?"

"I never made it to bed last night. What time is it?"

"Nearly eight."

Eight! Brandon had to be at school in twenty minutes. "Oh, dear. Brandon's going to be late. I'll grab my keys and be right over."

"You okay?"

Lauren wasn't sure. "I think so."

"Why don't you let me worry about getting Brandon to school this morning?"

"Don't you have any job interviews?"

"Not today. And Brandon's got his toothbrush, so that's not an issue."

"What about his clothes and backpack?"

"We'll swing by the house. Be right there."

"Sorry for the extra trouble, Kim."

"Don't be. I've got it handled."

She hung up and Lauren yawned once more, then sank back onto her arms. She wasn't ready to wake up because once she did, she'd have to face the day.

The phone rang again, and she eyed it dubiously. Probably her parents, wondering how things were going. She reached out to answer, then caught herself. She wasn't ready to talk to her father. She didn't know what to say. She knew he'd gladly give Harley the fight he was looking for, but she didn't want Brandon in the middle of a tug-of-war.

The ringing continued until the answering machine picked up. Lauren adjusted the volume so she could hear if the caller left a message.

"Lauren, this is Damien. My brother said Brandon's dad is in town, which has me a little worried. I know how you feel about Brandon and what your father thinks of Harley. And with you being there alone and everything, I just thought I'd call and see how you're getting on…."

He paused, and Lauren fought the urge to pick up the phone. She liked Damien a great deal, had once hoped to fall in love with him, but for whatever reason, her heart had refused to cooperate. She'd broken it off, and he'd finally stopped calling her. It probably wouldn't be wise to renew contact with him, but she was so lonely and confused. And he sort of knew Harley through Tank. Maybe he and his brother could convince Harley to back off.

"Call me when you get this mess—"

She grabbed the telephone before he could hang up. "Damien?"

"Lauren? You're home?"

"I am. Sorry about the delay. I wasn't quite awake."

"Doesn't school start soon?" he asked.

"Kimberly's driving Brandon for me today."

"Why, is something wrong?"

"I didn't get much sleep. Harley Nelson's pressing me to see Brandon, and I'm not sure what to do about it."

"Your father would have a coronary if you so much as let Harley in the door."

"I know, but my father's still in Europe, and Harley's

going to sue for custody if we don't come to some understanding.''

"Let him sue, Lauren. I'm a personal injury attorney; I don't know much about family law. But he abandoned Audra when she was pregnant with Brandon and has never paid a dime of child support. I don't think the courts will be very sympathetic to him."

Lauren moved her hands away from her mouth so she wouldn't be tempted to bite her nails. "I'm not so sure. Aren't judges notorious for favoring a child's birth parents?"

"That's in adoption cases."

"Exactly my point. I'm merely Brandon's guardian."

"I know, but I don't think you have to worry about that. I'm more worried about Harley taking matters into his own hands."

"What does that mean? You can't mean he'll try to *kidnap* Brandon?"

"Who can say? My brother doesn't think he'd go that far, but—"

"But this is the brother who ate thirty pieces of pie at a pep rally in high school, then threw up all over Kimberly, right?"

Damien sounded embarrassed when he answered. "That's Tank. But your father won't let anything happen to Brandon."

Quentin was halfway across the world. How could he stop Harley from snatching Brandon? How could he stop him from suing for custody? "Even if he was home, I don't see that my father has any more options than I do."

"Don't kid yourself, babe. He has options."

Lauren felt a headache coming on. Too many sleepless nights and worry-filled days. "If he has so many options, what are they?"

"He'd handle it like he did ten years ago."

"He'd threaten him with bodily injury? Have you seen Harley these days?"

Damien made a noise that sounded like a snort. "Your father wouldn't fight him, Lauren. He'd buy him off."

Buy him off? Lauren sat up tall, stunned because it was the first time she'd actually considered that Harley might be after something other than Brandon. He hadn't seemed insincere about wanting to meet his son. But he'd taken money from her father years ago. Maybe he was back for more.

"Just think about it," Damien was saying. "A few thousand dollars and the problem goes away."

"But Harley said he loves Brandon."

"If he loved him, he would've come around long before now, right? Cash is king with guys like him."

Lauren pictured Harley in his leather jacket, sitting astride his motorcycle, and remembered the neighborhood where he used to live. "He *could* probably use the money. I doubt he makes a very good living."

"What does he do?"

"He sells motorcycles."

Damien chuckled. "Just what I would've expected. Now I *know* he's after money."

Lauren played with the phone cord, relieved to have found a possible solution to her dilemma but sick at the same time—sick that Harley would use his own son for financial gain. Somehow, something in his eyes had made her believe he was sincere…. "How much should I offer him?"

"I don't know. Just remember that he'll probably take you for as much as he can get, so start low."

"Ten thousand?"

"Do you have that much on hand?" he asked.

"I can get it."

"Then start with five."

"Okay."

A pause. "Are you nervous about meeting with him? Do you want me to be there?"

Lauren was tempted to say yes but stopped herself. This was Damien, the Damien she'd broken up with several months earlier because she couldn't love him, the Damien who wouldn't give up. It wasn't fair to accept help from him now, not when it would only raise his hopes again.

"That's okay," she said as the door burst open and Brandon came charging into the house.

"Hi, Aunt Lauren!" he called.

Lauren smiled and waved as he jogged through the kitchen on the way to his room. Kimberly appeared a moment later wearing a tennis skirt, her face devoid of makeup, her streaked hair pulled into a ponytail beneath a navy visor. She selected a banana from the bowl on the table, then looked Lauren up and down. "Hey, weren't you wearing that last night?"

"Listen, I have to go, Damien," Lauren said, "but I really appreciate the call. I-I hadn't thought of things in quite this way."

"Glad I could help." He hesitated. "It's great to hear from you, you know. I really miss you."

She didn't want to hear the sentimental note in his voice, wasn't about to let him turn the conversation to anything personal. Not this morning. "Um, thanks," she said lamely. "I appreciate your...friendship."

"Friendship?" he echoed.

"Damien, I—"

"Forget it. I know."

She could tell he wasn't happy, but Lauren couldn't do anything to change the way she felt. Lord knows she'd already tried. "I'm sorry. I wish things could be different."

"Sure you do," he said, then the phone clicked and he was gone.

"What's up with you and Damien?" Kimberly demanded as soon as Lauren had hung up. "You told me you two were over for good."

Lauren sighed. "We were. I mean we *are*. He just called because—" she craned her neck to see down the hall that led to Brandon's room "—he heard You-Know-Who was in town."

"He did? How?"

She lowered her voice. "Because Harley's staying with his younger brother."

"Tank?"

"Yeah. They used to hang out together, remember?"

"How could I ever forget? We were ogling Harley when Tank threw up all over me on the way out of that assembly in high school."

Lauren grimaced. "Not a pleasant association."

"Definitely not." She opened the trash compactor and tossed the banana peel inside. "So?"

"So what?"

"Aren't you going to tell me what Damien had to say?"

Lauren checked for Brandon again, but found the hall empty. If he didn't hurry, he'd be late for sure, but she had bigger concerns this morning. "He said Harley's probably after money. He said I should buy him off like my father did ten years ago."

Kimberly's brows arched above her hazel eyes. "Has Harley asked for money?"

"Shhh," Lauren whispered. "Brandon will hear you."

"Well, has he?"

"No, but that doesn't mean he wouldn't accept it."

Kimberly crossed her arms and leaned against the counter. "Is that what your father thinks, too?"

"I don't know," Lauren said, shrugging off the question. "I haven't talked to him."

"Why not? Can't you reach him?"

"I haven't tried yet. I—"

"I'm ready, Aunt Kim," Brandon said, returning to the kitchen. "Oh, boy," he said, frowning at the clock. "We have to go."

"Did you get breakfast?" Lauren asked him.

"What, you think I'd send him to school hungry?" Kimberly said.

"Just checking." Lauren gave Brandon a hug and a kiss. "Have a great day, sweetheart. I'll see you when I pick you up this afternoon."

"Okay."

"Maybe we can play another game of Hearts."

"Cool." He hitched his backpack over his shoulder and started out. Kimberly followed a few steps behind but threw Lauren one last glance before disappearing into the living room.

"How much are you going to offer him?" she asked.

"As much as it takes, so long as I've got it," Lauren said.

"Well…" Kimberly gazed distractedly after Brandon. "Don't do anything till I get back."

"So what's the plan?" Kimberly asked as soon as she returned from taking Brandon to school.

Lauren sat at the kitchen table next to her friend, drinking the iced cappuccino Kimberly had brought her. The sun streamed in through the French doors that lined the back of the house, and the fresh flowers that normally graced the table were pushed off to the side. "I don't really have one yet," she said, speaking loudly enough to be heard over the vacuum. The maid service had arrived only minutes earlier, and a tall, lean woman was cleaning the bedrooms. "I went through my checkbook and savings account statements while you were gone, trying to figure out how much money I can lay my hands on right away."

"And?" The diamond tennis bracelet on Kimberly's

wrist slid partway up her arm as she took a sip of her own cappuccino. "What's the grand total?"

"Fifteen thousand seven hundred eighty-nine dollars." Lauren circled the figure beneath the column of numbers she'd added together on the pad she normally kept by the phone. "That is, if I don't break the Certificate of Deposit Nana gave me when I graduated from college."

"Fifteen thousand, huh?" Kimberly twirled her bracelet with two perfectly sculpted nails. "That doesn't sound like much, kiddo. You could get a lot more if you called your father. I'm sure he's got plenty stashed away."

"I doubt much of it's liquid. He keeps his money pretty tied up in investments. Besides, Harley's never had much. I think fifteen thousand will sound like a fortune to him."

"Does that mean you're not going to call your father about this?"

Lauren frowned as she pictured speaking with Quentin. Couldn't she wait until she'd cleaned up this mess she'd made? It would be so much more pleasant to tell him with a smile in her voice that he didn't need to worry any longer: Brandon was safe, they were all safe, she'd taken care of everything.

"What more can my father do than I'm already doing?" she asked.

Kimberly adjusted her visor. "It just seems like he'd want to be involved. What if your plan backfires?"

"It can't backfire," Lauren argued. "We offer Harley money, he rejects the offer, we sweeten the pot. It's that simple. Pretty soon, we'll reach a number he can't refuse."

"I don't think I'd accept any amount of money, not if it meant giving up my child."

"He's not you. He's always been dirt poor. And he's not 'giving up' Brandon. He did that a long time ago. This is just—" she shrugged "—insurance that he'll stay out of the way until Brandon grows to adulthood."

"Okay," Kimberly said, but she didn't sound very convinced.

"The problem is how to approach him," Lauren went on. "Should I call him and arrange a meeting? Or show up at Tank's apartment and hope to catch him off guard?"

Leaning back, Kimberly crossed her feet at the ankles and toyed with the white pleats on her skirt. "It would help if we knew him better," she mused. "Do you think Damien could tell you more about what he's like?"

Lauren propped her elbows on the table. "Damien doesn't really know him. He was out of high school by the time Harley was a freshman."

"Jeez, I didn't realize Damien's so old."

"He's eight years older than we are."

"Okay, so what about Tank? Do you think we can enlist his help?"

"Are you kidding? Harley's his friend."

"Wait, I got it." Clapping her hands, Kimberly shot out of her chair and did a palms up "ta-da." "We spy on him!"

"What?" Lauren cried. "No way!"

"Don't say *no* yet. I've seen it done in lots of TV shows. We simply get a pair of binoculars and stake out Tank's place. We watch what Harley does, get a feel for what he's like, and let that help us with our decisions. If he's drinking heavily or doing drugs or entertaining one woman after another, we can feel justified in buying him off, fighting him to the death, whatever. Because then we'll know his true nature, right?"

Lauren definitely saw the benefit of obtaining more information about Harley, but *spying?* "And if he's not doing any of those things? I've got to fight him anyway."

"Who says?" she demanded.

Lauren's father said. And she had to listen to him. It was her place in life to be the *good* daughter, the one who always tried to maintain peace in the family. She'd heard it as a constant litany the whole time she and Audra were growing up: *That lazy Audra, if only she was more like you, Lauren…If only she had her head on straight like you…Lauren knows what life's all about, don't you, my girl?…Lauren would never be so stupid…*

"*I* say," she lied. "We have to fight him because it's best for Brandon."

Kimberly frowned. "Then go to court if that's what you believe is best. But I think you're crazy to go into anything blind. You've got to know what you're dealing with, and if you see Harley in action again you might actually feel good about what you have to do."

There was nothing to lose. Harley was far from being a saint. Lauren knew he wouldn't be a good influence on Brandon, and confirming that could only help. "A man dressed in leather and riding a Harley is seldom a paragon of virtue," she said to battle the voice inside that whispered *Anyone can change…*

"Exactly! So come on." Kimberly scooped her keys off the counter and charged for the door. "We've got to buy a pair of binoculars and a plain-looking sedan and get set up before he starts moving around for the day."

"We're going to *buy* a plain-looking sedan?" Lauren echoed.

"No? Okay, you're right," Kimberly said. "That'll only eat into our bribe money. We'll borrow my cousin Georgia's car. It's a Chevy something or other, pretty nondescript, and she lives close by. Only you'll have to drive. I think it's a standard transmission and I don't know how to drive a stick."

Lauren shoved back her chair. As crazy as Kimberly's plan sounded, she thought that catching Harley in some transgression—doing something completely unacceptable—might be the perfect solution. At least it would eradicate the doubts in her mind. Plus, if she was keeping an eye on Harley, she'd know Brandon was safe at school. "We don't have any idea where Tank lives," she said.

"I've got my cell," Kimberly told her. "If he's not listed with information, we can always call Damien."

"Okay," Lauren said. Then she smiled. Harley had accused her of doing nothing more productive with her time than playing tennis. But she and Kimberly were going to be doing more than visiting the club this morning. A *lot* more.

CHAPTER EIGHT

"I'M HAVING A BLAST," Kimberly whispered, training her binoculars on Tank's apartment. "I've always wanted to do something like this."

"You don't have to whisper," Lauren told her, growing exasperated. "There's no way he can hear us."

"Our windows are down."

"Only because we can't run the air conditioning in this hunk of junk without burning up the engine. *His* windows are closed tight." May was hardly ever this hot in Portland. It felt like summer already.

"So, someone else could hear us," Kimberly said.

Lauren gazed around the deserted parking lot. "Who? There's no one around. The last sign of life we saw was that woman who carted her three children and several baskets of clothing to the laundry, and that was over an hour ago."

"Surveillance usually takes a while," Kimberly said. "Didn't you ever watch *Stakeout?*"

"I did, but Richard Dreyfus isn't here, and I'm getting bored, okay? This is a waste of time."

"Boy, did you wake up on the wrong side of the bed," Kimberly grumbled.

"Probably because I never made it to bed." Lauren sighed and tried to be patient. But after spending the next half hour tapping her fingers on the steering wheel, reclining her seat as far as the clothes and garbage behind it would allow, and leaning out the window to stare at

Harley's bike, which was parked in the shade of an old oak tree at the corner of the lot, she'd had it. "Aren't those binoculars hurting your eyes yet?" she asked when she couldn't take the boredom another minute.

"No."

"How long do you think we should stay here?" She depressed the cigarette lighter just to watch it pop out. "I mean, I admit this was kind of titillating at first. But I'm starting to feel silly."

"Consider it a background search," Kimberly said. "The do-it-yourself kind."

"Maybe if it was night, we'd see something. Probably Tuesday mornings aren't big drug-dealing hours."

"Tuesday mornings are as good a time as any."

"But we've been here for over two hours and we haven't caught sight of Harley once. He probably left the house with Tank this morning before we arrived."

"How do you know Tank's gone?"

"I'm guessing he works. Besides, there's only six cars in the lot and over fifty apartments in the complex. *Someone* has to be gone."

"Tank might be gone, but I don't think Harley is," Kimberly said. "He's probably sleeping. Drug dealers always sleep late. We just need to wake him up."

Lauren raised her brows. "We don't know he's a drug dealer. And how do you propose we wake him up? Knock?"

Kimberly handed over her cell phone. "Call him."

"What?"

"It's my cell phone, so even if Tank has Caller ID, Harley won't recognize the number."

"And if he doesn't answer?"

Kimberly hesitated.

"We leave, okay?" Lauren insisted. "If he doesn't answer, he's probably not home. And I don't want to be sitting here when he gets back."

Kimberly rolled her eyes. "Okay, don't get uptight."

Lauren figured she had good reason to be uptight. She'd never spied on anyone before, and she didn't feel like a particularly upstanding citizen doing it now. To appease Kimberly, she dialed Tank's number, which she knew by heart, and pushed the talk button.

Don't answer. Don't answer. Don't answer, she chanted to herself as it rang. She was starting to have a bad feeling about this. She was starting to think her time would be better spent playing tennis all day. At least she couldn't get into any trouble doing something so—

"Hello?"

Shit! It was him! Lauren nearly dropped the phone in her haste to punch the end button.

"He's home?" Kimberly asked, her eyes wide with excitement.

Heart racing, Lauren nodded.

"I told you," she said triumphantly. "He was sleeping, right?"

"I don't know. It's pretty hard to tell from *hello*."

"Yippee!" Kimberly clapped her hands. "Here we go." Using the binoculars, she watched the apartment while Lauren waited for any kind of reaction, but nothing happened. The minutes dragged on. A neighbor took out her trash. An old Corvette turned into the lot, idled while a young boy ran up to one of the apartments, then peeled off, but there was no sign of Harley.

"He must've gone back to sleep," Kimberly said, obviously disappointed. "Call him again."

"Why?"

"We need to stir him up, get him moving so we can see what he's up to."

Lauren looked at the phone she'd propped next to the gearshift. She didn't want to call him again. She wanted to go home. "No, we're leaving."

"Why? This is just getting good."

"Have you forgotten? We have a bribe to scrape together so I can get Harley out of my life. And I need to work on the fund-raiser for the women's shelter, and go to the grocery store, and—"

"Wait," Kimberly interrupted, her hand reaching out to catch Lauren just as she was about to turn the key in the ignition. "I think I see something."

Lauren saw it, too, even without binoculars. Someone was raising the blind a little higher on Tank's apartment window, but because of the brightness of the sun, she couldn't make out who it was.

"Is that him?" she breathed, her nerves jumping to attention.

"It has to be," Kimberly said. "Tank sure as heck never looked so good. And he wasn't the type to improve with age."

"What's he doing?"

"Nothing yet. He just looked outside, then walked away."

Lauren smacked the steering wheel. "Darn, that's it? Two hours out here in this heat and that's all we get? A glimpse?"

"I'm not complaining," Kimberly said. "He wasn't wearing a shirt."

"Give me those binoculars."

Kimberly reluctantly relinquished her new toy. At first everything was blurry and dark, but once Lauren had adjusted the focus, she saw a Coors poster plastered on the wall, a pinup of a woman with giant breasts wearing a string bikini, and an old lamp, obviously next to a couch or chair. "Which way did he go?" she asked.

"To the left."

Lauren scanned the area left of the window without seeing anything, then caught her breath when Harley loomed, larger than life, before her eyes. "Oh, my gosh. He's back. And he's wearing nothing but a pair of jeans."

At least, that was what Lauren guessed he had on. She couldn't see anything except a broad expanse of golden-brown chest and rippling muscle. "He must've just gotten out of the shower because his hair is wet."

"See? We probably woke him when we called. Party animals are always late risers."

Lauren didn't say anything. She was too busy staring at Harley as he paced in front of the window while using the telephone. He looked good enough to make her mouth go dry.

"He's a bum for sure," Kimberly went on, growing more committed as she spoke. "Who else would sleep until nearly eleven o'clock?"

"Sleeping late hardly makes him an unfit father," Lauren replied, watching Harley pinch the bridge of his nose, talk some more on the phone, then hang up. "We need something more, something that tells me Brandon's better off without him."

"We're going to have to get closer. You realize that, don't you?" Kimberly made a grab for the binoculars, but Lauren held them out of reach, so she leaned out the window, presumably to see what she could with the naked eye.

Harley disappeared, then returned carrying a cup. "Get closer? Why?" Lauren asked, still entranced by what she was seeing.

"Because you can't see if there's any drug paraphernalia on the coffee table from down here," Kimberly said. "You can't see whether there're any hard liquor bottles on the counter or whether there's a slew of adult videos stacked under the TV."

"All that stuff could belong to Tank. It's *his* apartment." Harley set his cup down, rubbed his face with one hand and picked up the phone again.

"If there're drugs up there, chances are Tank's not doing them alone," Kimberly said, and Lauren had to admit she was probably right. Still, sitting in the parking lot with a pair of binoculars, watching Harley through the living-room window, was one thing. Creeping up and peeking into other, more private rooms was something else.

"I don't think that's a very good idea," she said.

"Oh, come on. If you want to know what Harley's really like, you'll have to take a few risks, Lauren."

"Risks?" Lauren lowered the binoculars long enough to narrow her eyes at Kimberly. "You're going to get me arrested, aren't you?"

TANK'S CALL-WAITING BEEPED for the fourth time in an hour. Harley was still on the telephone with his dealership in Burlingame. He'd just spoken to his top salesman, helped him work out a deal for a customer who wanted a new hog but owed too much on his trade-in, and now he was talking to Joe, his manager, on another problem. But he was almost too tired to think straight. He'd worked most of the night, slept less than four hours, but there were things he needed to do that could only be handled during the day.

"It's a factory problem," he said after hearing about the many complaints they'd been receiving on the ignition modulator for the Softtail Deuce. "Call them and see what they're going to do to make it right."

"I've already talked to them," Joe said. "They'll guarantee the parts, but they won't cover labor. Which is a bitch because someone's got to change out the injectors, and people are getting royally pissed when we try to charge them for it."

"I don't blame them. They shouldn't have to pay for it. But I'm not going to eat the loss, either. It's not our fault the parts were bad. I'll call the factory myself and get back to you—"

Tank's call-waiting beeped again. "Gotta run," Harley said. "Someone's calling through and this isn't my phone.

I'll talk to you in a few minutes." He hit the flash button. "Hello?"

"Harley?" It was Tank.

"Hey, man. What's going on?"

"Reva, the neighbor who sometimes watches Lucy for me, just called me on my cell. I can't imagine there's anything to this, but she claims there's two women in a brown Chevy Corsica at the far end of the parking lot who are training a pair of binoculars on my apartment or someone else's close by. I can't imagine anyone would actually case *my* place, least of all two women, but whatever they're doing is making Reva pretty nervous. I was hoping you'd run down there and see what's going on."

Two women with *binoculars?* What was that all about? There certainly wasn't any good bird-watching around here, not in this cement jungle. "Sure thing," he said. "Call you back in a few."

Harley hung up and moved to one side of the front window, careful to stay in the shadows so he could gaze out over the lot without being easily observed. His bike was fine. He could see it parked under the oak tree where he'd left it yesterday. And the car he'd rented was still in its proper place, too, in a space marked Visitor. There was a brown Chevy Corsica parked on the street, tucked halfway behind the Springfield Apartments sign, but it appeared to be empty. He couldn't see anyone at all—until he spotted a slim woman in a tennis skirt slipping through the trees near the curb. A pair of binoculars hung around her neck, and she was casting furtive glances to either side while pulling someone behind her. But the pair didn't seem threatening. They just seemed out of place. He couldn't picture either one of them driving the rusted Chevy Corsica with the smashed front fender. Neither could he imagine them living in this mostly blue-collar neighborhood.

Then something about the second woman made him look closer. And he couldn't believe his eyes.

"I'M NOT GOING TO DO THIS," Lauren insisted, hanging back. She'd never scaled a fire escape before in her life, let alone one that rose out of the garbage and stench of a back alley that probably wasn't safe after dark. And she refused to start now.

"Come on. Don't be a poor sport," Kimberly said. "This is fun. It certainly beats the heck out of applying for jobs. It's like…it's like we're detectives."

"Detectives! We're acting more like criminals, if you ask me."

"We'll just take a quick peek. We're not hurting anyone. I mean, it's not like we're doing anything really bad, like breaking and entering."

Lauren squinted up at the small covered patio at the back of Tank's apartment. "The metal rungs on that fire escape are going to be hot," she said. "We'll burn our hands."

"It's not that hot yet." Kimberly felt the first rung. "Anyway, it's only ten steps."

"What if we get caught?" Lauren asked, catching Kimberly by the shirt before she could move up the ladder.

"We're not going to get caught, not if we're quiet."

"And if we're not quiet enough? How much jail time can a Peeping Tom get?"

"You're so negative," Kimberly complained, yanking out of her grasp. "I come up with this great idea, and all you can do is find fault with it."

"I'm not climbing up there," Lauren said in a loud whisper. "What if he's in the buff?"

"Oh, give me a break. He wouldn't parade in front of the window in the buff. We only want to know what kind of lifestyle he leads. We're not going to get five to ten for that."

"Do you really think he's a drug dealer? Very few junkies look as healthy as Harley does," Lauren said, but Kimberly couldn't hear her anymore. She'd already dashed up the steps and stood on the landing, giving Lauren a thumbs up.

Lauren searched one side of the alley, then the other as Kimberly edged closer to Tank's glass slider. "I don't want to be doing this, I don't want to be doing this," she whispered over and over to herself, her heart pounding so loud she felt like a walking time bomb. She wanted to run back to the car, get in and drive away—fast. If only Kimberly would come down...

"Hurry," she croaked when the minutes stretched on. "Let's get out of here!"

Kimberly must have heard because she waved a hand over the railing as if to say, "Not yet."

Was she seeing more than Harley's bare chest?

"Come on, Kimberly!"

Again, the little wave that said, "Just a minute."

"Kimberly!"

Nothing.

Biting her lip in frustration, Lauren eyed the ladder. She could stand and wait, and possibly have a heart attack in the meantime, or she could go up after her. Neither option seemed very appealing. But going after Kimberly had the advantage of bringing their adventure at Springfield Apartments to a close, which was motivation enough to start Lauren climbing.

"You girls get bored at the club or something?"

Harley! Missing the next rung, Lauren fell flat on her behind, but was too embarrassed to feel the pain of her landing. She immediately scrambled to her feet and found him standing at the edge of the building. He had on a T-shirt with his blue jeans now, but he was leaning against the brick corner as if he'd been there all along, watching their every move.

Oh, boy. This isn't good… This is really, really bad….

Kimberly came to the edge of the balcony and offered him a fake but very bright smile. "There you are! Would you believe I couldn't rouse anyone at the door, so I came around back?"

"No, I wouldn't believe that," he said, then turned his attention to Lauren. "You want to tell me what the hell you and your little friend are doing here?"

Lauren threw Kimberly an accusing glare, wanting to throttle her on the spot, then brushed off her shorts to buy some time. What did she say now? "Actually, uh, I came over because I have something I need to discuss with you."

He cocked an eyebrow at her. "I thought we said all there was to say last night."

"I've come up with a third alternative, one I hope we can both live with."

"And that would be…?"

"Whoa, hold on a minute," Kimberly said, climbing down the ladder. "I don't think I want to be here for this part."

"What part?" Harley asked.

"You'll see," she said. "Lauren, I'll be in the car. Harley, it was, um, good to see you again."

"Wait a second!" Lauren said. "You're not going to run out on me like that." But by the time she got the words out of her mouth Kimberly had already cleared the corner and wasn't turning back.

"Wasn't that the girl you used to hang out with in high school?" Harley asked.

Lauren nodded. "Her name's Kim."

"She hasn't changed much."

"She might look different tomorrow," Lauren suggested from between clenched teeth, but Harley wasn't in the mood to be distracted.

"So, what is it you have to say to me?" he asked,

shoving his hands in his pockets, which flexed the muscles
in his arms—something Lauren was determined to ignore.
A hormone spike like the ones he so easily inspired did
little to help her thought processes. "Because if you
haven't changed your mind about letting me see Brandon," he went on, "I don't want to hear it."

That sure didn't sound as though he was after money....

Taking a deep breath, Lauren straightened her spine.
Her father would have barreled through this somehow.
He'd done it once, hadn't he? And she was twenty-seven
years old. Certainly she could manage without Quentin by
now. "I was thinking that the cost of living is probably
pretty high in California."

"The cost of living?" he repeated skeptically.

"You know—" she licked her lips "—it takes a lot to
get by these days, and, well, I was thinking that if you
wanted to make some sort of deal, I could help you
out…with that."

He scowled at her. "With what?"

"With the cost of living."

Her words hung suspended in the air like smog and
seemed to have the same stifling, distasteful effect.

"You're offering me money to go away?" he said at
last.

She swallowed hard and nodded. "But more than ten
years ago. Five times as much."

His expression didn't improve.

"Ten times as much," she said, even though Damien
had cautioned her to start low. So much for negotiating.
She was already five thousand dollars past her limit,
which meant she'd have to cash Nana's CD, and Harley
hadn't given her an answer yet.

"That's a lot of money—twenty thousand dollars," she
said to fill the uncomfortable void. "It could buy you a
new car, depending on what kind you wanted, or a boat
or…or whatever."

"A car? Or a boat? That's disgusting," he said. "*You're* disgusting if you think twenty thousand dollars is worth what I would lose."

Lauren felt as disgusting as he said she was, but she'd committed herself and couldn't back down now. "What about more?"

He shook his head. "You don't get it, do you? Spoiled little Lauren who always gets her way. If she wants something, Daddy just buys it for her. Well, it won't work this time. There are some things in life money can't buy, and I think you'd damned well better learn that Brandon is one of them."

"I'm *not* buying Brandon," she cried. "I'm only trying to ensure his—"

He raised a hand to stop her, and she shrank from the scorn on his face. "Go home and explain it to a good lawyer, Lauren, because you're going to need one," he said, then he turned and stalked away, leaving her standing in the alley feeling lower than an ant.

CHAPTER NINE

"THANKS A LOT for your help back there. I really appreciate it," Lauren said sarcastically to Kim. She was behind the wheel and they were, thankfully, several blocks from Tank Thompson's apartment and chugging successfully toward the Southwest, despite the car's initial reluctance to start.

Kim kept her face averted, as though suddenly fascinated by the rundown apartments and government housing projects flying past them on the right side of the road. "I thought you might like a little privacy," she said, but there was a sheepish quality to her voice that told Lauren she knew exactly what she'd done when she bailed out.

"Right. Privacy," Lauren echoed. "It's always best to humiliate oneself in private."

Kim sent her a fleeting glance. "You humiliated yourself?"

"No, actually you got me halfway there before you left. I wasn't exactly coming from a position of strength, considering that we'd just been caught pressing our noses to his back window. But I certainly finished up with a flourish." *Not that I didn't have a little help from "Now I Know He's After Money," Damien,* she added mentally.

"I take it that's a 'no' to the fifteen thousand," she said with a wince.

"That's a 'no' to the *twenty thousand.*"

"You offered him that much? And he still refused?"

He'd done more than refuse. He'd regarded her with

such disdain she'd never forget it if she lived to be a hundred years old. It had to be the first time she'd ever encountered such a look. It had to be the first time she'd ever deserved one. "The amount didn't seem to matter."

"Jeez, what a guy," Kimberly said, her voice dreamy.

Lauren nearly ran up on the curb. "*What a guy?* He's determined to fight for Brandon, which means I'm in real trouble, and you say, 'what a guy?'"

"Well, you have to admit he's pretty cute." She folded and unfolded the pleats on her skirt as she talked. "And the fact that he won't take twenty thousand dollars to walk away from his son is admirable, considering he's always been so poor. I mean, he can't be all bad, right? Look at this neighborhood. I'd do anything to get out of here."

"He's only staying here!" Lauren snapped. "How many times do I have to tell you that? We don't know anything about where he lives."

"We know where he came from."

That, at least, was true. He'd grown up just a block or so from the Springfield Apartments in a government-subsidized duplex. Kimberly and Lauren had occasionally driven past it when they were in high school, but they hadn't made a habit of traveling to the other side of town. They didn't typically cruise Broadway, like the popular kids, or hang out at Harley's house afterward, where, according to Audra, the music was always blasting and the beer flowed.

"I can't believe I let you drag me over here," Lauren complained. "If we'd stayed home, this would never have happened."

"You would've offered him the money, anyway. I'm not taking the blame for that."

"The bribe should've worked," Lauren retorted. "It worked ten years ago, for my father. And he only gave him a couple grand, just enough to pay rent for a few months."

"Evidently Harley's grown up," Kimberly said.

They'd certainly seen evidence of that through the binoculars. As hard as Lauren tried, she couldn't erase the vision of his bare torso from her mind. Nor could she convince herself that his wasn't the most gorgeous body she'd ever seen.

"What do I do now?" she asked.

"Call your father?" Kimberly suggested.

"I don't want to do that."

Her friend raised her brows in obvious surprise. "What's going on? You and your father have always been close."

Lauren shrugged because she couldn't explain. She knew what Quentin would say, and she didn't want to hear it. Probably because she wasn't sure she agreed with him anymore.

"What *do* you want to do?" Kimberly asked.

Deep down, Lauren wanted to let Harley see Brandon. She'd wanted it ever since that night in the restaurant, ever since Brandon had responded with such eagerness when she mentioned his father, ever since Harley had shown up in a suit with that silly stuffed snake. She'd ended up giving the snake to Brandon, telling him Grandpa Worthington had sent it from England. But she wasn't going to admit any of that to Kimberly. At least not yet. Their visit to the Springfield Apartments might have been a complete disaster, but there was, possibly, another way to gain a few insights into Harley Nelson.

"I'm just going to sit tight for now," she lied. She couldn't say what she was about to do or Kimberly would never let her do it alone.

THE DOOR TO THE ATTIC creaked as Lauren opened it and stared apprehensively at the narrow stairs that led up, then turned and went up farther still, to a large room with sloping ceilings and a single double-paned window. Because of the deep eaves on the house, she could see only a few slivers of sunlight. They filtered through the gloom overhead, casting everything in shadow and creating, if not an eerie place, a room that felt pregnant with closely guarded secrets and old memories.

Or maybe it wasn't the strange color of light or the musty smell or anything physical at all. Maybe this place made Lauren uncomfortable because, as children, she and Audra loved to play with the antique cradle that had once belonged to their great-grandmother, and the trunk of dress-up clothes that had come from her, too. As the years passed, and she and her sister lost interest in playing "house" and grew apart, they rarely came back here. Occasionally, Audra had tried to punish or scare Lauren by locking her in the attic and claiming it was haunted. But Lauren hadn't spent any time here in the past ten or fifteen years, except for the hour it had taken her and her father to carry up the boxes of Audra's belongings a few days after the funeral. The holiday decorations and sewing and craft supplies were stored in well-labeled cupboards in the garage, along with anything else that needed to be accessible, so there generally wasn't any need to go rooting around in the attic. Only things that could be put away and forgotten for years at a time were ever stored here.

When Lauren walked up the stairs, they complained as loudly as the door had. Before she reached the top, she heard the phone ringing downstairs and wished she'd brought the cordless with her, but she didn't turn back. She couldn't get stuck on the phone, anyway. Brandon was only in school for another two hours. She needed to make good use of the time.

Lauren and her father had stacked Audra's things against the far wall, beyond the draped furniture and paintings that crowded most of the attic. She made her way through the clutter and pulled the chain on the bulb overhead. Then, taking a deep breath, she started digging.

Sweaters, yearbooks, pictures, the wrist corsage Audra's first prom date had given her, the star lamp that had sat on her dresser... Each item brought her sister back more poignantly than the one before, until Lauren half expected to see Audra coming up the stairs behind her. She found the card she'd made for Audra when she was only eight and for the first time since Audra's death, Lauren felt something more than sadness. She missed Audra, truly missed her, and mourned the little girl she used to play dolls with.

"Audra, why did you sell yourself so short?" Lauren asked, burying her face in her hands and finally letting the tears come. Audra's accident had put a stop to her constant unhappiness and ended her painful decline. That alone had brought some relief to Lauren and her father. But Lauren felt guilty for feeling that relief, guilty for not being able to help her sister find some glimmer of happiness, especially in the later years, and guilty for being okay when Audra never was. What had made the difference between them? Why had Lauren been able to cope with life while Audra retreated into drugs and alcohol? Even for Brandon, her sister hadn't been able to stay clean.

Audra's death was a tragedy Lauren would always regret. But the way her sister had lived was the greater tragedy by far.

Time was getting away from her. Lauren checked her watch, realized she had to pick up Brandon in just thirty minutes and tried to distance herself from her emotions so she could search the boxes more quickly. But her heart was heavy, and the close, still room seemed too full of memories.

Probably this was a waste of time. She was opening old wounds for nothing, she decided, and was about to pile everything back into the boxes so she could leave when she found what she'd been looking for all along—

Audra's journals. Every rehab her sister had ever attended told her to record her feelings, and Audra had definitely done that. She mostly wrote when she was in recovery, but she'd kept journals since she was in her early teens. There were at least a dozen notebooks here, neatly packed away. Lauren had never read them before—she'd respected her sister's privacy, even in death—but Brandon *was* Audra's son. It was time Lauren found out exactly how her sister had felt about his father.

If she'd ever mentioned Harley...

Sitting cross-legged in the warm, dusty attic, she thumbed through each notebook, trying to put them in chronological order. She might never learn anything more about Harley, but maybe she'd gain something that would prove even more valuable. Maybe she'd get to know the sister who had become a stranger to her.

LAUREN WORTHINGTON WAS just like her father, Harley thought with distaste. His desire to tread lightly, to work peaceably with the Worthingtons, had slowly faded away. They didn't want peace, not unless it came on their terms. Neither did they want to share. Nothing, really, had changed in the past ten years. They still thought they could flick him away like some kind of insect and keep Brandon to themselves, but now that Lauren had shown her true colors and united with her family, Harley felt perfectly justified in doing everything in his power to gain custody. The move to California might be difficult on Brandon at first. Harley understood that. But he could no longer allow the boy to grow up in the Worthington household. There were more important issues at stake than providing food and clothing. His son needed to be taught that a real man didn't rely on money or status, that he didn't bribe or intimidate his way out of difficult situations, that he acted upon the convictions held in his heart and stood behind those convictions no matter what.

Like now, Harley told himself. The legal process would be slow, could take a year or longer. Quentin would put up one hell of a fight, which meant the battle would become incredibly time-intensive and expensive. And Harley still had a business to run. But the doubt that had undermined him from the start was finally gone. He might not be the perfect dad for Brandon, but he *was* his dad. And it was his prerogative to do whatever he could to ensure that his son knew he loved him.

Which was all well and good—for later. For now he was stuck in Tank's apartment, trying to run his business by remote control, in between telephone calls to various family law attorneys. It was going to be a long year or two....

Propping his feet on the couch, Harley leaned back and closed his eyes. After last night he should probably try to grab a nap, but he was still too wound up from catching Lauren and her friend creeping around the apartments, peeking in his windows. What had they been looking for, anyway?

Suddenly remembering that his mother had called while he was on the phone with the dealership, he sat up and punched her number into his cell. Beverly Nelson-Hallifax-West, who was single again after the failure of her third marriage, probably needed money. Harley paid all her bills and gave her a small allowance every month. She had enough to get by, but ever since she'd taken up bingo, she was always after him for more. And it was pretty hard to refuse an old woman the pleasure of a night at the bingo parlor. Except that Harley feared she'd meet someone there and get involved in yet another doomed relationship. At least now that her financial needs were met, she was slowing down on the boyfriends. She hadn't let a man move in with her for the past three years, which saved Harley the trouble of moving him out when things fell apart.

"Mom?"

"There you are," she said in her deep, smoker's voice. "I thought you were going to call me back."

"I am calling you back. What's up? You need money again?"

"Why do you always think I'm calling about money?"

Because most of the time you are. "Bingo's tonight, isn't it?"

"It is, but I've already got the money. I won $250 last time. I called 'cause I want to know what's happening with Brandon. You've been gone four days and haven't checked in with me once."

He rubbed his temples and didn't mention that he hadn't even considered contacting her. Their relationship was changing now that she was growing older. She was much more mindful of him and eager for his attention, but old habits were hard to break. "Sorry. I would've called, but I haven't even seen him yet."

"Why not? What've you been doing?"

Not much, unless you include getting arrested for an old speeding ticket and buying a suit. "Lauren Worthington hasn't been very happy to see me."

"So? Who is she?"

"Audra's sister."

"Where's Quentin?"

"In Europe."

"Brandon's with his aunt, and you're letting *her* stop you?"

Harley couldn't help chuckling. "What do you want me to do, break into their house?"

"You don't have to break into anything. Brandon goes to school, doesn't he? A school is public property."

"Not the kind Brandon would attend," Harley said, but his mother had started him thinking. Why *was* he sitting in Tank's apartment waiting for some judge to award him his son several months, maybe years, down the road? He needed to go the legal route, of course, and certainly planned to do so, but the only thing stopping him from seeing Brandon now, today, was Lauren's refusal. And after what had happened a few hours ago, he didn't think that anything she said or did should matter to him.

"If I showed up at school, Brandon would tell Lauren. And she'd probably get the entire faculty and staff up in arms. She might even serve me with a restraining order."

"Let her. Wouldn't it be worth ruffling a few feathers to meet your son?"

Definitely, Harley thought, smiling at the role reversal between them. It was a sad day when his mother had to tell him to take a risk. He used to be a hellraiser. What was happening to him?

"Maybe I'll stop by there tomorrow," he said.

"And then you'll call me? Tell me about Brandon? He's my only grandchild, you know. And it doesn't look like you're in any hurry to give me more."

Harley rolled his eyes. Interesting that she'd be so concerned about her grandson when she didn't spare her own son a second thought unless there wasn't another man in her life. "I'll let you know how it goes," he said, then he hit the end button and got up to shave, picturing Lauren and her friend Kim running through the parking lot with a pair of binoculars. Maybe it was time he did some sneaking around of his own. After all, the battle lines had been drawn, and all was fair in love and war.

"Is BRANDON HOME from school?" Kimberly asked, her voice tinny as it came through Lauren's speakerphone and into the Worthingtons' vaulted kitchen.

Lauren glanced across the room at her nephew, who was sitting at the table doing his homework while she stood at the island making cookies. "Yeah. He's right here."

"You guys want to come over and go swimming?

May's usually too cold, but with the weather we've been having…''

''Yeah!'' Brandon said, but Lauren spoke at the same time, saying, ''Not today. I've got too much to do.''

''Like what?'' Kimberly asked. ''I thought your father's new vice-president was handling most things at the office these days.''

''He is, but I have a lot of calls to make for that fundraiser.''

''The women's shelter event?''

''That's the one.''

''Then Brandon and I will go swimming later. You're still coming over tonight, aren't you, Brandon?''

Lauren looked at her nephew, hoping for a positive response instead of the reluctance she'd encountered yesterday, and was relieved when he didn't argue with her. ''Yeah, I'm coming,'' he said, but he didn't sound particularly excited about it and quickly bent over his homework again.

''You sure your parents won't mind?''

''Not at all.''

''I'll bring him after dinner then,'' Lauren said.

''What are you doing right now?'' Kimberly asked.

''Baking cookies.'' Lauren's hands were busy dropping spoonfuls of dough onto a baking sheet, but her mind was still on Audra's journals. She'd only had a few minutes to read before it was time to retrieve Brandon from school. What she'd seen so far was promising, though, and she was dying to get back to it. Just before she left, she'd found a volume that began at the start of Audra's junior year, judging by the date. She hoped her sister's senior year—the year she got to know Harley—would follow. But anxious as Lauren was to find out, she couldn't pore through the journals in front of Brandon. She wasn't sure they were something he should see.

"You're acting funny," Kimberly said. "Are you still mad at me about today?"

"A little," she admitted.

"Come on, Lauren. I said I was sorry."

"I know. It's okay, I guess. I'm just a little... preoccupied."

Brandon frowned up at her. "You were mad at Kim? What for?"

"Nothing," she told him, and grabbed the handset off its cradle despite her flour-covered hands before Kim could say anything that might generate more questions.

"Want me to bring you some cookies?" she asked so they wouldn't have to talk about the fiasco at the Springfield Apartments. Lauren had been completely humiliated, and she didn't feel much better thinking back on it.

"That'd be great," Kim said. "Has You-Know-Who called?"

You-Know-Who? For some reason, calling Harley that made Lauren think of Harry Potter's "He Who Must Not Be Named." She hoped the two had nothing in common. "No. And you're off speakerphone."

"I can tell. I'm just being careful."

"I appreciate that."

"So you haven't heard anything?"

"Nothing."

"What about your father? Have you talked to him?"

There was a message on the answering machine from her parents. Theirs was probably the call she'd heard in the attic. Or maybe it was Damien's. He'd left a message, too, saying he'd talked to Tank and didn't think Harley would take a bribe. A bit late on that piece of information. "No. It's after midnight in London. I'll get in touch with my dad in the morning."

"Okay. So you'll be coming over soon?"

"Yeah. See you in a little while."

"Why were you mad at Kim?" Brandon asked when Lauren had hung up.

"I wasn't mad at her, not really," she said. "Are you sure you're okay with staying over there again tonight?"

He rested his chin in one hand and studied the tip of his pencil. "Yeah, I guess, if you need me to. I mean, Kimberly's pretty cool. She lets me eat all the ice cream I want. But she doesn't like to play Hearts." He made a face. "She wants me to watch television while she talks on the phone forever. And too much television's not good for kids."

Lauren smiled. That sounded like his schoolteacher talking. "You don't watch too much television. I make sure of that. And Kim doesn't enjoy Hearts because she always gets stuck with the queen of spades. No one likes to stack up thirteen points almost every hand when the object of the game is to get as few points as possible."

"She's not a very good player?"

"Let's just say I've seen better."

"Great," he said happily. "If I can talk her into playing with me, maybe I'll have a chance to shoot the moon and actually make it work this time."

Lauren laughed as she took the first batch of freshly baked cookies out of the oven. "I don't know anyone more dedicated to mastering everything they learn than you are," she said, putting two good-sized cookies on a plate and carrying them to the table, along with a glass of milk.

He eagerly pushed his homework out of the way and smiled up at her. "Shooting the moon isn't easy," he said. "But I think it's going to be worth it."

CHAPTER TEN

PRIVACY AND TIME. AT LAST. Forgetting all the calls she needed to make on the fund-raiser, Lauren dashed to her room as soon as she returned from taking Brandon to Kim's and scooped Audra's journals out from under the bed. Piling them on her nightstand, she arranged her pillows, then settled back to read the one that started with her sister's junior year.

October 14, 1989
Johnny Dakota asked me to the Homecoming Dance today. I don't really want to go with him, but hey, it's better than saying yes to some geek. Kevin already asked Melissa. (Boo hoo!) And Gary's taking LeAnn. I guess I shouldn't have broken up with him until after Homecoming. I'll be lucky if Johnny doesn't get stoned at the game and forget to pick me up, which just can't happen because I have the most incredible dress...

Lauren recognized the names and remembered the faces. Johnny, eyes red-rimmed and glazed almost all the time. Kevin, handsome, rich and completely stuck-up. And Gary, sweet, friendly Gary, who'd followed Audra around like a puppy. The journal went on to tell all about Homecoming Night and how Audra had started out with Johnny but ended up leaving the dance with Kevin. They went to a party, got drunk and slept together—even

though, according to the journal, Audra wasn't really interested in Kevin anymore. By then, she'd figured out he
was too conceited. However, she seemed to like the idea
that Quentin would be shocked by her actions. Lauren
frowned when she read a whole paragraph dedicated to
how much their father would hate what Audra was doing.

Other than that, the journal was almost completely
filled with what the boys at school said or did and which
one Audra liked at the moment. It wasn't difficult to find
Harley's name. He figured in earlier than Lauren had expected, appearing for the first time right after Homecoming.

November 2, 1989
    Harley Nelson is *so* gorgeous! What a babe! And
he smiled at me today, right in front of Marie and
all my friends. They nearly turned green with envy.
Hillary's been trying to get his attention for months,
but he didn't even look at her, which was the best
part of all because she's stabbed me in the back way
too many times. Rhonda said she's been calling Gary
and telling him he's better off without me. Like *she'd*
be perfect for him? Give me a break…

The entry veered off on a tangent, about Hillary stealing
a blouse out of Audra's locker, which was part of the
reason Audra didn't like her. Then it detailed an argument
Audra had had with their father over whether or not she
was grounded for the weekend. There weren't any entries
for the next few weeks and no mention of Harley again
until the Christmas holiday, when Audra went to a party
and actually danced with him.

Shaking her head after reading the details of another
sexual encounter with a cousin of the Robinson boys
who'd lived down the street, Lauren skipped forward. She
and her sister had been so different, even way back then.

Audra had been consumed with garnering male attention, being the most popular girl in school and getting high. Lauren had been too busy getting good grades, establishing a relationship with her teachers, excelling at debate and working in her father's video stores. She'd admired a couple of boys, of course. One who wore glasses as thick as hers but consistently challenged her in debate and would probably go on to become a United States senator or something. And Harley, a poor boy with grease under his nails who drove a motorcycle and got her sister pregnant. He was hardly the type an achievement-oriented girl would aspire to marry and yet Lauren couldn't deny that there'd always been a mysterious allure about him that appealed to something very basic in her.

Maybe she wasn't so unlike Audra, after all. What would she have done if Harley had given her even a crumb of his attention?

Lauren smiled wistfully as she remembered a barbecue she'd attended in the spring of her sophomore year. It was Elaine Scofield's end-of-year party and over a hundred kids, as well as several neighborhood families, had been invited for hot dogs and hamburgers and swimming. Harley had been there. For an hour or so, he'd played pool and Lauren had watched him from the dimmest corner of the game room, where she and Kimberly had been talking when he and his crowd came in. He hadn't done particularly well at croquet earlier—according to Kevin, who was taunting him about it when they poured into the room—but then croquet probably wasn't a game Harley played much at home. Pool was another story. He could shoot like a hustler, and he proved it by beating all takers and winning all bets. His skill, coordinated movements and rugged good looks riveted Lauren and Kimberly until he went out to swim and started flirting with Audra. Then Quentin, already angry because Audra had defied him by wearing a shockingly revealing bikini, dragged the entire family home, and they were treated to yet another of Audra's and Quentin's many arguments.

So much for the end-of-year party, Lauren thought. But then she chanced upon an entry recording some of the events of that very day and had to pause long enough to read it. Audra wrote that her father had gotten upset over nothing, that he'd tried to ruin her fun just because she wore a swimsuit he didn't like and flirted with a boy he considered beneath them.

Forget the fact that she'd been making a fool of herself in front of everyone they knew....

With a sigh, Lauren thumbed toward the back of the book. This wasn't getting her anywhere. The details Audra felt were important enough to record were merely highlighting the vast differences between them and making Lauren feel more distant from Audra than ever. Why couldn't Audra understand how cheap wearing that suit had made her look? Especially combined with the way she'd been brushing up against Harley in the pool?

Lauren was ready to give up and tote the journals back to the attic so Brandon wouldn't find them when she caught sight of Harley's name again. Almost six months had passed without mention of him, but then he appeared at the beginning of Audra's senior year. She hadn't written for most of the summer so it was a long entry, mostly concerned with the boys she'd met at Nana's in Colorado, where she'd spent the summer. At the bottom of the page she said she'd seen Harley after second period and thought he was totally and completely hot and that she was determined to make him her new conquest.

From there, Lauren was riveted because almost every entry was centered on Harley. Audra had started calling him the first week of school and begun arranging meetings with him at the houses of different friends. Soon he was calling her, too. Or rather, he'd let the phone ring once and hang up so Quentin couldn't answer. Then Audra would slip away and phone him back, and they'd set up their next rendezvous. It was a classic example of forbidden love, except that Lauren got the impression Audra was more interested in spiting her father than in loving anyone.

November 9, 1991

I slipped out of the house after dinner last night and went to Harley's. Dad thought I was studying, but I couldn't read a word, not with him in the house. He makes me sick. What a hypocrite! He's always handing me all these brochures on the dangers of drinking and smoking, as if *he* lived a monk's life when he was in school! Just because my little sister's the perfect nerd, straight As, long skirts and not a horny bone in her body, he wants me to be the same. Well, they can have each other. I'm not like Lauren. I can get any man I want and make him grateful to have me....

Lauren winced at that entry. It was one thing to know what her sister had thought of her and another to see it so baldly stated. But Lauren was more concerned with the underlying problem that had always come between them. Audra was jealous of Lauren's relationship with their father. It was obvious and, yet, Lauren found Audra's jealousy ironic considering the fact that Lauren hadn't possessed the looks or the popularity Audra seemed to prize so highly.

December 23, 1991

Harley made love to me tonight for the first time. After everything I've heard about him, I was pretty surprised it took him so long to get around to it. He wasn't a virgin or anything. He said the thirty-year-old woman across the street came on to him when he was only fifteen. But he moved very slowly with me. I think he wanted it to mean something, but I'm not sure how I feel about him. He's certainly different from any other boy I've known. And he's damned good in bed. I can't get enough of him. If every guy could screw like him, I'd stay on my back all day. Too bad Daddy doesn't know I'm banging the boy he met at the Scofield picnic....

December 28, 1991

Harley gave me a motorcycle helmet for Christmas with my name on it. I guess that's the same as a ring to him. I wasn't too thrilled with it until Daddy saw it and got really pissed off. Then it was the best present I've ever received. I gave Harley five hundred bucks to buy parts for his engine. He acted offended that I'd give him so much money and wouldn't take it even after I told him he'd be doing me a favor, that I was trying to spend as much of Daddy's money as possible. He said he didn't want anything from my father. Isn't that hilarious? Daddy thinks Harley's a gold digger, and Harley won't even accept my Christmas present!

January 21, 1992

I'm so mad at Harley. I went over there tonight with some of the best crack I've had in a long time, stuff I had to go clear across town to get, and he flushed it down the damned toilet! I don't know why he's so uptight about me getting high once in a while, but he's starting to treat me like he's my dad or something. He even threatened to break up if I didn't get my shit together. Maybe all guys are alike, little clones of the great Quentin, thinking they know what's best for everyone else....

February 14, 1992

I let Harley make love to me today, then told him I'd skipped my birth control pill. Loved the look of panic on his face. I swear I laughed for nearly an hour, but he was a typical jerk and got angry. "That's not funny," he said. So I had to tell him I was only joking. The joke's on him, though. A girl's got a right to do *something* exciting on Valentine's Day. I'm sure Lauren had fun. She went out with *Daddy and Mommy* again. The three of them go out for Valentine's every year because Mom and Dad know Lauren will never be able to get a real date....

Lauren put a hand to her stomach, which was starting to churn. Her sister's words were personally painful, but they were disappointing in other ways, too. It seemed that Audra had slept with Harley merely to punish their father. Where were her sister's emotions in the relationship? Other than the physical pleasure Harley brought her, she didn't make their intimacy sound very special. On the contrary, she'd obviously felt the need to add greater risk to the situation to make it more stimulating.

"Audra," she whispered. "Why were you willing to settle for such a poor substitute for real happiness?"

March 4, 1992

Daddy caught Harley and me in my room together a few minutes ago. Harley didn't want to come up here. Guys can be so weird. But he doesn't like my dad any more than I do, and when I told him we'd just had another fight, he came anyway, saying he wouldn't let anyone hurt me. What I really wanted was to let him screw my brains out right here in my own bed with my parents just down the hall and innocent little Lauren studying her heart out in the room next door. Only Harley wouldn't even let me unzip his pants. I took off my top and everything, and he just kept shoving my shirt at me, telling me to put it back on. He can be so stubborn sometimes. "Not here," he kept saying, "no way." I guess I'm kind of glad now, because my dad opened the door right afterward to tell me good night, and when he saw me without my shirt and Harley standing right next to me, he came unglued. I swear I've never seen him get so red in the face. He told me if I ever see Harley again, I'll be cut off from the family. Like I'm not already cut off from this family. Harley was trying to stick up for me, though. He told my dad he loved me and planned to make something of his life, as if that would make a difference to my father. Daddy doesn't care about love. Probably because he doesn't believe anyone can love me. The only person he really cares about is Lauren. Little Miss Goody Two-shoes, who wouldn't know what to do if a guy ever touched her—

Lauren covered her mouth with her hand and closed the journal. She couldn't read any more. What Audra wrote might be her version of reality ten years ago, but it wasn't pretty. And Lauren had had more than enough for one night.

She glanced at the phone, wanting to call someone with whom she could share the burden of what she was feeling, hoping it would dispel some of the terrible pain in her heart. Audra had purposely messed up her life, over and over again, and for what? To prove that she could? To prove herself unworthy of her family's love? Lauren hadn't majored in psychology. She couldn't explain the motivations behind her sister's self-destructive behavior. But she didn't need an expert to tell her it was a gut-wrenching, unnecessary loss.

If only...

She eyed the phone again. It was nearly midnight. Who could she call? Damien wouldn't mind, but she didn't want to talk to him. What she was going through was too personal, too painful to share with someone she didn't love. She could call her father—except that, at this moment, she almost blamed him for what had happened to Audra more than she blamed her sister. He should've backed off somehow, convinced her she was loved.

But how? Lauren hadn't been able to manage that, either, and hated the helplessness it had always engendered.

Kimberly. Kimberly would understand. She always did, but since her divorce, she was living with her parents again, and the phone would probably wake them. Besides, the person she most wanted to call was Harley.

Picking up the phone, she dialed Tank's number, then held her breath, wondering whether or not she'd have the nerve to say anything if someone answered.

"Hello?" It was him. Lauren immediately recognized his deep voice, but for a moment, she couldn't speak. She kept picturing him trying to stand up to their father back in 1992 as a tall but scrappy and spirited youth. "I love her, dammit," he'd cried and Quentin had shouted back at him, "You rotten little son of a bitch. You don't know anything about love. Who the hell do you think you are, sneaking in here? What are you trying to do? Get in my daughter's pants? You think I want the likes of you for a son-in-law? You stay the hell away from her, you hear? I don't want you within twenty feet of her!"

Lauren cringed. Was that really eleven years ago? It seemed like only yesterday.

"Hello?" Harley said again.

Lauren opened her mouth and managed to draw a small breath of air. *I'm sorry,* her mind whispered, *I'm sorry.* But the words hadn't reached her tongue before Harley hung up. And she couldn't have explained why she felt like she owed him an apology, anyway.

SO THIS IS WHERE the kids from Hillside Estates go to school these days. K to 8, huh?

Harley pulled his rental car to the side of the road at the far corner of the schoolyard and watched Lauren's late-model Lexus continue down the street several cars ahead. Because he didn't know what time Brandon started school, he'd had to sit outside the gates of Hillside Estates for over an hour before she'd appeared this morning, but it turned out to be quite fortunate that he'd gotten an early start. She'd been alone when she left. That had puzzled him at first, but then he'd followed her to another neighborhood of expensive homes where she'd picked up a young boy. And though he'd been too far away to get a good look at the boy's face, Harley knew it had to be his son. Especially when the friend who'd visited Tank's apartment with Lauren yesterday came out in her robe and walked them to the car. Did Kim have a child Brandon's age for him to play with? Or was Brandon staying with her for other reasons?

At least now he knew where Brandon probably was the night Lauren had stood him up and come home alone. And, if he had his guess, he knew where Brandon was going to be staying for the next few days....

"Nice try, Lauren," he murmured, "but a wasted effort at this point."

Her Lexus turned into the school's circular drive, crawling along because of the number of other cars, and she let Brandon out at the front steps. Harley instantly lost sight of him because of the crush, but only moments later picked out his red backpack and watched as he met up with a couple of friends and moved onto the playground.

Lauren exited the lot and headed straight toward where

Harley was parked, and Harley ducked so she wouldn't see him. When he sat up again, he caught her taillights in his rearview mirror. She turned at the stop sign and was gone. Then it was just him and his son, who was only about fifty yards away.

Brandon... Harley had told himself he'd follow Lauren, catch a glimpse of his boy and drive away. But his heart was pounding so hard he could scarcely breathe. He knew he couldn't leave now if his life depended on it. He had to get closer. He might run the risk of looking like some perverted stalker skulking around the school grounds, but he had to get a better glimpse of his own flesh and blood.

Taking a deep breath in an attempt to slow his racing pulse, Harley got out and walked beside the chain-link fence that separated him from Brandon. His son was setting his backpack on the ground and getting involved in a soccer game.

Harley stopped as he drew even with him and casually leaned against the fence as though he belonged there—as though he was waiting for someone or making sure a child got to school safely—and watched as Brandon began to chase the ball.

His kid was tall. Brandon stood an inch or two above most of the other boys his age. And he had dark hair, like Harley's. Harley could definitely see a hint of Audra in his face, especially around the mouth, but his thin build and carriage were reminiscent of pictures Harley had seen of himself at a similar age.

A woman walked by holding the hand of a little girl with at least four purple bows in her hair, and eyed him suspiciously. He supposed he didn't blend in very well despite his nonchalance, not at a private school where most of the children's fathers wore Armani suits and drove Mercedes to work. But at this point he was having a tough time caring what anyone thought. Brandon was so close. Harley wanted to watch him all day, to memorize every line of his face and listen to his laughter—

"Excuse me."

Harley turned impatiently to the woman who'd just passed him.

"Yes?"

Her eyes flicked over his jacket, jeans and boots. "I don't recognize you. Do you have a child who goes to school here?"

"I do," he said.

This seemed to surprise her, which was no more than Harley had expected. "And that child's name is…"

"None of your business," he finished frankly.

Her eyes widened and her lips pursed, then she gripped her Gucci bag closer to her body and dragged her child down to the corner, where she threw him another reproachful glance before continuing at light-speed toward the school.

Harley knew he should go. With all the dangers children faced these days, he couldn't really blame the busybody for being protective, but neither could he force his feet to carry him back to his car.

Just another minute or two…

Brandon had the ball and was running toward him, closer and closer. Harley could see the sweat running down from his hairline and was caught by the intensity on his face.

Look up, he thought, *look at me.* He didn't want to upset Brandon or bother him in any way, but at the same time, he longed for eye contact, for…something.

But Brandon was too intent on the game. He tried to kick the ball past the goalie, only to have it deflected. Then someone from the other team started moving it in the opposite direction. The ball changed hands several times, but then Brandon's team scored a point, which brought him close to the fence again.

"That was awesome! Way to go, Scott," Brandon called, cheering the boy who'd managed to slip the ball past the goalie.

Harley smiled at the camaraderie, completely enamored with his son, but then the boys ran back the other way and a man wearing a tweed sport coat came out of the huge red brick school and interrupted their game. When he pointed at Harley, everyone turned and Harley started hedging away. Evidently, his time was up. He was making people uncomfortable; he needed to move on.

But, man, it had been great to see his son!

Grinning like a boy himself, he shoved his hands in his pockets and strode to his car. And he was still wearing that same silly grin as he drove off.

CHAPTER ELEVEN

"HAVE ANY OF YOU seen that man before?" Mr. Haggerty asked.

Brandon shaded his eyes and watched a guy in a black leather coat get into a white car and drive away. His English teacher's question followed the two he'd already posed: "Who is that man?" and "Did he say anything to any of you?" But it received a similar response.

"I don't think so."

"Who?"

"I've never seen him before."

"Me, neither."

"No one knows who he is or what he was doing here?" Mr. Haggerty pressed.

"Why? Do you think he's a drug dealer or something?" Johnny Lindstrom wanted to know.

"I have no idea," Mr. Haggerty replied, "but he sure seemed to be taking an interest in your game."

"He never said anything to us."

The bell sounded and everyone scrambled to line up at the front entrance, everyone except the soccer players. They hesitated, wondering if the mysterious man was significant in some way, but Mr. Haggerty waved them on. "Go ahead, boys. There's no need to be late. He's gone now. But I want to be informed if he comes back, okay? Especially if he tries to approach any of you."

"Why?" Travis Peltier asked.

"Because we have to be careful of strangers."

"Maybe he's not a stranger. Maybe he used to go here," Travis said.

"I sincerely doubt that," Mr. Haggerty replied.

Sean Covey made a disbelieving face. "I don't think so, either. He looked too cool. Did you see his jacket? I bet he has a tattoo. He probably has lots of tattoos."

"Just remember that we don't talk to anyone we don't know regardless of how 'cool' we think they look," Mr. Haggerty said. "There are some very dangerous people out there."

"My mother told me about this guy who planted a bomb at Southside School," the boy next to Brandon told the boy standing on his other side. "He ended up shooting himself, brains all over the mirror and everything. And then they didn't know where the bomb was. But they sent in a bomb squad, and one guy found it under the bleachers in the gym."

"That only happens at public schools," Theo, the other boy responded, but Brandon wasn't really paying attention to the conversations that had started buzzing around him. He was still picturing the man by the fence.

"What do you think that was all about?" he asked Scott as they hurried to the back of the line.

Scott shrugged. "I don't know. I didn't even see that guy until Mr. Haggerty pointed him out, did you?"

"No." Brandon had been too wrapped up in the soccer game to notice anything else. But when he'd seen the man standing there, watching them, he'd felt sort of singled out even though he couldn't explain why.

He kicked a small rock and focused on the way it skittered across the pavement while the other children's voices droned in his ears. *Singled out.* How dumb. Why would a complete stranger be any more interested in him than in the other boys? Maybe he was imagining it. The odd tingle that had zipped down his spine was probably just more of the weird feelings he'd been having about all the stuff going on at home. His grandparents were still gone, Aunt Lauren was acting strange and Kim was whispering about him when she talked on the phone. People used to whisper in his presence all the time, when his mother was alive. They thought he didn't know about the pipes she was always trying to hide, but he'd been good at finding them, much better than anyone else. She used to get so angry with him for throwing them away, but he hated the stuff she smoked with them, hated what it did to her. And sometimes he hated her. Once he found a baggie in her purse while they were driving in the car and he'd tossed it out the window. She'd slapped him then, but he'd never given up trying to save her. That was probably what made him the angriest of all. No matter how hard he tried, she always managed to get more, to hide it in better and better places, to smoke it with those pipes.

But that was what people *used* to whisper about. The grayish rocklike stuff and what it was doing to his mother. The whispering wasn't so bad when he understood the reason behind it. He would simply act as if he hadn't heard it. But these new secrets really bothered him. There wasn't anything to whisper about now. Was there?

"LAUREN? Where are you? I thought I could catch you before you left to take Brandon to school. This is your father. Your mother and I are wondering what's going on and why you haven't called us. Are you okay? Let us hear from you. We're planning to visit the Tower of London today, but we'll wait till you call." *Click. Beep.*

Lauren hit the erase button on the answering machine and slumped down on the stool by the kitchen desk. She'd finished making her bed and straightening her room and getting showered and making a grocery list. She'd even placed a few calls on the fund-raiser and recruited Jennifer Pratt to help her, since she was so behind. But now it was time to talk to her parents and level with them about her thoughts. She couldn't put it off any longer. Her father wouldn't appreciate a dissenting opinion, especially where Harley was concerned, but she felt she owed it to Brandon to voice one. Especially after reading Audra's journal last night. Her sister's words painted a very vivid picture of the way Audra had behaved in high school, lending credence to Harley's assertion that he didn't exploit her or intentionally get her pregnant. It was Audra who'd been playing games, Audra who'd used Harley.

Rubbing sweaty palms on her khaki capris, Lauren picked up the telephone and dialed the eleven-digit number that would connect her to The Ritz in London.

"Room 311," she said when the hotel operator answered.

"One moment please."

Lauren drummed her fingers on the desk while she waited, but it was only a moment before she heard her father's voice.

"There you are. We've been worried about you. What's going on? Why haven't you tried to reach us?"

"I haven't had a chance," she said. "I've been busy."

"With what?"

Standing Harley up, spying on him, hiding Brandon—take your pick. "I've got a fund-raiser coming up. For the women's shelter," she hedged.

"Oh. Well? What's happened with Harley?"

Straight to the point. Her father was so predictable. Rock-solid, confident, determined…authoritative, overbearing, closed-minded. "Nothing."

"Did you talk to him?"

To distract herself from her nervousness, Lauren doodled on the telephone message pad, scribbling out the fifteen thousand dollar figure she'd originally offered Harley until it was completely obliterated. "He stopped by here, but I'd already sent Brandon to Kimberly's for the night, so it wasn't a problem."

"What did he say?"

Lauren hesitated, then decided there wasn't any point in hiding the truth. "He's going to fight for custody."

"That son of a bitch! Who does he think he is, appearing out of nowhere after all these years?"

Lauren winced at her father's reaction, wondering why hearing him call Harley a *son of a bitch* bothered her.

"He'll do no such thing!" her father was saying. "I've already placed a few calls. Vince, at my office, is going to follow up on this until I can get home. He'll line up the best lawyers in the state. You don't need to worry about any of this, Lauren. It might take some time, but—"

"Actually, I'm not so sure that drawing a hard line is the best thing for Brandon," she said, interrupting before he could go too far down that road.

"What do you mean? We're not going to sit back and let—"

"Brandon *wants* to meet his father," she said.

"I don't care what he wants. We've already talked about this. There isn't any need to go into it again."

Lauren took a deep breath and blurted out what she'd been dying to say for days. "Actually, I'm afraid there is. *I* think letting Harley see Brandon could be a good idea."

Silence. Dead silence. She curled her fingers into her palms and waited for the explosion, the disappointment, maybe even a few accusations of disloyalty and betrayal. What her father said hit even lower.

"I thought you loved that boy."

"I do love him! That's why I want to give him the opportunity to meet his father. Harley doesn't seem like such a bad guy, Dad. I've—"

"You've what?" her father broke in. "Gotten to know him in the past three or four days? How can you possibly assess his character in so short a time?"

"How can you be any more sure of his character than I am?" Lauren responded before she could stop herself.

"How can you be so confident that you're always right? That it's fair to play God with other people's lives? What if Harley's just what Brandon needs? Brandon had a mother who chose crack over him, who purposely destroyed herself before his eyes. And he's never had a father."

"He's had us. How could a child possibly need any more than we've given him?"

"We can't replace his father," she said. "I don't think we've got the right to try."

"Are you serious?"

"Completely!"

He laughed, but it was a harsh, denigrating sound. "I can't believe this. What is it about that bastard that turns my daughters' minds to mush?"

Fresh anger surged through Lauren. Audra might've said some things in her journal that had made Lauren think more kindly of Harley than before. And he was an incredibly attractive man. But her decision to let him see Brandon had much more to do with her nephew than it did with Harley. "My mind isn't mush just because I disagree with you, Dad. Maybe *you're* the one who has a problem. Maybe you're afraid of losing control of everyone around you."

"Now you're acting like Audra," her father accused. "And I thought you were better than that."

Better than that? Lauren hung up because it was the only thing she could do to stop the conversation from getting even worse, but she was shaking and crying and so angry she could scream. When was her father going to stop treating her with such condescension, as though his opinion mattered so much more than her own? When was he going to stop treating her like a child?

When she quit acting like one, she decided, and dialed the phone again.

"Hello?" Tank. Lauren took a deep breath, so she could speak, and asked for Harley.

"This Lauren?" Tank asked.

"Yes."

"You and Kim aren't after my color TV, are you?"

"What?"

He chuckled. "Nothing. Just a minute."

She heard him say something in the background, then Harley came on the line.

"Hello?"

"It's me."

"I know."

He didn't sound particularly happy to hear from her. Swallowing hard, she forced herself to speak while she still had the nerve to take a stand against her father. *I have to trust myself now or I never will.*

"You can see Brandon," she said. "Come over tonight at six."

Stunned silence. Then, skeptically, "Are you going to be there this time?"

"We'll both be here."

More silence, but finally, he asked, "What's changed?"

I have. "Everything," she said, "and I'm afraid it'll never be the same again."

LAUREN TOLD HERSELF she didn't care what she looked like. She didn't care whether or not Harley thought she was a good cook. She wasn't trying to impress him. But she spent all afternoon making salmon steaks, new potatoes, asparagus pasta salad and stuffed mushrooms, and she changed outfits three times before settling on one.

Feminine pride, she told herself. Harley had considered her beneath his notice in high school. She wanted to make sure he realized she could hold her own now, that was all.

Brandon had called her from school two hours ago to see if he could go home with his and Scott's other friend,

Winston, and she'd let him to buy herself more time. It had saved her the half hour it would've taken to pick him up from school—and all the questions he would've asked when he saw her preparations. Which was good, because she wanted to have everything ready so she could focus completely on him when she told him the news. Only now that the edge was gone from her anger, and her nephew was supposed to be home any minute, she felt nervous and doubtful again, and wondered how he was going to react when he learned his father was coming to dinner.

The aroma of cooked mushrooms and the sausage she'd used to stuff them permeated the house. Elegant china and fresh flowers graced the table, and she was wearing a sleeveless summer sweater and wraparound skirt that made her appear more shapely than she was.

The house smelled and looked great, but with only a clock ticking in the background, it was too quiet. Lauren felt as though she was holding her breath, waiting, waiting, waiting. She needed music, something to distract her from her thoughts and calm her nerves. Especially since Brandon was late. If her nephew didn't arrive soon, she wouldn't have the time she wanted to discuss Harley with him.

She put on a Faith Hill CD and poured a glass of wine. *He'll be here any minute,* she told herself, but time kept slipping away, and there was no sign of Brandon. Maybe he needed a ride. Although Mrs. Reynolds had agreed to drop him off, something could've happened. Lauren called to check, but after a few rings, the answering machine came on. She left a message and hung up.

"They're on their way," she said aloud. "I'm sure they're on their way. God, they'd better be on their way!" Keeping one eye on the clock, she sipped her wine and paced the floor and sipped her wine some more. Five-forty. Five-forty-five. Where was he? Harley was supposed to arrive in fifteen minutes.

She called Winston Reynolds's house again, with no luck, then tried Scott's.

"Scott wasn't able to go to Winston's today," his mother told her. "He hasn't cleaned his room for a week, so I made him come home."

"Has he heard from Brandon?"

"Not since school. He hasn't been out of his room. I won't let him come out until it's clean, so it might be a while."

"Thanks," she said and hung up to call Harley. She needed to put him off for a few minutes, needed to find Brandon and—

The roar of a motorcycle intruded on the music. He was here! He was here ten minutes early when she needed him to be ten or even twenty minutes late!

Lauren set her empty wineglass down and stood to the side of the window so she could watch Harley approach without being seen. He wasn't wearing a suit today. He wasn't carrying any presents. He was wearing the faded blue jeans that looked so good on him and a simple T-shirt. No frills. No fuss. No jacket. The temperature had soared into the lower nineties this afternoon, prolonging the unusual heat wave that made it much too hot for leather, even when riding a motorcycle.

He stood on the porch for a few seconds before ringing the bell and Lauren wondered what he was feeling. Was he as nervous as she was? She doubted it. Given the circumstances, he probably felt some apprehension, but he looked as cool and calm as a deep, still lake. On the other hand, he always looked cool and completely in control. That was part of his appeal.

The doorbell sounded, and Lauren took a shaky breath. So he was a little early. It wasn't the end of the world, right? Brandon would be home soon, and then…and then she'd just have to see how the two of them got on. She wouldn't have the chance to prepare her nephew for his surprise, but he'd already told her he wanted to meet his dad. Tonight he was going to get that wish—in spite of her father.

"Hello, come in," she said, opening the door and stepping back to admit him.

He hesitated for a fraction of a second, as though he felt like Daniel about to step into the lion's den, but then he angled his shoulders to fit past her and stood in the living room, making the whole place feel smaller for his dominating presence.

"Where's Brandon?" he asked, his eyes quickly scanning all points of entry.

"He's a little late, but he'll be home any minute."

He nodded, his right hand fiddling with the keys to his bike, and Lauren realized he *was* nervous. The implacable Harley Nelson felt as uncomfortable as she did.

"I hope you're hungry," she said, trying to make small talk so they could both relax. "I've got dinner ready."

"I ate before I came over."

Great. Well, that was probably her fault. She hadn't mentioned dinner, and he'd gone without the last time she'd invited him. Tonight he'd obviously prepared for the worst.

"Why don't you sit down?"

He glanced at all the furniture cluttering the room—the Victorian settee and matching chairs, the marble-topped side tables her mother had had flown in from Italy, the mahogany secretary and rococo mirrors—and, if Lauren was reading him correctly, felt a measure of contempt at the excess. But he sat on an antique Chippendale chair and continued to jingle his keys.

"Can I get you a drink?" she asked. "A glass of wine or something stronger?"

"No, thanks."

He wouldn't even look at her. He wasn't going to eat

dinner. And Brandon wasn't home. They certainly weren't getting off to a very good start.

"Look, I know you're angry with me about what happened at Tank's apartment. And I'm sorry. I-I was just trying to solve the problem any way I could."

"Don't worry about it. You were just following in your father's footsteps, right?"

Lauren knew that wasn't a compliment. "Maybe. You took his money readily enough last time."

He scowled, his anger showing now, but Lauren preferred this response to the tightly leashed disdain of before. "There wasn't any point in *not* taking it," he said. "No matter what I did, your father wasn't going to let me be anything to Audra or our baby. He'd already decided I was nothing more than a bum, and without her support, I had nothing to work with."

"My father wasn't trying to hurt you or anyone else. He just wanted to ensure his daughter's happiness."

"From what I'm hearing, he did one hell of a job."

"That's not fair," Lauren said. "We did what we could."

"Maybe. Maybe not."

Lauren was on the verge of launching into a tirade about how difficult it had been to live with Audra and witness her steady decline, how helpless they'd all felt when they couldn't save her. Harley had no right to condemn them, she thought. But then she remembered what he'd said when the shoe was on the other foot—*You and your family have made judging me a national pastime*—and knew, if they were ever going to get anywhere, attitudes had to change on both sides.

Taking the seat beside his, she placed a hand on his forearm, hoping he'd feel her sincerity through her touch. "I'm sorry I stood you up last time," she said. "I'm sorry I tried to bribe you and, regardless of fault or blame, I'm sorry for what happened ten years ago. I love Brandon with all my heart. I want what's best for him. I also love my parents and I want to protect them. Isn't there some way we can work this out peaceably?''

His gaze settled on her hand, then shifted to her face. ''You didn't have anything to do with what happened ten years ago,'' he said.

''But I'm the one who's in the line of fire now. Will you work with me instead of against me, Harley?''

HER EYES WERE shockingly blue. Harley hadn't wanted to notice—he didn't want to find *anything* about Lauren Worthington attractive—but the beauty of her eyes was tough to ignore when she was staring up at him so beseechingly. She was sitting close enough that he could even catch her sweet, clean scent, and although he might not have paid much attention to her in high school, he was certainly aware of her now.

Don't trust her. She's just like her father, remember?

But she had a certain magnetism Quentin Worthington did not possess, and it had nothing to do with the canned sex-appeal so many men found appealing in a woman.

''I'm willing to let bygones be bygones,'' he conceded, but he moved his arm so that she was no longer touching him. He was too anxious about seeing Brandon to maintain much of a defense against liking her right now, and he felt safer keeping his distance—a strange reaction, considering he'd never felt threatened by a woman before.

''I haven't had a chance to warn Brandon that you're coming,'' she said in an apologetic tone. ''He was supposed to be home forty-five minutes ago, and I'd planned to sit down with him and—''

The door flew open and Lauren's words were lost as the boy Harley had watched at the school—*his* boy—came in yelling for Lauren. When he saw both of them in the living room, he froze, his backpack still slung over his shoulder, a wary expression clouding his face.

"What are *you* doing here?" he asked, as soon as he noticed Harley.

Harley's stomach clenched with the worst kind of fear he'd ever known. Never had he felt more vulnerable than at this moment, when he was gazing at the child he'd dreamed about for so long. "I came to see you," he admitted.

"How come?"

Harley stood, as did Lauren. She went to Brandon while he searched his son's face, hoping for some sign that he might be accepted. *Please, God, after ten years....* He'd told himself not to expect too much. His son had never had any contact with him. Brandon could resent him, hate him or be ambivalent. The boy had lived with the Worthingtons all his life, so it was too much to hope he'd be open-minded, wasn't it? And yet Harley couldn't help hoping with everything inside him.

"Brandon, do you know who this is?" Lauren asked, sounding slightly confused.

Brandon didn't give away Harley's visit to the school, although Harley could tell from his reaction that he'd seen him. "No."

Lauren took him by the shoulders so that he'd have to meet her eyes. "This is your father, sweetheart," she said. "He's visiting from California."

"My *father?*" he echoed weakly. And suddenly Harley regretted that he hadn't worn his suit. Maybe Brandon was disappointed. Maybe Brandon wanted a father who dressed and behaved like all the other kids' dads...

But then his son looked at him and smiled, and Harley's knees went weak in relief.

CHAPTER TWELVE

LAUREN STOOD in the driveway next to Harley as Brandon sat on his motorcycle and pretended to drive it. They'd had dinner together, taken a tour of Brandon's bedroom and played Nintendo for over an hour. They'd fed the spectacular tropical fish that filled the giant tank in the game room, talked about Brandon's school, his favorite movies and his friends. Everything had gone much more smoothly than Harley had dared to expect. Even Lauren had been pleasant. More than pleasant. She'd been supportive and responsive. Only now it was time for him to leave. Already. It was nearly ten o'clock and Brandon had school in the morning.

"This is so cool," Brandon said, still admiring the bike. "Will you take me for a ride sometime?"

Harley looked at Lauren, knowing instinctively that she wouldn't like this idea. For one, it required a great deal of trust, and she was still too wary to watch him take off with Brandon on the back of his bike. Harley was even a little worried about what he might do with such an opportunity. If he did what he *wanted* to do, he'd keep driving and take his son to California without a backward glance. "Maybe another time," he said. "Motorcycles are dangerous, and I'm afraid we'd worry your aunt Lauren."

"I'd rather you didn't," Lauren concurred.

"Aw, she worries too much," Brandon complained, but he didn't put much conviction in it. Harley got the impression he was distracted by something he deemed more important. And he found out what it was a few seconds later.

"Are you gonna go back to California soon?" he asked. Judging by the way he had his head down and was playing with the gauges, Brandon had meant to sound casual. But something in his voice revealed his fear that Harley would leave before he was ready to let him go. With their history, Harley could certainly understand why he'd be worried.

"Not for a while," he said, careful not to state anything too strongly for fear of spooking Lauren. He didn't want to lose her cooperation now.

His son found the switch to turn the headlight, which came on automatically with the key, to bright. *Click, click. On, off.* "So I'll see you again?"

"I hope so," he said. "But that's up to your aunt."

Brandon turned his attention to Lauren, who was silhouetted in the moonlight and looking prettier than Harley had ever seen her. Or was his exaggerated appreciation just more of the euphoria he was feeling?

"Pleeeease, Aunt Lauren?" Brandon pleaded. "Can he come back? Can he come back tomorrow?"

Lauren smiled. "Okay, Bran." She tousled his hair lovingly, then turned to gaze at Harley. "Tomorrow's Friday. Why don't you come over and go swimming with us after Brandon gets out of school? It's certainly hot enough."

"What time will that be?"

"Three o'clock."

He nodded, feeling so warm and good inside that he hardly knew how to react. *He'd met his son.* Brandon liked him and wanted him to come back. And Lauren was going to allow it. "I'll be here. Any chance you'll let me take you both out to dinner afterward?"

"Aunt Lauren?" Brandon asked with the same hopeful expression.

She laughed. "How can I say no?"

"Great." Harley reached out to help his son off the bike and nearly pulled him into his arms. But he knew it was too much too soon. He needed to wait until Brandon was more familiar with him, until they'd built a relationship.

"Good night, squirt," he said, giving him an affectionate squeeze on the shoulder instead. Then he looked at Lauren and had the crazy impulse to hug her, too.

He was just high on happiness, he decided, and tossed her his most carefree grin. "Thanks."

WHEN HARLEY RETURNED to the apartment, Tank's brother Damien was sitting on the couch with Tank, having a beer. Even though Damien was already living away from home, starting his law practice, when Tank and Harley were in high school, Harley recognized him from the family functions he'd attended with Tank ten years ago and the photographs that had hung around the Thompson household.

"Tank told me you were in town," Damien said as soon as Harley had let himself in and shut the door.

Harley smiled. Smiling seemed to be all he could do since meeting Brandon. "Good to see you again, Damien. What's up, man?"

"Just thought I'd stop by and say hello. Want a beer?"

Harley had stopped drinking years ago, in his darkest moment, when he knew that if he continued on the path he was treading, he'd end up a drunken failure. Barring the night Lauren had stood him up, the most he ever drank now was an occasional glass of wine, which he'd already had with dinner. "No, thanks."

"Sit down. I'm anxious to hear what's going on with you. Tank says you're doing pretty well for yourself in California."

"Well enough," Harley said, but he didn't want to talk about the dealership or how he'd gotten his start by buying used cars and bikes out of the newspaper or at auctions, fixing them up and reselling them for a profit. His mind was still one hundred percent focused on Brandon.

"How'd it go with Lauren?" Tank asked, following him across the room with his eyes.

"Good," he said, even though Lauren had been much better than good. She'd made a fabulous meal he'd eaten even though he wasn't hungry and she'd been accommodating, sweet, even friendly. Harley had enjoyed her intelligent comments and her laughter when she couldn't figure out how to play the Nintendo game and kept causing her little guy to jump off a cliff. Brandon and Harley had both beaten her again and again, but she'd sure been fun to play with. And the memory of her cool fingers when she'd touched him right before Brandon got home was—

Harley jerked himself out of his thoughts long enough to realize where they were leading and made a quick and decisive correction. It was nothing. Lauren's touch was nothing.

"Well? You gonna tell us what happened?" Tank asked.

Taking the easy chair across from the couch, Harley put his feet up and linked his fingers across his abdomen. "I met Brandon," he said simply.

Tank smiled, but Damien nearly choked on his beer. "You did?" he managed to say after a sputtering cough. "When?"

"Tonight. I had dinner with Lauren and Brandon."

"I told you," Tank said, grinning. "She invited him over this morning."

"But what about her father?" Damien asked.

"He wasn't there," Harley said.

"I know he wasn't there. He's not even in the States. But he's not going to stay away forever."

"When's he due back?" Harley asked.

Damien didn't answer immediately. He stared at his beer as though deep in thought.

"When's he comin' back?" Tank repeated.

Finally Damien glanced up. "I don't know. I tried to reach Lauren yesterday, but she hasn't returned my call." He paused. "I can't believe she'd cross him."

"How do you know she crossed him?" Tank asked. "He's getting on in years. Maybe he doesn't have the energy to hate Harley anymore. Maybe he's ready to put the past behind him. Audra's gone, after all."

"Quentin Worthington isn't the type to give up a grudge that easily," Damien said. "Besides, he holds Harley responsible for Audra's death."

"Her *death?*" Harley cried.

"If not her death, then her ruin. She was never the same after you left," Damien said. "At least, that's the way Quentin tells the story. I used to date Lauren, so I heard a lot of it. The whole family blames you for starting Audra on drugs."

"I had nothing to do with the drugs," Harley said. "That was all Audra. I hated it when she got high. I didn't like how it made her act."

Damien shrugged. "You might know that, but Quentin believes otherwise. And I thought Lauren did, too." He took a pull of his beer. "Even if she doesn't blame you, I'm surprised she'd let you see Brandon and risk losing her father's goodwill. She's always thought Quentin could walk on water."

Harley had known all along that he probably wouldn't be seeing Brandon if Quentin was home. But he'd been so caught up in finally meeting his son that he hadn't really considered the price Lauren might pay for letting him come over tonight. Somehow that cast her in a different light entirely.

"You don't think he'll cut her off or anything, do you?" he asked.

"Who can say? He's got more pride than most men. But I wish he *would* cut her off. Then maybe she'd need someone."

Tank chuckled. "Someone like you?"

Damien finished his beer and set the empty can on the coffee table. "Yeah. Someone like me."

"So? How'd it go?" Kimberly asked.

Lauren stretched and shoved the pillows against the headboard so she could sit up. She'd gone to bed shortly after Harley left, but she hadn't been able to sleep. She'd been too busy thinking about Brandon's almost instant adoration of his father, the way Harley smiled every time he looked at his son and how it made her feel to see the two of them. Regardless of what Harley was or wasn't, something about him fit Brandon perfectly. She could feel it when they were together and she enjoyed watching her nephew bask in his father's attention, which was, she had to admit, a pretty nice thing to have.

"It was fantastic," she admitted. "It was the first time I've ever found Harley easy to read. Whenever he looked at Brandon, it just melted my heart, you know?"

"Really? What about Brandon? How did he respond?"

Lauren laid one arm across her forehead and stared up at the ceiling. "He took one look at Harley and fell in love. It was that simple."

"Did Harley treat *you* okay?"

"He was a little cool at first. But we decided to bury the hatchet for Brandon's sake. After that he seemed to forget we were ever enemies. He teased me every time I lost a game of Nintendo, had seconds of everything at supper even though he'd already eaten, and was really the perfect date."

"*Date?*"

"I mean guest," she said quickly.

"Right."

Lauren chose to ignore the disbelief in Kimberly's voice. She was still too excited about the events of this evening. "He even deferred to me when Brandon wanted a ride on his motorcycle," she went on. "He knew I wouldn't like it."

"Sounds like we've misjudged him."

Lauren sighed wistfully. "Yeah, I think maybe we have."

"Lauren?"

"Hmm?" She was picturing Harley lounging back on the leather couch in the game room, easily beating her at Nintendo, then nudging her and winking as he pointed out the huge difference in their scores. He had such a disarming grin—

"Lauren!"

"What? What's wrong?"

"Nothing's wrong with me. It's you I'm worried about. You're not...you know, *interested* in Harley, are you?"

Lauren laughed incredulously. "Of course not. I'm just happy for Brandon that things went so well, that's all."

"Uh-huh."

"Stop it. Why are you being so skeptical?"

"Because you're acting a little giddy."

"What are you talking about? I never act giddy. I skipped the giddy stage altogether."

"You're acting giddy now. You're absolutely gushing about Harley."

"That's not true! You asked me how things went, so I told you."

No response.

"Kimberly!"

"Okay, but just keep this in mind: it's in Harley's best interests to win you over, and he has some pretty powerful tools at his disposal."

"I know that. Don't you think I know that?"

"I don't think you realize how vulnerable you are.

You're twenty-seven, single and you have no love life. And he's one of the sexiest men I've ever met. He knows how to appeal to women. Don't let him use you to get what he wants.''

"What is it you think he wants?"

"Brandon."

Of course. What had she been thinking? He wouldn't want anything more than that. Not from her. "I won't let him or anyone else take Brandon away from me. Jeez, wasn't it you who said 'what a guy' when Harley refused my bribe?"

"I can admire him, Lauren. I don't have anything to lose. You, on the other hand, have to be careful."

Lauren's call-waiting beeped, and she glanced at the digital alarm clock by her bed. It was after eleven. Who would be calling this late?

Her parents. *Oh, no...not yet.*

"I mean, he could really cause some problems if he wormed his way into your heart, you know?" Kimberly was saying. "Think what it would do to your father. And think where it would leave you if Harley was only interested in exacting a little revenge."

"I've never fallen head over heels in love. I'm not sure I can. So don't worry about it. But now that the afterglow of the evening has been completely destroyed, I have to go," Lauren said. "I have a call coming through."

"This late?"

"It's probably my dad," Lauren said with a growing sense of dread.

Kimberly told Lauren to call her in the morning, then hung up so Lauren could switch over, and Lauren hesitated for only a second before doing so. She had to tell her father what she'd done sometime. She'd known that before she'd ever let Harley come to the house. Now she had to stand by her opinion and her actions. And it was better to do it sooner rather than later, right?

Get it over with. You can do it. You're a woman full-grown....

"Hello?" she said, her heart pounding.

"Lauren?"

Harley. Lauren could tell by the immediate thrill the sound of his voice sent down her spine. Or was that merely the relief she felt that the caller wasn't her father?

"Did I wake you?"

"No, I was just—" *praying it wasn't my father* "—thinking."

"About what?"

You. "Tonight."

"Tonight was great."

Lauren could picture the expression on his face when he made that statement and felt her heart soften even more. "It *was* great. Brandon really enjoyed you." *I enjoyed you.*

"He's such a good kid. He's everything I ever hoped he would be."

She paused, waiting to hear what he was calling about. But he seemed to have difficulty coming out with it.

"Listen, I'm sorry to trouble you so late," he said at last. "I just couldn't sleep and wanted to...you know, thank you. For tonight."

"You're welcome."

"Well, I'll let you get some sleep."

"Good night, Harley."

"Good night, Lauren," he said and hung up, but the sound of her name on his lips stayed with her until she fell asleep several hours later and it was the first thing on her mind when she woke up the next morning.

HARLEY WAS DEAD ASLEEP when Tank came in and woke him.

"Harley, man, wake up. I think your kid's on the line."

His kid? For a moment, Harley thought he had to be

dreaming. But then he remembered last night and everything that had happened, and jumped out of bed to grab the phone.

"Hello?"

"It's me." Tank was right. It was Brandon.

"Hi, buddy. How are you today?"

"Good. Did I wake you up?"

"Yeah. I got to bed late. But that's okay. I like hearing from you. What are you doing?"

"Getting ready for school."

"Is it that time already?"

"Uh-huh. We're leaving in a minute. I just wanted to make sure you're still coming over today."

"Of course I'm coming over."

"Good." He paused. "Sure wish I didn't have to go to school..."

Harley was pretty groggy, but there was no way he could miss a hint of that size. "Sorry, bud," he said, laughing, "I can't get you off the hook there. But all that studying's going to come in handy later. I promise."

"And I'll get to tell my friends about you," Brandon added, as though doing so would make a nice consolation prize.

"There you go."

"They'll all be pretty excited. You don't have any tattoos, do you?"

"Any what?"

"Tattoos."

What made Brandon think of tattoos at eight o'clock in the morning? "Just one."

"That's awesome! Where?"

"On my shoulder blade."

"Is it a heart or an animal or something?"

Harley was wearing only a pair of boxers. Rolling his shoulder forward, so he could see the tattoo that had always carried such significance for him, he said, "No, it's a name."

"Really? Whose? Whose name is it? My mother's?"

He smiled. "No. It's yours."

"HE IS TOO my dad!" Brandon whispered harshly, growing angry when Travis Peltier and Theo Price, the two boys sitting on either side of him in English class, wouldn't believe him.

"You didn't even know him," Travis said. "When Mr. Haggerty pointed him out, you said you'd never seen him before."

"Mr. Haggerty thought he looked like a bad guy," Theo added. "You're telling us that's your *dad?*"

"He's not a bad guy," Brandon said. "He just drives a motorcycle. There's nothing wrong with that. And I didn't know him 'cause he's lived in California for ten years."

"My mom says motorcycles are dangerous," Theo said.

"So?" Brandon replied.

"She also says your mom was a whore and you're a bastard who had to be taken in by family. She said you're lucky you have grandparents who are so good to you."

Theo's words caused Brandon's ears to burn with embarrassment. Most of the kids at Mt. Marley treated him well and didn't seem to care that he didn't have the same type of family they did. But every once in a while, someone said something—though it was usually a teacher—that reminded him he was different, that he had more reason to be grateful than everyone else. Which was why he'd been so eager to tell his schoolmates that his father had appeared at last. He wasn't going to be different anymore. He wasn't going to be the kid who needed others to feel sorry for him.

"You just want that guy to be your father because Sean said he was cool," Travis persisted.

"That's not true!" Brandon cried.

Scott was sitting a few desks away. Mr. Haggerty had moved him and Brandon apart a few weeks ago for talking, but he was still close enough to hear. He kept twisting around in his seat, frowning. "Why don't you guys leave him alone?" he whispered at Travis and Theo while Mr. Haggerty was busy writing on the blackboard.

All the students in that part of the room looked up from their work and started to stare, and Brandon felt his blush deepen.

"Shut up," Travis said. "You don't even know what we're talking about."

"You're talking about his dad."

"So? We weren't talking to you."

"I don't care," Scott said. "If Brandon says his dad's in town, then his dad's in town."

"After ten years?" Travis laughed. "He's a little late, isn't he?"

Theo joined in the laughter and a few of the other kids snickered, too. One of them was Melissa Hayes, who Brandon thought was the most beautiful girl in the world. "I predict he'll disappear for another ten years. What do you think, Travis?"

"He's going to stick around now," Brandon announced, loud enough for Melissa to hear, although he had no way of knowing whether or not his father planned to stay until morning, let alone make any kind of permanent move. "He wants to be a real dad to me."

"Right. And my dad's the president of the United States!" Travis scoffed.

"Bastard, bastard, bastard," Theo taunted. "What would a tough dude like the one we saw yesterday want with a bastard like you? Only your grandparents want you. Or maybe they're taking you 'cause no one else will."

"Leave him alone." This time Scott didn't keep his voice low enough. Mr. Haggerty turned just before Brandon slugged Theo in the stomach and knocked over Travis's desk. The three of them went down in a pile of arms and legs, groans and grunts, with a cry from Melissa when they nearly toppled her desk, too.

A few seconds later, a red-faced and puffing Mr. Haggerty pulled them apart. "What's going on here?" he asked angrily. "Who started this?"

Brandon pointed at Theo. Theo and Travis pointed at him.

"Tell me why you did this," Haggerty demanded. He was looking at Brandon, but Brandon could see Melissa out of the corner of his eye and didn't want to tell the whole class what Travis and Theo had said. He wasn't really a *bastard*. Was he? At least not the kind Theo meant. His parents might never have married, but that wasn't something *he* could help. And the way Theo said *bastard* made it sound so…awful.

"It was Theo's fault," Scott announced, elbowing Theo in a move that was obviously meant to go unnoticed but was too blatant to avoid Mr. Haggerty's attention.

"That's enough," he said, giving Scott a stern look that warned him to stop immediately. "I'm asking Brandon what happened."

Brandon stared at his teacher for a few seconds, wondering what to say, but the faces of his classmates were all turned toward him, expectant, curious. What had happened didn't bear repeating. When he said nothing, he saw Scott open his mouth, but quickly silenced him with a glare. Then Mr. Haggerty grabbed him by the scruff of the neck and hauled him out of class.

"Well, if you don't want to tell me what happened," he said, "you can explain it to your parents—I mean your aunt—while you sit home on suspension."

CHAPTER THIRTEEN

"DAD?"

Harley couldn't believe his ears. Brandon was calling him again? Already? It wasn't quite noon. Shouldn't he be in school? "What's going on, buddy?"

"I'm in the principal's office. I...I got in a fight during English."

This surprised Harley. He'd gotten the impression from his son's speech and manner, and Lauren's attitude toward him, that Brandon was a pretty mild and obedient kid. "You did? Over what?"

A weighty pause. "Nothing," Brandon said at last.

"I've fought over some pretty stupid things, but I always felt I had a reason," Harley said. "Who started it?"

"Theo and Travis."

"Are you okay?"

"I hit my face on something when we fell and got a bloody nose. But it's stopped now."

"And where's your Aunt Lauren?" Harley was flattered that Brandon would think to contact him—and that he'd remembered his number after dialing it only once—but he was also a little curious as to why *he* was getting this call.

"She's not home. They tried to call her, but she's not even answering her cell phone."

"Do you need a ride home? Should I come to the school?"

This time when his son spoke, Harley thought he heard tears in his voice. "Will you?"

"Sure, bud. I'll be right there. Just hang on for a few minutes, okay?"

"Okay."

Harley doubted anyone at Mt. Marley Academy would let him take Brandon and leave, at least not without prior authorization from the Worthingtons, but they sure as heck couldn't stop him from sitting with his son. Hanging up, he scooped his keys off the counter and headed outside. He'd returned his rental car that morning, so he had only his motorcycle as transportation, but he would probably have chosen to ride it, anyway. When he was in a hurry, he liked the maneuverability of his bike.

He reached Brandon's school only fifteen minutes later. Unlike yesterday, he parked in front, where the faculty and other parents parked, then cut the engine, set his helmet on the seat and jogged to the entrance.

"Can I help you?" A redheaded woman with curly hair looked up from her computer as soon as he darkened the threshold of the principal's office. Not quite as Spartan as the principal's offices he'd visited so often in his youth, this one had attractive paper on three walls and mahogany bookshelves lining the fourth, a jewel-toned rug and heavy, quality-looking furniture.

"I'm Harley Nelson. My son called. He said he's been in a fight."

The woman blinked up at him, the freckles on her face only partially hidden by a thick layer of powder. "And your son is…"

"Brandon Worthington."

"Oh!" She swiveled toward him. "He mentioned that he'd called his father, but I…well, I assumed he meant Quentin Worthington. Quentin and his wife, and Lauren, of course, are the only ones listed on Brandon's card. I don't even have an emergency number for you."

"I've been living out of town. Can I see him?"

Her eyes slid to the closed door of an inner office before she looked him over once again. "Have a seat," she finally said.

For some reason, Harley doubted she'd have told Quentin Worthington to "have a seat." He shook his head. "I'd rather not. I told Brandon I'd come right away, and I mean to keep that promise."

Her eyebrows shot up, making the blue of her eye shadow look as though it extended almost to her hairline. "That isn't how we do things here," she muttered.

"There's always a first," Harley told her. "Will you knock, or shall I?"

"Just a minute." She stood and made a show of closing her cardigan over her blouse and skirt—why she was wearing a cardigan in ninety-degree weather, Harley couldn't fathom—and stalked to the principal's door, where she rapped lightly.

"Yes?" came a voice from within.

Mrs. Wells, according to the name plate on her desk, shot Harley another disgruntled glance and poked her head inside the room. "There's a man out here who claims to be Brandon's dad," she said, the incredulity in her voice apparent.

"Have we heard from Lauren Worthington?"

"Not yet."

"Well, have him wait."

"He won't. I asked him to wait already, and he—"

Harley gently pushed the door out of Mrs. Wells's grasp. She whirled, but he was standing in the way so she couldn't close the door again, and she barely came to his collarbone. There wasn't a lot she could do to contest his actions. At least on her own.

Inside the smaller room, Brandon and a white-haired man who seemed to be in his late fifties sat facing each other across a wide desk. They both stood at his appearance, the principal in surprise, if Harley had his guess, and Brandon in eagerness, considering the way he grabbed his backpack and announced that he was ready to go.

"Slow down a second, bud," Harley told him. "And tell me what happened."

Brandon scowled. "I just got in a fight. It was nothing."

"Nothing?" Harley echoed. "Does this kind of thing happen very often?"

"No, which is what confuses me," the principal volunteered. "I'm Dr. Vincent Vanderloch."

Harley accepted the hand extended toward him. "Harley Nelson."

"This is Brandon's first altercation," Dr. Vanderloch went on. "He's always been a model student, which prompts me toward leniency, but we have an automatic suspension for fighting. He and the other boys won't be allowed to return to campus until next Wednesday."

Harley nodded. "I understand. Do you know what caused the fight?"

Vanderloch frowned at Brandon. "I'm afraid your son won't say."

"What about the other boys?"

"They claim the fight was unprovoked. They say Brandon came at them, swinging for no reason at all, but with Brandon's history, I have a difficult time believing that."

"Where are they?" Harley asked.

"Their parents picked them up just a few minutes ago."

The phone rang, and Mrs. Wells stepped over to her desk to answer it. "Thank goodness," he heard her say. "I'll get Dr. Vanderloch." She put the phone on hold and came back to the inner office. "It's Lauren Worthington," she said.

Dr. Vanderloch raised a finger, indicating to Harley that

he wouldn't be long, and picked up the phone. "I'm afraid that's true, Miss Worthington," he said. "Yes, he's fine. He had a bloody nose, but that was sort of an incidental injury, and the bleeding has stopped now... Uh-huh, that's right... No way around that, unfortunately. Yes, well, we have a small complication beyond the automatic suspension. Brandon's *father* is here."

Harley held his breath as he waited to see what Lauren's reaction would be. It wasn't as if he'd come to school to create problems. Brandon had called him because he needed someone. But she wouldn't know the background and might take exception to his involvement.

"I'll let you speak to him," Vanderloch said.

"What are you doing there?" Lauren asked the instant Harley took the phone.

"Brandon called me when he couldn't get hold of you, and I came for moral support."

"What happened?"

"Brandon won't say."

"Who did he fight with?"

"Two other boys—Travis and Theo. I don't know their last names."

"Travis and Theo have played on Brandon's soccer team before. I can't believe he'd fight with them."

"Well, according to Dr. Vanderloch, he doesn't have a history of making trouble, so let's give him the benefit of the doubt and deal with it once we get him home, okay?"

Jeez, that sounded fatherlike, Harley thought, marveling at how quickly and easily that role seemed to be coming to him. Maybe he could be a good father to Brandon, after all. He *wanted* to be a good father to him....

When Lauren didn't answer right away, Harley feared she wasn't happy with his slightly commanding tone. But what she said next was short and sweet and gave him no indication of any kind.

"I'm on my way."

"I'd offer to bring him," he told her. "But I only have my motorcycle."

"That's okay! We'll be careful!" Brandon cried, but Lauren's response was immediate and unequivocal.

"No, there's no need to take the risk."

"Okay, we'll be waiting," Harley said, but he suspected it wasn't the physical danger of Brandon riding on the back of a motorcycle that frightened Lauren. It was the risk of letting Brandon go anywhere alone with him.

LAUREN HUNG UP and dashed out of the house, feeling guilty for not answering the telephone earlier. Audra's journals had drawn her back to them, and she'd been so caught up in the events of ten years ago that she hadn't wanted to be bothered. Besides, with the way the phone kept ringing, she'd been positive it was her father. He didn't give up easily, and he hadn't called or left any messages since their argument. She was bound to hear from him eventually. But when she'd finally wandered out of her bedroom and checked the answering machine, she'd felt horrible. The calls had been from Brandon and Mt. Marley—all of them. Brandon had needed her, and it was Harley who'd been there for him. "Serves me right," she muttered, racing down Terwilliger Boulevard, where she turned left on Barber. Some of the explicit details of her sister's past made her feel like a voyeur, but she was learning a few interesting things about Harley. Like the fact that his mother wouldn't let him come home if she was entertaining a man, so he was forced to sleep where he could. Sometimes he slept on the front lawn of a friend's house. Sometimes he slept on a neighbor's couch. If it was very late, he slept on a park bench.

She also learned that his mother had managed a cheap dry cleaner and worked long hours, usually seven days a week, just to put bread on the table. Audra hadn't liked Mrs. Nelson much, who was actually Mrs. Hallifax by then, because her house always smelled of greasy fried foods and because she did nothing after work except smoke.

Aside from that kind of detail, Lauren had learned what Harley's reaction to the pregnancy had been. Audra had found out about the coming baby on April 3, 1992. She'd taken an in-home pregnancy test, which had come out positive, and had instantly tried to call Harley. But they'd just had an argument. She couldn't get him at home, and she was on restriction, so their father wouldn't let her leave the house. She had to wait until the next day, but then she'd sprung the news on him right before classes started. He'd grown angry and accused her of being care-less, had caused quite a scene in the halls, according to Audra, who'd been upset by his reaction. But remember-ing Audra's Valentine's Day entry, Lauren had to admit he had some justification for his accusations. Lauren har-bored a few of her own and even wondered if Audra hadn't relished the thought of getting pregnant by some-one like Harley as a form of revenge against their father. Harley had told Audra he didn't have anything to give the baby, didn't have any way to support them if they decided to run away, and demanded to know why she hadn't been taking her pills. She'd insisted she *had* been taking them and had gotten pregnant anyway, which seemed highly unlikely. In any event, Audra had called him a selfish pig and told him she never wanted to see him again. After that, he didn't phone for several days, which scared Audra and made her think he really was going to let her go. But then he finally called and told her he was willing to do the right thing by both of them. He'd never known his father. He didn't want a child of his suffering the same fate.

And that was where Lauren had left off to check the answering machine.

The school was coming up. She veered into the parking

lot, saw Harley's motorcycle parked in a visitor slot and angled her Lexus next to it.

Brandon and Harley were waiting for her in the principal's office. Mrs. Wells showed her inside; Dr. Vanderloch immediately stood, Brandon wore a contrite look, and Harley gave her a hesitant smile.

"Thanks for staying with him," she said to Harley. It was difficult to see him in a role she considered her own, but she could hardly blame him for being there when she wasn't.

He nodded, then she turned to Dr. Vanderloch. She was used to dealing with Brandon's teachers and Mt. Marley's administrative staff. She wasn't used to dealing with Brandon's dad. "When can he return to school, Dr. Vanderloch?" she asked.

"He's supposed to be suspended for three days. But as I was telling his father here, Brandon has always been an excellent student, so I'm willing to count today as one of the suspension days."

Harley comes back on the scene, and I argue with my father, defy him, and Brandon gets suspended from school. Was the life she'd known gone for good? "Thank you. I'm sorry it took me so long to get here."

"No problem. He had his father," Dr. Vanderloch responded. "Would you like me to have Mrs. Wells put Harley on Brandon's emergency card so he can pick Brandon up from school occasionally?"

Pure panic hit Lauren at this suggestion. She knew Dr. Vanderloch was only trying to be accommodating. He was a good, fair man and had no way of knowing that she was terrified of doing any such thing. Allowing Harley to pick Brandon up from school relinquished some of her control. It assumed that Harley was safe, that she trusted him and was willing to share Brandon. And she wasn't sure of any of that.

"We'll talk about it," she hedged. "I'll call you later, if that's the case."

Harley jammed his hands in his pockets but said nothing. Dr. Vanderloch smiled and nodded patiently.

Lauren took Brandon's hand and hurried out of the office, feeling as though she couldn't escape the school fast enough. Or Harley, either. Brandon was her responsibility, her child in almost every sense of the word. She couldn't help feeling that Harley had no right to be here, quietly discussing Brandon's problem with Dr. Vanderloch. He had no right to be on the emergency card, no right to be anything more than she was willing to let him—

"Lauren."

She turned and finally noticed that she was walking so quickly she was nearly dragging Brandon along behind her. "Yes?" she said, forcing a polite smile.

Taking her by the arm, Harley stopped her just before she reached her car. "Don't be spooked."

How could she not be spooked? She was more than spooked. She was frightened of what she'd started and where it might lead, how easily it could spiral out of control. She wanted to do the right thing, but the situation seemed to be getting more complicated by the minute.

"I just—" she cleared her throat "I just…" She was going to ask for some time away from Harley, a few days to settle her mind again, but the words wouldn't come. She knew if she banished Harley now, Brandon would be crushed. And Harley seemed to care just as deeply.

One of the tears she'd been trying to hold back slid down her cheek. "Come here," Harley said softly, and Lauren surprised herself by letting him pull her into his arms. He tucked her head under his chin and whispered that everything would be okay, and for the briefest moment, Lauren let herself relax. Closing her eyes, she heard his heart beating from the pulse point at his throat, smelled the faint scent of cologne on his T-shirt, felt the pressure of two strong, sure hands lightly rubbing her back—and found that she believed him. At least for today.

ONCE THEY WERE HOME and outside at the pool, it wasn't difficult for Lauren to put the uneasiness she'd felt at Mt. Marley behind her. There'd been no message from her father, which enabled her to continue ignoring the fact that she'd have to deal with him at some point. And in such familiar surroundings, she felt safe and in control again.

Harley was wearing swim trunks and a T-shirt, and sat on the lawn chair across the pool from her, blowing up a beach ball he'd stopped to purchase on his way over. Brandon kept calling him to watch while he showed off this dive or that, picked up a quarter on the bottom of the pool or did a handstand.

We're all just having a little fun, Lauren told herself. There wasn't anything to worry about. Even Brandon's trouble at school seemed to be more minor than she'd first feared. According to her nephew, he and his friends had had a misunderstanding of some sort about their morning soccer game. It had led to raised tempers and eventually come to blows, but he'd promised it would never happen again. And with his impeccable track record, Lauren didn't think it fair to punish him too severely. She had talked to him about the need to have patience and treat others kindly, and she'd stressed the importance of excelling in school, but that was about it. Since they'd arrived home, Brandon hadn't been able to focus on anything besides Harley. He was too taken with having his father around, too eager to spend every moment with him.

Lauren felt herself relax even further as she watched Harley plug the ball and toss it into the pool. A lawnmower hummed in the distance, bees flitted about the flowers along the fence, and a gentle breeze swayed the trees. It was so warm outside—a perfect, clear spring day.

She had her mister, filled with cool water, on the table beside her, but she wasn't ready for a reprieve from the heat. Soaking up the sun felt so good. She smoothed a mild sunblock on the skin her bikini didn't cover, then settled her sunglasses farther up her nose and adjusted her visor so she could lean back and rest. She wasn't going to watch Harley when he took off his shirt. She didn't need to see his bare chest again....

She heard his chair scrape the cement and knew Harley had stood. He was probably lifting his shirt over his head this very minute, she realized—and opened one eye.

Sure enough, the shirt was off. She watched, refusing to succumb to the appreciative smile that was tempting her lips, and admired the view from behind the safety of her dark lenses.

Brandon, if you look half as good as your father does when you're an adult, you'd better carry a stick, she thought as Harley dived in. Then she closed her eyes and would have drifted off to sleep if not for Brandon.

"Aunt Lauren! Aunt Lauren! Have you seen my dad's tattoo?" he asked, blocking the sun and dripping all over her.

She sat up to give Brandon the attention he wanted and to avoid the cold drops of water, moving her sunglasses to the top of her head. She'd seen a blue mark on Harley's shoulder blade when she'd been admiring him a few minutes earlier, but she'd been feigning indifference and didn't want to admit she'd noticed such a small detail from across the pool.

"No, I haven't," she lied. "I didn't see any tattoos."

"Well, he has one. Guess what it is."

Lauren shrugged. "A Harley Davidson logo?"

Her nephew smiled broadly. "Nope. Guess again."

"An anchor? Hearts and flowers? A rose? I don't have any idea," she said. "Why don't you tell me?"

"Dad, show her," Brandon urged.

"She's resting right now," Harley told him from where he was floating on his back in the water. "She can see it another time."

"Come on. I want to show her," Brandon rejoined.

The muscles in Harley's arms flexed as he flipped over and hoisted himself out of the pool. His suit was now wet and clinging to every curve and bulge as he approached, and Lauren quickly covered her eyes with her sunglasses again so he and Brandon wouldn't notice the difficulty she had in looking away.

"Where is it?" she asked, to distract herself as much as Harley and Brandon.

Harley turned and gave her a closeup of the blue mark she'd seen on his shoulder blade. It was a name and a date: Brandon, 11/92.

"When did you get that?" she demanded, surprised.

"As soon as I heard his name," Harley said.

"Which was when?"

"Audra stopped by my mother's place just after he was born."

"So you've had it for ten years?"

He nodded.

Harley had no other tattoos, at least none Lauren could see. Just his son's name, permanently etched into his skin. That told her Brandon's birth had meant something to him from the very beginning.

"Cool, isn't it?" Brandon said.

Lauren didn't know what to say. Meeting Harley and reading her sister's journals were changing everything she'd believed about what had happened ten years ago. "It's cool," she agreed.

"Hey, what about you?" Brandon asked her. "Will you put my name on your back, too?"

"Sorry, kiddo," Lauren said. "I love you, but I'm not the type to get a tattoo."

"Come on, Aunt Lauren. It'd look awesome. You don't

have to put it on your back. You could put it on your arm or your ankle or somewhere else.''

Harley stepped closer. He didn't have the benefit of sunglasses, so Lauren could tell exactly where he was looking—and it wasn't at her face. ''I think it would look good right here,'' he said, his finger grazing the indention just below her collarbone and leaving a drop of water that rolled down between her breasts.

Goose bumps immediately pimpled Lauren's flesh and, judging by the grin twisting Harley's lips, he noticed.

''Forget it, guys,'' she told them. ''Nothing's going to mark this body.''

They finally went back to swimming and Lauren's goose bumps disappeared. But she grabbed her mister. It was definitely time to cool off.

CHAPTER FOURTEEN

IT BOTHERED HARLEY that Lauren wasn't swimming. He and Brandon were having a good time, but they'd already played with the beach ball, dived for plastic oysters and competed to see who could swim the fastest, float the longest and swim the farthest without taking a breath. Meanwhile, Lauren hadn't said a word. She'd stayed on her back, then rolled onto her stomach. That was it.

Harley didn't understand what anyone saw in tanning. He could nap for a few minutes, but then he had to get wet and cool off or do *something*.

He regarded her for the hundredth time, gauging the chances of waking her with a well-launched splash. Wasn't she ready to join the fun? How much longer could she sleep?

"Doesn't your aunt ever get in the water?" he asked Brandon.

Brandon was busy blowing more air into the beach ball, which was already going soft from an unfortunate landing in the rose bushes. "Sometimes," he said. "Mostly she just lies in the sun and watches me."

"How exciting," Harley said.

Brandon shrugged, taking his words at face value. "I guess that's what girls like to do."

"What if we threw her in?" Harley asked.

A devilish glint entered Brandon's eyes, but then he shook his head. "We'd better not. I'd rather have you stay for supper."

"Right. Better to stay and eat," Harley agreed.

"Hello? Anybody home?" a male voice called from the front yard.

Flinging his wet hair out of his eyes, Harley started toward the steps to see who it was when Damien Thompson let himself through the gate and came into view.

"Hi, Damien," Brandon said. "You want to play volleyball with me and my dad?"

Judging by his tailored suit, tie and expensive loafers, Damien hadn't come over to swim. He shot Harley a look that surprised him, one Harley didn't quite understand or appreciate, considering they'd spoken like friends only yesterday.

"Not today," Damien told Brandon.

"Did you know this is my dad?" Brandon pressed.

"Yes, I know."

"He has a tattoo with my name on it."

"Good for him," Damien said, and turned to Lauren, who was finally sitting up, rubbing the towel impression from her face and righting her sunglasses.

Obviously, she'd been dead to the world. Harley might have been ultra-conscious of her, but she'd tuned *him* out completely, which, he decided, wasn't particularly good for his ego.

Not that his ego or anything else mattered. He was here to see his son. Brandon was a great kid—warm and loving and bright—and Harley had nine years to make up for. He began a wrestling match between them and pretended to let Brandon overpower and dunk him, again and again, but it wasn't long before Harley's attention wandered back to Damien and Lauren.

Damien was sitting close to her chaise, too close in Harley's opinion. Tank's brother was crowding her, and he was speaking in low tones, as if he didn't want Harley or Brandon to hear what he was saying.

For her part, Lauren didn't appear pleased. She wore a

frown above the fabulous swimsuit that revealed her stunning figure. Harley would never have guessed she hid a body quite like that beneath her conservative clothing, and he didn't care for the way Damien's eyes kept flicking over it.

"Want to have a diving contest?" Brandon asked, wiping his swimming goggles and interrupting Harley's growing irritation.

"Sure," Harley said. He tried to ignore Damien and Lauren as he climbed out of the pool, but Damien started running his fingers up and down Lauren's arm and leaning even closer, as though trying to convince her of something. She shook her head and pulled away, but he grabbed her arm again—and Harley did a cannonball.

When he surfaced, he found Damien glaring at him and brushing water droplets off his suit. "Do you mind?" he snapped.

"Sorry," Harley said without any real effort to sound sincere.

Damien shook his head in apparent disgust, but returned to his conversation with Lauren, so Harley encouraged Brandon to try his best cannonball. When his son's splash didn't travel nearly far enough, Harley showed Brandon how to tuck and jump for maximum water displacement and succeeded in drenching Damien again.

"What the hell's wrong with you?" Damien demanded, coming to the side of the pool to confront Harley as soon as he broke the water. "This happens to be a two-thousand-dollar suit. Maybe you could be a little more careful."

"And maybe you could go back to work," Harley told him, lifting himself out of the water to sit on the edge of the pool.

"This isn't a public pool, Harley," Damien said, stand-

ing over him. "For your information, you're not even supposed to be here."

Harley gave him what he hoped was an infuriating
smile. "That's funny. Seems I remember being invited."

"Damien, please go," Lauren said, getting off her
chaise and coming toward them.

Damien ignored her. "If you *were* invited, it was only
because Quentin Worthington isn't here," he retorted.
"As soon as he gets back, you can kiss your visits goodbye. Tank and Lauren might think you're an okay guy,
but Quentin and I know the real story."

Harley felt a muscle twitch in his cheek, but the way
Brandon was watching the confrontation gave Harley the
incentive he needed to resist the anger building in his
blood. "And what is the real story, Damien?"

"You left Audra holding the bag ten years ago. Now
you're trying to see if you can get in her sister's pants."

"Damien!" Lauren cried. "Brandon's here!"

It was easy to tell that Damien wasn't too concerned
about Brandon. Hands clenched into fists, he kept his eyes
riveted to Harley. "You're not going to get anywhere with
her, you hear me?"

"Unless you want to take a swim in that suit you like
so well, I suggest you listen to Lauren and go," Harley
said. He made no move to get up, but something in his
voice must have convinced Damien he was serious. After
another tense moment, Tank's brother jerked a hand
through his hair, released his breath in a huff, and stalked
off.

"Wow," Brandon breathed in the echo of the slamming gate.

Harley looked at Lauren, who was standing with her
hands on her hips, frowning. "I didn't know Damien was
such a pleasant guy."

"He's usually not so bad. He's just convinced I'm making a big mistake," she replied, sounding resigned.

Flashbacks of ten years ago assaulted Harley's mind.
Quentin, fired up because he'd just caught Harley meeting
Audra outside the Hillside gates: "What the hell do you
think you're doing with my daughter? You're not even
good enough to carry her books!" Audra, laughing: "I
didn't take my birth control pill today. Don't you love
living dangerously?" And Mrs. Worthington, weeping
when she ran into Harley and Audra at the mall: "How
can you do this to us? Why won't you just leave my
daughter alone?" He even remembered Lauren walking
with her head down, moving through the halls of Oakmont
High unnoticed, or almost unnoticed. One of his friends
had once nudged him to remark about how odd it was
that Audra was such a fox while her sister was a brainy
nobody, but back then Harley hadn't thought enough
about Lauren to decide whether or not he considered her
a nobody. Other than her connection to Audra, she simply
wasn't part of his universe. But he would've been amazed
to know that in ten years, he'd find her one of the most
attractive women he'd ever met.

Picking up a plastic oyster on the edge of the pool,
Harley tossed it into the water. "Do you think you're
making a mistake?" he asked, hoping *somebody* in the
Worthington family might finally show a spark of faith in
him.

Lauren held his gaze. "I don't know."

LAUREN FOUND Harley's voice soothing. Brandon had
read the first chapter of *Holes* by Louis Sachar and grown
too sleepy to continue. He'd asked his father to read, then
proceeded to doze off on the bed between them. Even
though Brandon was asleep, Lauren wasn't in any hurry
for Harley to close the book. She was full of the Mexican
food he'd bought them for dinner and her face still tingled
from laughing when she and Brandon had teamed up to
beat him at darts. He'd rallied during the second and third

games, but Lauren was still quite pleased with herself, pleased with the evening as a whole, in spite of Damien's surprising visit at the pool and his insistence that she stay as far away from Harley as possible. He said she should think about what her father would want and everything they'd already learned through Audra's experience. But it was difficult to feel the necessity of keeping a safe distance from Harley when she was enjoying his company so much—and Brandon was enjoying it even more.

"Are you asleep?" Harley asked softly, lifting his head to peer at her over Brandon's sleeping form.

Lauren gave him a lazy smile. "Almost."

He retrieved the folded quilt at the foot of Brandon's bed and started to cover her and her nephew, but Lauren sat up. "I'll walk you to the door," she said, helping him tuck Brandon in.

"Are you sure? I can find my way out."

"That's okay. I slept enough in the sun today. I'm not in any hurry to turn in. I was just relaxing."

He nodded, but he was looking at Brandon, gazing down at him as though he was afraid his son might disappear. "You're such a great kid," he murmured.

Lauren stepped into the hall to give him some privacy but couldn't help turning at the entrance to see what he might do. When he brushed back Brandon's hair and kissed his forehead, she thought, "Damien, you're wrong," and for the first time since Harley had arrived in Portland, the knot of worry in her stomach completely eased. She was letting two people who loved each other be together; she was even chaperoning them. What could be so terrible about that?

Moving beyond the portal, she waited for Harley to join her, then snapped off Brandon's light and led the way to the living room.

When they reached the entry hall, she found herself

strangely reluctant to say goodbye. "I had a nice time tonight," she said, opening the door.

The porch light came on automatically, and Harley stepped outside, then turned and grinned at her. "I never dreamed you'd eat that entire combination plate at La Mision. I was kind of hoping for a bite of your tamale."

"You should've said something. I ate it because I didn't want it to go to waste."

He raised his eyebrows. "So tonight was an exception and you normally have a petite appetite?"

Lauren laughed. "Okay. The food was good and I stuffed myself and I loved every minute of it. But I would've shared."

"I know you would." The levity was gone from his words, and Lauren knew he was referring to something deeper.

Smiling at the compliment, she almost reached out to squeeze his arm. She would have, if he were anyone else. A little pat or squeeze was a natural gesture of friendship. But she was feeling more than friendship for Harley and because of that, she didn't dare touch him at all. Odd thing was, she'd stood at this door a thousand times with Damien, and her heart had never beat so hard.

"You're nothing like Audra, are you," Harley said, studying her.

Did that mean he found her lacking? Probably. She'd been passed over a lot of times in favor of her sister and had mostly taken it in stride. She'd countered the disappointment by focusing on all the things that were so much more important than looks, like achieving her goals and developing her talents. But it bothered her that, as far as Harley was concerned, she was still the homely little bookworm she'd been in high school.

Trying not to wince, she leaned against the doorframe. "No, I'm not," she admitted, hoping she appeared casual and unaffected. "I'll never be like Audra. She was the swan. I'm the ugly duckling."

He didn't say anything for a moment, but then he lifted his hand and ran a finger over the curve of her cheek. "Not on the inside," he said, "and not anymore."

Their eyes met and Lauren felt chills chase down her spine. She wanted to kiss Harley Nelson. It came as a sudden and very powerful revelation. But somehow, it didn't come as a surprise.

After all these years, after everything that's happened…

His fingers slipped around to the nape of her neck and exerted just enough pressure to draw her toward him.

Lauren had a fleeting memory of Damien, earlier today, telling her how easily she could get caught in Harley's web, but she told herself she'd think about that later. One kiss…just one… Surely she could indulge herself that much.

Letting her eyelids slide closed, she felt her breathing go shallow and hoped her heart wouldn't pound its way right out of her chest. Harley's face was so close, she could almost feel his lips on hers. Any second they'd touch, and she'd melt and then—nothing.

Dropping his hand, he stepped back from her, and Lauren opened her eyes to see him shove both fists in his pockets.

"I'm sorry," he said. "I don't know what got into me, but you don't have to worry. I mean, I won't…" He swallowed. "It won't happen again. A lot's been going on, that's all, and…well…I'm really sorry," he finished quickly, then turned and strode to his bike as though he couldn't get away fast enough.

Lauren watched him leave, feeling numb and unreasonably disappointed. She'd never wanted a man to kiss her so badly. And not just any man. Harley. No one else had ever made her knees weak. In the past, she'd thought something was wrong with her, that she wasn't capable of feeling the kind of desire others experienced, but now she knew better. She *could* want a man. That was the good news. The bad news was that she wanted Harley.

Kimberly's car pulled into the drive, changing Lauren's disappointment into a quick and sudden relief. If Harley hadn't left when he did, her best friend might have come upon them kissing—and then Kimberly would've been absolutely certain Lauren had lost her mind.

With a deep sigh, she dropped her head in her hands. Wasn't it only minutes earlier that she'd decided she was on the right track? That the world was as it should be? And now...

"Hey, how'd it go?" Kim asked, slamming her car door and rushing up the walkway.

Lauren put on her best poker face. "Good," she said. After the telephone conversation in which Kim had accused her of acting giddy, she hesitated to elaborate. Giddy was nothing compared to how she was feeling tonight. Tonight she felt as if she was experiencing her first crush.

"So? Tell me what happened. I passed Harley on my way in and waved at him, but I don't think he saw me."

If he was as shaken as she was by what had almost happened, Lauren could understand that kind of obliviousness. But a near kiss was probably nothing to a man who could have almost any woman.... "We swam earlier. He took us out for Mexican food. We came back here, threw some darts and read with Brandon. Then Bran fell asleep and Harley went home."

"That's it?"

Lauren held the door for Kim before heading inside. "Well, not exactly. Things heated up for a little bit when Damien stopped by earlier."

"*Damien* stopped by? Does he think you two are back together or something?"

"I don't know. He claims he's trying to be my friend, but he's being pretty aggressive in giving me advice and insisting I take it."

"What sort of advice?"

Lauren walked into the family room, where she sank onto the soft leather sectional that arced around the big-screen television; Kim joined her. "He told me not to let Harley come around, that I'll regret it later. He says someday I'll thank him for his advice, but I'm not feeling much gratitude at the moment."

"Damien loves you, Lauren."

"Damien and I aren't even dating anymore. He doesn't have the right to tell me to do anything. And I resent the fact that he's taking my father's side."

"Your father knows Harley's been seeing Brandon?"

"I haven't talked to him since yesterday morning, but I told him I thought we should allow Harley to meet his son. He probably has a good idea of what's going on," she said, picking up the remote and turning on the television.

"Wait a second." Kimberly crossed the room and turned it off. "He didn't get angry?"

"He accused me of acting like Audra," Lauren said, putting down the remote and folding her arms.

"Oh, boy. That isn't good. I've never heard him do anything but sing your praises."

Lauren grimaced, hating the reminder that she was doing something terribly wrong by abandoning her proper role as "the good daughter." "I'm entitled to my own opinion," she insisted. "I don't have to agree with my father on everything."

"Does Damien know the two of you argued?"

"No. He just knows my father wouldn't be happy with Harley hanging around. When he came over today, it was almost as if he thought he could win me back by stepping into my father's shoes and becoming the voice of reason and good judgment. He kept saying I wasn't thinking clearly, that when I returned to my senses I'd regret what I was doing, and on and on.''

"Where was Harley when Damien was saying all this?''

"We were at the pool. I was lying on a chaise, Harley was swimming with Brandon.''

"Did Harley know what Damien was saying?''

Remembering the cannonballs, Lauren finally cracked a smile. "I think he had an inkling,'' she said, then she waved Kimberly over to the couch and told her all about the engineered splashes, the confrontation that followed, how quickly Brandon seemed to be bonding with his father and the tattoo on Harley's shoulder blade. The only part she left out was the very end, when Harley had almost kissed her. She didn't want anyone to know about that.

"So what do you think your father's going to do?'' Kimberly asked when she'd finished. "Let you handle this thing with Harley on your own?''

Lauren shook her head. "No way.''

"Then what?''

"I haven't heard from him, so I'm guessing there's a reason. I'm guessing he and my mother are on their way home.''

Kimberly kneaded her forehead. "Three weeks early? I'm glad I'm not you.''

Lauren rolled her eyes, attempting to shrug it off. "It's not like I'm going to get grounded or something. We're all adults.''

"A family feud is a family feud. It isn't pretty at any age,'' Kimberly said.

And you don't know the half of it, Lauren thought.

CHAPTER FIFTEEN

"I SAW HIM," Harley said as soon as his mother answered the phone. He realized he'd probably awakened her—it was almost eleven o'clock at night—but Harley couldn't make himself wait. For the first time in a long, long time, possibly since he was a kid, he really wanted to talk to her.

"Brandon?" she said.

"Yeah."

"What's he like?"

"He's..." Harley tried to explain how wonderful his son was, but found himself at a loss for words. "He's cool," he said.

Her usual hacking cough sounded in his ear. "Does he look like the Worthingtons?" she asked when she could speak.

Harley put one arm over his eyes and pictured his boy. Tank was already in bed, but Harley was out on the couch watching an old karate movie because he couldn't seem to shut down for the night. He was too wound up, too excited about the past couple of days. "He looks a little like the Worthingtons. He's got his mother's mouth, but I'd say he looks more like me than he does Audra."

"Did you get to talk to him?"

"I spent several hours with him last night and most of today."

"I thought his aunt wouldn't let you come around."

"She changed her mind," he said, hoping his mother

wouldn't press for a more detailed explanation. He didn't want to think about Lauren. Every time he did, he remembered those last few minutes on her doorstep and what he'd been feeling when he looked at her—gratitude, respect, friendship...and desire. Which was the one thing he didn't want to feel. He was hoping it was merely a natural reaction, given the gamut of emotions he'd experienced in the past few days.

"So? Was seeing Brandon everything you thought it would be?" his mother asked.

"It was better."

"Really?"

He heard the excitement in her voice and smiled. "Somehow my life wasn't complete without him," he admitted. "Now I feel...I don't know. Good."

"Does that mean you're going to bring him home with you?"

"I'd like to. But I'll have to cut through a lot of red tape first. I can't just take him and walk away. I may have to go home for a while, then come back."

"When are you filing for custody?"

"I just found an attorney yesterday. We'll probably file sometime next week."

His mother let out a triumphant laugh. "That's my boy! After the way Quentin Worthington treated you, I can't wait to see his face when you take Brandon away from him. He deserves a little of his own medicine, don't you think?"

"Maybe," Harley said, but he wasn't nearly as happy about the possibility of turning the tables on Quentin Worthington as he would've been a week earlier. Because anything that hurt Quentin would hurt Lauren, too.

April 9, 1992

I hate Harley. Or maybe I love him. I don't know. I'm so confused. One minute I'm throwing up, the

next I'm crying. I don't know how I'm going to tell
Mom and Dad about the baby. Lauren just won some
kind of community service award, and here I am,
flunking out of high school. Mrs. Merimack called
the house today to tell my parents that I haven't been
in class for over a week. Fortunately, Mom and Dad
were at the golf course and I erased the message. But
she'll only call back tomorrow or the next day. And
then I've got to come up with an excuse for where
I've been and why I'm failing—at everything.

The old grandfather clock in the hall outside Lauren's
room chimed midnight but she couldn't stop reading. She
needed something to distract her from Harley's near-kiss
and hearing about her sister's involvement with him
helped. Or was the truth that she had as much interest in
getting to know Harley as she did in learning more about
her sister?

April 17, 1992
     Sometimes I think about getting an abortion. It
would be so easy just to put an end to the worry and
the sickness and the fear. But I don't know if I could
live with that decision. Harley is definitely against it.
He keeps talking about what we'll do after school
gets out. He thinks we should get married. At eighteen. Wouldn't my father just love that? Daddy
would never speak to me again.

April 21, 1992
     Harley and I went to the free clinic today to have
an official pregnancy test. It came back positive, of
course. The lady there gave me some pamphlets, one
on abortion and two on adoption. But Harley tossed
them all in the trash. He said he's not like his father—that nothing's going to happen to his baby.

Maybe I'll just make my own arrangements without telling him.

April 22, 1992

Mom and Dad heard from Mrs. Merimack today. They were waiting for me when I came in the door. They started with the usual—what the hell is wrong with me? What am I trying to do, screw up my future? Why can't I be more like Lauren? And something inside me just snapped. I told them. I told them about the baby. Dad looked as though I'd shot him. He went completely white, and sat down. He wouldn't say anything. He wouldn't even yell. And then he started to cry. I'd never seen Dad cry before, and I've never hated anything worse. I felt filthy, horrible, more unworthy than ever before. I wanted him to yell and tell me how foolish and stupid I was. I wanted any kind of a reaction but the one I got. I told him I'd get an abortion, do anything he wanted, if he'd only love me again. He didn't respond at first, but I could hear him and Mom talking in their room later. Then he came to see me and said I could keep the baby. He's pulling me out of school, since I'm not going to graduate, anyway. And he told me to stay away from Harley. I didn't need to ask him what would happen if I didn't. I know Dad. He's offering me one more chance. Just one.

April 28, 1992

Harley's been calling and hanging up, again and again, but I can't call him back. If I call him back, I'll want to see him, and if I see him and Dad finds out...

April 29, 1992

Harley came to the door tonight. I never dreamed he would, not with everything Daddy's already said to him. When Dad answered the door, Harley demanded to know if I was okay, as if he thought Dad might have beaten me or something. Dad let go of all the anger I think he's feeling toward me, and they had a huge argument. I thought it might actually come to blows, but when I told Harley to leave, that it was over between us, he backed off and stared at me for several seconds, then said, "So you're choosing him over me." What does he expect me to do? Live a life of poverty? What about our baby?

April 30, 1992

I'm dying to see Harley. I've never hurt like this before. It's my punishment for always being so bad, I guess. What I wouldn't give to go back in time!

May 3, 1992

I slipped out of the house last night and went to Harley's, just after midnight. I couldn't help myself. I'm so miserable without him. I needed him to hold me one more time, and I almost didn't come home. He begged me to run away with him, to trust him, but I was too scared. What would we do? What kind of life would we have? I can just see myself barefoot and pregnant...

May 5, 1992

Harley isn't calling anymore. Last time I saw him, he told me if I went home again, it was over between us for good. I want to call him, want to hear from him, but I'm so scared Dad's going to find out. I can't see him, anyway. It only makes things worse. The wanting fights with the fear, until it feels like my head's about to explode. I can't take it. I just want to check out....

May 15, 1992

Harley's kept his word. I haven't heard from him, but I think about him all the time and I wonder what he's doing. I want to tell him I'm sorry, but even that seems pointless. Dad won't even allow me to mention his name.

Lauren closed Audra's journals, rolled over on the bed and buried her face in the pillows. What had happened between Audra and Harley was so sad. Despite the belligerence and, sometimes, the indifference of her sister's earlier entries, Lauren now believed Audra had loved Harley. At least, as much as she was capable of loving. And judging by Harley's repeated attempts to contact Audra after finding out about the baby, she could only believe he cared about her, too. Or maybe it was the baby he cared about, but even that did him credit, especially since Lauren had always assumed he'd been reluctant to live up to his responsibilities in that regard. The fact that he'd taken her father's two thousand dollars made him look greedy and eager to benefit from the situation, but Lauren was beginning to believe the money had very little to do with anything.

Burrowing deeper under the covers, she pictured Harley at eighteen and tried to feel what he must have felt then. How did he get through those first few years on his own? He hadn't had a parent willing to step in and help him. And unlike Audra, he hadn't turned to drugs, hadn't allowed such substances to destroy him. He might only be a motorcycle salesman, but he managed to get by, and that in itself was a marvel.

Strength. He had an inner strength Audra had lacked, and that was what pulled him through. He hadn't grown up with many advantages, but he'd survived and now he was back.

Slowly the tightness in her chest that had come from reading her sister's journals eased, and Lauren actually smiled into the darkness. After ten years, Harley had returned to face his past—and all the things that had been thought of him and said about him and were still, by most, believed to be true. His appearance in her life threatened her, because so much of her happiness depended on Brandon, and yet Harley's courage and determination evoked an unexpected sense of pride.

I'm just tired. I don't admire him. I don't want to kiss him. But when she finally drifted off to sleep, she dreamed of kissing Harley and more—and then she was pregnant and carrying his child, feeling it kick inside her womb, and strangely enough she was excited about it.

"AUNT LAUREN!"

Lauren awoke with a start and immediately put a hand to her belly, expecting to find it round and extended. Instead she felt the soft, flat surface beneath her ribs and exhaled in relief. She wasn't pregnant. Mercifully, she'd been spared having to tell her family that the man who'd gotten Audra pregnant ten years ago had returned and done her the same favor. If she felt a trace of disappointment, too, she wasn't willing to think about it.

"Aunt Lauren," Brandon persisted. He was holding the cordless telephone in one hand while shaking her arm with the other. "My dad's on the phone. He wants to know if we can go on a picnic with him today."

Oh, boy. Yesterday it was swimming and dinner. Today it was a picnic. Quentin wasn't going to be pleased that she and Brandon had become so friendly with the enemy. She'd feared that letting Harley see Brandon would spiral out of control, but she'd never thought it would gather momentum quite so swiftly. Or lead to such vivid and very personal dreams...

"You just saw him last night," she said, stalling because she thought maybe she should slow down the relationship now, while she still could. But Brandon looked so eager and excited, she couldn't bring herself to tell him no. "What about your karate lesson?" she asked, covering a yawn.

"Can't I miss it, just this once?" he asked.

Lauren struggled into a sitting position, already regretting that she'd stayed up so late…and afraid that when her parents returned, she'd be suffering even worse regrets. But she was in too far to back out now. "I have a better idea. I'll take you to a morning class, and we'll meet your father afterward. Okay?"

Brandon put on his begging face. "But I want to see him *now*. I don't want to go to karate. What's one time? I go every week."

"Exactly. That's how you learn and improve."

"Aunt Lauren, I can't wait to see my dad."

"Brandon…"

The warning in Lauren's voice was enough to make him back off. "Okay," he grumbled. "He's on the phone. You want to talk to him?"

As Lauren accepted the handset, she rubbed her stomach again, just to be sure. No baby. She hadn't even kissed Harley. She'd only *wanted* to kiss him. And dreamed about kissing him. And still felt a certain flutter in her chest at the mere thought of kissing him…

Those were thoughts that would only lead her into trouble, she reminded herself and tried to say hello, but her voice caught and she had to clear her throat instead.

"Lauren?"

For some reason, hearing Harley on the other end of the line made her clutch the telephone closer to her ear. "Brandon says you want to have a picnic today."

"I thought we could go to the park and barbecue some

chicken, maybe throw a football around or get a volleyball game going.'' He sounded almost as eager as Brandon. ''What do you think?''

''Volleyball takes more than three people,'' she pointed out.

''Tank has his little girl today. He's divorced and only gets her on weekends. She just turned four, so she's pretty little, but I thought they could join us. Maybe your friend Kimberly would like to come, too.''

A group activity? What a brilliant idea. There was safety in numbers. Surely she'd forget all about kissing Harley if Kimberly was along to remind her that he was the one man she could *never* kiss. ''Sure. I'll check with her. What time?''

''Noon?''

''Noon's good.''

There was a brief hesitation, then, ''I heard you say something to Brandon about karate lessons.''

''Brandon takes karate. He's a blue belt. We usually go in the afternoon, but they have a few morning sessions, too, so we'll go early today and get it over with.''

Another pause, then, ''Would you mind if I tagged along?''

''To karate?'' Lauren imagined the interest of the other mothers, especially that of Kara Fletcher, and decided she'd rather Harley didn't come. Quentin and Marilee traveled in a pretty tight circle; she didn't want everyone gossiping about Brandon's dad and what was going on at the Worthingtons', especially before she had a chance to work things out with her father.

''Actually, it's really…'' she was going to say ''boring, nothing you'd want to bother with,'' but she couldn't offend her nephew, who was still standing by the edge of her bed, hanging on every word, ''…not that big a deal,'' she finished lamely.

"Sometimes it's the little things that matter most," he said.

Great.

"Is he going to come?" Brandon asked, easily catching the drift of the conversation.

Lauren groped for something else she could say that might put Harley off, but she couldn't think of anything with Brandon jumping up and down and pleading, "Please, Aunt Lauren, pleeeease?"

"I guess that'll be okay," she said at last, then she told Harley the class started at ten-thirty and gave him directions, hung up and immediately dialed her parents in London to see if they were on their way home. Now that she and Brandon were going to be spending the entire day with Harley, she had to know what to expect.

"Quentin and Marilee Worthington, please," she told the hotel operator when he picked up. "I think they're in Room 311."

There was a pause while he checked. "Just a moment, please."

The telephone rang in short bursts, again and again, then Lauren was transferred to her parents' voicemail. "This is Quentin and Marilee," her mother's voice lightly intoned. "We're off seeing something wonderful and historic, so leave a message and we'll call you back as soon as we get in."

Lauren breathed a sigh of relief and hung up without leaving a message. She had a reprieve. Her parents hadn't called her, but they weren't on their way home, either. Maybe they hadn't been able to get a plane out.

Telling Brandon to put on his karate uniform, she dialed Kimberly.

"Don't tell me. Your father's home," her friend said, omitting the usual hello.

"No, not yet. They haven't even checked out of their hotel. I just called to see."

"Thank God. Are you relieved, or what?"

"I'm relieved. Any chance you'd be interested in a picnic today?"

"What kind of picnic?"

"The kind that includes Harley, Tank, Tank's little girl, me and Brandon."

"Tank has a little girl? Is he married, then?"

"Divorced."

"Boy, that makes me feel really bad," Kimberly said. "Even Tank has more to show for his marriage than I do."

"You hooked up with a guy who was raised on steroids, shaved his entire body twice a day and insisted on three different forms of birth control every time you made love. What did you expect?"

"Some women like body-builders," Kimberly said. "The thing that really hurt was the way Jim kept staying up all night looking at porno on the Internet, instead of coming to bed with me."

"You mean his growing obsession didn't inspire fidelity, trust and love?"

Kimberly laughed. "Try going to your father and telling him you need to borrow money because your husband's spending a thousand dollars a month at a site called 'Wet and Wild with Candy.'"

"I think splitting up was a better idea."

"I did the right thing, but it isn't easy trying to live the single life again. There are actually days I'm tempted to go back to him."

"You've got to be kidding! He pinned up Playboy Playmates on your kitchen calendar."

"You never liked him because he hated that we were such good friends. You thought that's why he decided we should move away."

"That *is* why."

"I know, but it wasn't just you. He wanted to cut me off from my family, too."

"Such a great guy. Well, I can't promise Tank will prove to be a pillar of the community. But we could spend the afternoon together for old times' sake."

"Old times' sake? In high school, Tank and Harley didn't even know we existed." She paused. "At least Harley didn't. Tank might've realized it the day he threw up on me."

"Harley knows we exist now," Lauren said.

"He knows *you* exist," Kimberly corrected. "But I'm not so sure that's good."

Lauren thought about it for a moment. "Neither am I," she admitted, her mind conjuring up Harley as he'd been last night, his breath gently fanning her face as she'd tilted her head back and closed her eyes in anticipation. She had to put some distance between them, had to take a step back or things could easily get out of control. And it didn't help that, even though she was reluctant to be seen with him in front of people who would most certainly say something to her father, she was excited about the prospect of Harley's company. Excited enough to be planning what she was going to wear.

Distance, she told herself sternly. She had to treat Harley as indifferently as possible. It was the only way to foster his relationship with Brandon while keeping herself—and her family—safe from further emotional turmoil.

"Don't worry. I think I have a plan that might make everything work out. Just meet me here at eleven-fifty," she told Kimberly.

After hanging up, Lauren put on something quite different from the flattering shorts and sleeveless sweater she wanted to wear. Then she scrounged around for her old glasses and pulled her hair into a simple ponytail. After all, she'd been invisible to Harley in high school. Maybe she could be invisible to him now.

THERE WAS A WOMAN wearing skin-tight satin pants, six-inch heels and a halter-top sitting next to Lauren. Her bleached blond hair was teased high on top of her head, and she kept leaning over and pointing a long, red-lacquered nail toward the class of ten or twelve children who were following the karate instructor in front of the mirrors. Like most of the other mothers in the place, the woman looked as though she had money. But not "old" money. She was too garish and bold to fit in with the conservative Worthington crowd.

Lauren glanced back and saw him, and Harley moved eagerly toward the empty seat on the other side of her. He'd spent the past twelve hours being amazed at how badly he'd wanted to kiss her last night. And was still absolutely shocked that she'd acted as though she might let him. Yet the same crazy desire hit him now, the moment he laid eyes on her, even though she wasn't wearing any makeup, had donned glasses that were obviously years out of date and hadn't bothered to fix her hair.

"There you are," she said when he approached, but a self-conscious glance at the woman beside her gave him the impression she didn't really want to claim him.

Harley hesitated, suddenly wondering if he should have stayed in the back. He'd assumed she'd saved him a seat, but maybe he was wrong.

"Is this chair for me?" he asked.

She shrugged. "It's free, if you'd like to take it."

If he'd like to take it? What had happened to the friendly Lauren he'd known last night? She'd been replaced by a woman dressed in a pair of black slacks and a flowery, button-up shirt that resembled something an old lady might wear, and she was acting as though...as though she didn't want to be seen with him.

Suspicion tightened Harley's chest, leaving a dull, solid ache. Lauren was just reacting to yesterday's near kiss, he tried to tell himself. It was his fault for what he'd almost done.

But the memories of her father's sneering comments— "You little bastard, you aren't worth the time of day," —made him think it might be more than that.

"Is everything okay?" she asked, her eyes searching his face.

Harley removed the scowl he hadn't realized he was wearing until that moment and forced a smile that was halfhearted at best. "Fine. Great. Slept like a baby last night. You?"

She nodded a little too vigorously and turned back to the karate class. "Me, too."

"How's Brandon doing?" he asked, pulling the chair slightly away from her before he sat down. Fortunately, his son was more excited about his arrival than Lauren was. Brandon's smile stretched from ear to ear, and he kept turning to wave—until the instructor said something to him about paying attention.

"He's doing pretty well," Lauren said. "He just has to learn a few more moves, and then he'll get his green belt. I think he'll be testing for it next week."

Harley's court hearing for his unpaid speeding ticket was on Tuesday of the following week, so he knew he'd be in town. But he didn't ask to come and watch. He almost wished he hadn't come today.

"Is this your new boyfriend, Lauren?" the woman in the tight pants cooed when neither of them acknowledged her even after she'd craned her head around several times to stare at Harley.

"Oh, no," Lauren said, and something about the quickness of her answer made the throbbing in Harley's chest grow stronger. He raised a hand and tried to smooth it away, but it was no use.

"We sort of knew each other in high school," she explained, fiddling nervously with her nails.

"Really? You go back that far? I just returned from my fifteen-year reunion, and boy, was it a lot of fun. We visited Washington D.C. on the way—I grew up in Virginia," she added as an aside for Harley. "I'm Kara Fletcher."

Lauren hesitated, but finally introduced him. "This is Harley Nelson," she said. "A…a friend."

Harley mumbled something polite, but Kara Fletcher had already charged past "nice to meet you" and was back on the subject of her trip to Virginia.

"I got to see all my cousins and other relatives while I was there," she was saying. "I have twenty nieces and nephews now. Mallory, my sister's oldest daughter, is just starting law school at McGeorge. I can't believe she got in. When she was growing up, she was so absent-minded." Kara shook her head.

"My sister has a lot of kids, but Richard and I got started late," she told Harley. "That's our little guy over there, with the blond hair. He's our only child. I don't know how my sister does it. Besides Mallory and Tommy, she's got three more who are younger. Kids are such a handful. Honestly, there are days I don't think I'm going to fit it all in, what with homework and baseball and…"

Though Lauren nodded and punctuated the conversation with an occasional, "oh, really?" and "that's nice," Harley thought he saw her eyes glaze over as Kara rambled on for another five minutes. But when she returned to her original subject—him—Lauren sat up straighter, still fidgeting with her nails.

"So you and Harley knew each other in high school?" Kara asked.

"Sort of," Lauren replied.

Kara grinned and nudged her knowingly. "Did you two ever date?"

"No, never," Lauren said, her words once again brisk enough to make Harley rub his chest. Was Lauren really that afraid her friend might think her romantically interested in someone *like him?* A man who'd been born on the other side of the tracks, still worked on his own cars and, heaven forbid, had no college degree and only one suit? If she was as much like her father as Harley had once thought, it was certainly a possibility. But yesterday in the pool, and last night at the restaurant, and then at her doorstep later, he'd been so sure she was different...

"Too bad," the woman was saying. "You'd make a good-looking couple. Don't you want to marry and settle down, Lauren?"

"I'm not in any hurry," Lauren said, but Harley detected a slight blush.

So Lauren was in the market for a man, only she was making it quite clear that someone like him didn't appeal to her. That he didn't *want* her to be interested in him suddenly seemed beside the point.

"Harley, do you have a wife?" Kara asked.

"No," he said shortly.

"Well, it won't take you long, I bet. I like a man in leather. There's something so titillating about the Hells Angels look, you know? Last night Richard and I dressed up in our biking clothes—I got them out of the attic after we talked about it last week, Lauren—and just wearing them made us want to head down to the dealership to buy another bike. But we didn't make it out of the house, if you know what I mean." She giggled, then added in a conspiratorial tone to Lauren but loud enough for Harley to hear, "Doesn't a man in leather turn you on?"

"Not particularly," she murmured, sitting ramrod straight and blushing again, but Harley didn't remember her being so opposed to a man in leather last night. Granted, he'd made the first move, but she hadn't exactly pulled away in disgust.

"Dad, watch me do the Kimono Grab," Brandon sang out, interrupting the conversation.

Harley turned his attention to his son, who proceeded to demonstrate a series of memorized movements that, evidently, constituted something called a Kimono Grab. "Good job, buddy," he said.

"Want to see the kata I made up on my own?"

"Sure."

Harley kept his eyes on his son's performance, even though Kara was staring at him, silent for almost the first time since he'd arrived.

"You're Brandon's *father?*" she asked when Brandon ran off to get a drink of water.

Harley sent a glance at Lauren, wondering if she wished he'd deny the connection. But she wouldn't look at him. She picked up her purse and started digging around inside it.

"I am," he said.

"Oh!" The woman's red lips formed a perfect circle, which matched the roundness of her eyes, then relaxed into a smile even more eager than the ones she'd flashed before. "How long have you been in town?"

Another glance at Lauren told Harley she was concentrating her entire mental energy on unwrapping a stick of gum. He didn't like her cool reserve, he decided. He didn't like the way she'd been acting ever since he arrived. It reminded him too much of her father. And though he might regret it later, if she was going to be embarrassed by him, he was going to do his best to give her reason.

"Including jail time or not including jail time?" he said to Kara, and when they left thirty minutes later, he had the whole place staring after him as though expecting to see his mug on *America's Most Wanted.*

CHAPTER SIXTEEN

"WHAT THE *HELL* was that all about?" Lauren demanded as soon as she and Harley reached the house and Brandon ran down the hall to straighten his bedroom so they could go to the park.

"All what about?" Harley responded, taking the seat in the living room that was closest to the window, ostensibly to use the sunlight streaming through the sheers to read the newspaper he'd carried inside.

"You know what I mean. All that stuff you said to Kara Fletcher. Don't you realize that what you say and do reflects on your son?" Not to mention the fact that she'd been trying not to make too many waves in her father's small pond and now he'd be inundated with calls from appalled friends and acquaintances.

"Brandon doesn't have a problem with who I am. You do," he said. "Besides, I was just having a little fun with your friend."

"A little fun. You made Kara believe you're some kind of dangerous criminal," Lauren cried.

He unfolded the paper. "Maybe she hasn't had enough dangerous men in her life. You heard what she said about men in leather. She fantasizes about them. But you wouldn't understand a fantasy if it bit you on the ass. You've probably never even had one. In any case, a man in leather doesn't appeal to you. You like a different sort."

"Really!" she said. "And you think you know what kind of man that is?"

"The kind who doesn't like to get dirty," he replied smugly. "The kind who speaks through his nose and would never tackle you in a soft meadow and roll around kissing you in the grass, or tickle you until you could barely breathe. You certainly wouldn't want anyone who made you laugh out loud."

"You don't know *anything* about me," she retorted. "How do you know I wouldn't like to be tumbled in a meadow? By a man I admired and loved, I mean," she added so she wouldn't sound quite so eager.

He dumped the paper onto the coffee table and stood. "How many men have you admired and loved?"

"That's none of your business."

"Has anything spontaneous ever occurred?"

Lauren backed up a step because he seemed to fill the room. "Maybe not often, but being tackled in a meadow is not the type of thing that happens to everyone. And it doesn't mean there's anything wrong with me—"

"It means you surround yourself with the type of people who are as worried about wrinkling their clothes as you are."

"I'm not worried about wrinkling my clothes!"

He looked her up and down with obvious distaste. "Not *those,* anyway."

Again, Lauren felt hyper-conscious of her big-framed glasses and ugly clothes and wished she hadn't been so determined to make herself unattractive this morning. But now that Harley had her primed for an argument, she wasn't about to let him change the topic. "Appearances are nothing in the overall scheme of things. I know what's important in life."

"Sure you do," he said. "You and your father are so busy being *proper* and *properly* annoyed when someone else isn't *proper* enough, that it's a wonder you don't explode."

Lauren stared up at him. Where was this coming from? A grudge that was ten years old? Well, she'd been an innocent bystander back then, and she wasn't about to put up with Harley's residual anger now.

"You think you know everything, don't you?" she said. "The boundless wisdom of the common man. Well, so what if you've gone without? So what if you've had it rougher than I have? It's not *my* fault you've always been poor, and you're not going to make me feel guilty for it. Being deprived doesn't make you a better person. And it doesn't mean you're any more in touch with all that pure and simple stuff than I am."

"Oh, yeah?" he countered, stepping toward her. "What if *I'm* not the one who's been deprived? What if you are?"

He was crowding her, but Lauren refused to back away. "What's that supposed to mean?"

Gripping her upper arms, he glared down at her. "Have *you* slept outside on the ground, far from the city, just so you could see the stars? Or gone mountain-biking in a spring shower, when the rain's so warm and gentle it feels like tears bathing your face? Or swum naked in the ocean at night, with the waves roaring in your ears and the moon shining off the water? Or made love on a beach in the light of a bonfire?"

She blinked at him, her chest heaving, but it was difficult to remain angry when he was so close, and when her soul ached for the very things he described. "No," she said.

"No, what?"

"No, I've never done any of those things. I've never gone biking in the rain or swum naked in the ocean. And the few times I've made love haven't been very special. But that doesn't mean my life isn't a good one," she said, only her voice cracked, and she prayed Harley wouldn't be able to tell that she wasn't half as confident as she wanted him to believe.

"Why?" he said, his expression softening.

"Why what?" she repeated, taken off guard.

"Why haven't the times you've made love been special?"

It was a very personal question, something she'd never imagined discussing with him, but it struck at the heart of her insecurities and therefore demanded an answer. Why hadn't she ever experienced the kind of intense emotion others described? She'd wanted to fall in love, especially with Damien. The commitment, the *"you're the only one for me"* just hadn't been there, so she'd put off a physical relationship with him and most of the other men who'd been interested in her.

"You know what I looked like in high school," she said with half a smile, to divert him from glimpsing her real, underlying fear—that she wasn't capable of feeling as deeply as he was.

"I know what you look like now," he said. The pressure of his fingers eased and his hands fell away from her arms, but neither of them moved apart and the intensity in his face didn't change. The nearness of his body, the warmth of it, beckoned her....

"I might not have looked so bad after high school, but there's always been my father's expectations, and..." She let her words drift off as she gazed up at him, noting the clarity of his green eyes and the thick lashes that framed them, and the cowlick that forced his dark hair up and off his forehead. He had a single mark on his temple that might have been something left over from the chicken pox, and white even teeth that flashed at her when he spoke. In high school, his hair had been long, and he'd habitually shoved it out of his eyes....

"And what?" he prompted, his voice now as soft as a caress.

"And the fact that I've never found the right man," she admitted.

He tilted her chin, then hesitated as though assessing her response. When she did nothing, he slowly traced the outline of her lips, making them tingle and part, almost of their own accord. "So you're holding out," he breathed.

Lauren nodded mutely and put a hand to his chest. Now that he was no longer holding her by the arms, she felt unsteady, as if she might fall if she didn't hang on to him. But touching him only made her sway toward the heart that was beating so strong and sure beneath her palm.

"I'll have it all or nothing," she managed to say over the rushing of blood in her ears, but before he could reply, Brandon came charging down the hall, and they jerked apart.

"I'm finished," her nephew announced, carrying a football in the crook of one arm. "Let's go to the park."

THE PARK WAS ONLY fifteen minutes from Hillside Estates. Large and wooded at the south end, it smelled of damp earth and pine despite the heat.

"Lucy is *so* cute," Kimberly said, watching Tank help his daughter down the slide in the play area.

Lauren nodded and stretched out on the blanket, hiding a smile. Considering Kimberly's behavior over the past hour, Lauren had the sneaking suspicion Lucy wasn't the only member of the Thompson party Kimberly found attractive. Despite the traumatic vomit incident in high school, Tank seemed to be running a close second. "Tank hasn't changed much, has he?" she said to gauge her friend's reaction.

Kimberly shrugged, but Lauren knew her too well to buy into her indifference. "Not a lot," she said. "He's certainly not as handsome as Harley, but his look suits him. He reminds me of the guy on *Roseanne*."

"The guy who played her husband?"

"Yeah. He's a little overweight, but I can't imagine him any other way."

Lauren bit the inside of her cheek to avoid a grin. "Um-hum."

"Why are you acting so odd?" Kimberly demanded. "Like you're hiding some sort of secret?"

"I'm not hiding a secret," Lauren told her. "You are. You like Tank."

Kimberly waved a dismissive hand at her. "Get out of here. No, I don't."

"Oh, yes, you do. I haven't seen you this starry-eyed since we met those two brothers in college, and you made me go out with the ugly one so you could date the cute one." Lauren shivered in revulsion. "That guy had to be the worst kisser on earth."

"Well, I dated a few lemons for you, too," Kimberly retorted.

Lauren laughed, remembering some of the men in their lives. There'd been times when they hadn't been nearly selective enough. "Come on," she said. "Tank's no body-builder, but if he asked you out tonight, you'd go."

"No, I wouldn't," Kimberly said, "He's not my type." But she kept her eyes on the chip she was about to eat and wouldn't look up.

"*Lucy's* your type," Lauren prodded.

Kimberly arched her brows and crunched the chip while gazing wistfully at Tank's four-year-old. "That's true. Lucy is *definitely* my type. I'd love to have a little girl just like her."

"Maybe you could get two for the price of one."

Kimberly's face reddened, but the corners of her mouth started to twitch. "What about you?" she asked after a moment, in a voice that said she was impatient with her own transparency. "I'd accuse you of having the hots for Harley, but if you really liked him, I know you wouldn't be caught dead wearing that hideous outfit. Where'd you get that blouse, anyway? A secondhand store?"

Lauren frowned at the outfit her Aunt Myrtle had sent her for her birthday. She'd regretted choosing it from the first moment she'd put it on, but she wouldn't let herself change—because then she'd be admitting that she cared what Harley thought, that she wanted to impress him.

At least she'd given up on the glasses and put in her contacts. "It doesn't matter what I look like," she said, unwilling to explain that the outfit was actually part of her plan to distance herself from Harley. Especially since it didn't seem to be working.

Kimberly shrugged. "Suit yourself. At least Harley and Brandon seem to be getting on well."

In between frequent interruptions when Harley turned the chicken cooking on the grill, father and son were throwing the football back and forth on the grass between the blanket and the play area. Lauren had been enjoying the sound of their voices as they called to each other and sprinted or dived for the ball. "Did you see that spiral?" Brandon would cry. "It was *beautiful*, Dad."

"See? You've got a good arm," Harley would say, but from Lauren's vantage point, it was Harley who had a good arm. And a great body. Watching him run around in shorts, his arms and chest flexing beneath his T-shirt as he caught and threw, made for an enjoyable show— one that left her feeling too warm, even though a cool breeze had started filtering through the shady trees.

"I'm glad I let them be together," Lauren said.

"Even though you'll have to pay the price?"

"Even still."

Kimberly shoved the bag of chips away and leaned back to cross her legs at the ankle. "Your parents might not have checked out of the hotel this morning, but they could still be home as early as tomorrow. You know that, don't you?''

''I know.''

''Well, for what it's worth, I think you did the best thing for Brandon.''

''Really?'' Lauren smiled at her friend and reached over to squeeze her arm. She felt bad that Kimberly's marriage hadn't worked out, but she was delighted to have her back in Portland. Life just wasn't the same without her.

''How's the job hunt?'' Lauren asked, hoping to distract herself from drooling over Harley.

A pained expression crossed Kimberly's face. ''I'm afraid that in order to get a job, I'm going to have to actually apply.''

''That's the general idea.''

''But there's no hurry, right?''

''I thought you wanted to be busy. I thought your parents were driving you crazy.''

''Not as crazy as putting on a pair of panty hose and going to one interview after another. In another couple of weeks, I think I'll go back to Baer, Bower and Horton, anyway. They might be a little stuffy for my tastes, but most accountants are. And they like me well enough there. I think I can eventually make partner. When I left, they said the door would always be open.''

''At least you've got that as an option.''

''Aunt Lauren, come and play with us,'' Brandon called.

Lauren considered Harley and Brandon, who had both turned expectantly toward her, and glanced at Kimberly. ''Do I really want to get out there and make myself look like an uncoordinated dork?''

''Naw. You'll get grass stains on your pants.''

''I'm not afraid of getting dirty,'' Lauren protested.

Kimberly blinked at her in surprise. "I admit that ruining those pants wouldn't be much of a pity, but—"

"But nothing," Lauren said and hopped up to prove to Harley that she could be as carefree as the next woman.

LAUREN COULDN'T THROW worth anything. Harley scratched his head, then loped over to give her a few tips. If she could only remember to put the opposite foot forward when she extended her arm, she'd probably be able to throw a lot farther. It was definitely apparent that she'd spent her childhood reading books and not climbing trees.

"Look, try this," he said, modeling a solid throw. "See? You're right-handed, so step forward on your left foot. That way you won't throw your shoulder out trying to get the ball to me."

"Give it a try, Aunt Lauren," Brandon yelled.

Lauren wound up and heaved the ball to her nephew, but it was about the ugliest throw Harley had ever seen.

"Was that any better?" she asked hopefully.

"Er, yeah," he said. "Just try to keep your elbow closer to your body." Taking her arm, he started guiding her through the proper motion so she could get a feel for what she should be doing, but Tank looked up from swinging Lucy just then, and Harley let go of Lauren as quickly as if she'd burned him. While they were preparing the grill, Tank had mentioned that Damien had stopped by the apartment earlier and ranted and raved about Harley using Brandon to get close to Lauren. "He thinks you have a thing for Lauren," Tank had said, laughing in amazement, "and you don't even think she's cute." Harley had laughed, too, but he knew the joke was on him. After what Lauren had said in the living room about her love life, he'd imagined a hundred different ways to show her what she was missing—and that conversation had taken place only five hours ago.

What I feel for her is just physical, and as fleeting as

it is ironic, he told himself, but he had a hard time believing his interest was just physical when she was wearing old-lady clothes and no makeup and was such an embarrassment to women's athletics.

Brandon threw her a long spiral, and Harley backed
away to give her room to field it. Lauren managed to catch
it, with her arms and the aid of her body. She gave him
a triumphant smile.

"I catch better than I throw," she explained, but Harley
wasn't too impressed with her ability on either end. He
liked her enthusiasm, though. He liked that a lot. And he
thought her smile was pretty damn cute.

"Good job," he said, wishing he was half as taken with
any other woman in the park—or any other woman in the
world, for that matter.

She lobbed him the ball, he threw it to Brandon, and
Brandon heaved her another long, spiral pass. Only this
one was pretty far over her head. She started running
backward and was so intent on the ball, Harley had the
impulse to warn her about the uneven ground. But before
he could get the words out, she reached up, bobbled the
ball, dropped it and fell on top of it.

"Aunt Lauren, are you okay?" Brandon cried, running
toward her.

Harley was the first at her side. "Are you hurt?"

"I don't think so. At least not seriously," she panted,
but her brow was creased. *Something* hurt, and seeing her
in pain was making Harley feel queasy himself.

"What is it?" he coaxed.

She didn't answer for a moment. Rocking back and
forth as though waiting for the pain to ease, she finally
indicated her right ankle. "I wrenched it."

"Kimberly! Aunt Lauren broke her leg," Brandon
called.

"Should I call an ambulance?" Kim asked, hurrying
over, Tank and Lucy right behind her.

Harley shook his head. "No need for an ambulance. I'll carry her to her car and take her to the emergency room to have an X-ray. Any chance you could stay here with Brandon? The chicken's not quite done, and there's no need for the rest of you to miss the picnic."

"Is that okay with you, Lauren?" Kimberly asked.

Lauren nodded, her face now pale, but Brandon immediately protested.

"I don't want to stay here!"

"You haven't had anything to eat," Harley told him.

"I don't care. I want to go to the hospital with you."

"I'm not going to the hospital," Lauren said. "I just sprained my ankle, no big deal. I'll take it easy for a few days, and everything will be fine." She tried to get up but collapsed back onto the ground when her ankle wouldn't support even a portion of her weight.

Harley bent to examine the injury. "I think we should have a doctor look at it."

"It's better to be safe," Kimberly chimed in. "You want it to heal right, Lauren. Let Harley run you over to the hospital. Tank and I will take good care of Brandon while you're gone." She put a hand on Brandon's neck. "You'll stay with us, won't you, Bran? And help us keep an eye on Lucy? Your father and Lauren will be back before you know it."

"Okay," Brandon relented.

Lauren blew a stray wisp of hair out of her face. "I guess a trip to the hospital is what I get for trying to show off my football prowess," she said with a smile, but it seemed to Harley that her attempt at humor was aimed at keeping them from realizing just how much pain she was in.

"You nearly had the ball, too, Aunt Lauren. You were doing really good," Brandon told her, which was an absolute lie and everyone knew it. But his son's desire to make Lauren feel better brought a smile to Harley's lips.

Lauren had done well by Brandon. He might not have had much of a mother, but he had a great aunt, and it was obvious they loved each other very much.

A second later, Harley's smile disappeared as he remembered the conversation he'd had with his own mother just last night. "I can't wait until you take Brandon away from those snooty Worthingtons," she'd said gleefully, an echo of his own feelings—once. But everything had changed. How could he take Brandon away from Lauren now?

Then again, how could he leave him behind?

CHAPTER SEVENTEEN

"I DON'T SUPPOSE you'd let me take you to the hospital on my bike," Harley said, the devilish glint in his eyes telling Lauren he was teasing, possibly to distract her from the pain. But he didn't need to do anything special by way of distraction. Being carried in the cradle of his arms was more than enough.

Lauren purposely kept her arms loose around his neck; he seemed to bear her weight quite easily and she didn't want Kimberly and Tank to see her clinging to him as they made their way across the grass. But the impulse to tighten her grip, and snuggle closer shot from her brain to her arms every few seconds.

"I think I'll be more comfortable in my car," she said, twisting to catch sight of the sleek, diabolical machine parked next to her Lexus at the far end of the lot. That motorcycle was going to be the death of her. Before the picnic, Brandon had spent a full fifteen minutes begging her to let him ride on the back, "just to the park." By the time she'd convinced him that her answer wasn't going to change, she'd felt absolutely pummeled by his verbal onslaught. And Harley hadn't helped much. He hadn't interfered or tried to override her decision, but she could tell he wasn't happy with her refusal.

"Are you ever going to let me give you a ride?" he asked.

"Maybe," she said, so she wouldn't have to deal with the repercussions of a solid "no" right now. Her ankle was hurting too badly. She just wanted to get to a doctor and take some painkillers.

And she wanted to snuggle closer....

"Is that a yes?"

"Since when does 'maybe' mean 'yes'?"

"It doesn't. But it means I have a good chance at a yes."

"You have a better chance at a no."

"Come on," he said, giving her an adorable, little-boy scowl. "Really?"

Lauren had never wanted to ride on a motorcycle before, but the thought of clinging to Harley held a certain undeniable appeal. Maybe she'd injured more than her ankle when she fell; maybe she'd hit her head.

"I don't know," she said. "Maybe means maybe. I can't promise you anything."

"Why not?" he asked, his feet now crunching on the loose gravel in the lot as they wove through the parked cars.

"Will you stop pressuring me?" she said with a groan. "You sound like Brandon. I can't take it from both of you. Besides, you have me at a disadvantage. I'm injured."

"And I'm going to take care of you," he said. "Just like I'd take care of you if you ever got on the back of my bike."

"That's a completely illogical argument," she complained. "You can't control what other drivers on the road might do, so you can't guarantee my safety."

He shifted her to get a better grip, and Lauren could tell from the perspiration on his brow and neck that hauling her such a long distance was starting to tax him. "Forget about being the Queen of Debate for a minute," he said. "Some things aren't logical. They're instinctual."

Lauren's instincts were telling her all kinds of things about Harley. She just didn't know whether or not to trust them because they were telling her to trust *him.* "If I go for a ride with you, Brandon will never quit begging me for a turn," she pointed out.

"Then you and I will go some night when Brandon's in bed. We can have Kim come over and sit with him. He'll never even know."

Lauren hadn't intended to spend *any* evenings alone with Harley. Limiting their contact was all part of her "distancing" plan. "Are you trying to show me it's safe so I'll eventually let Brandon enjoy the experience?" she asked. "Are you trying to break me down?"

"It doesn't have anything to do with Brandon."

"Then why does it matter whether or not I go?"

A look of irritation, or maybe it was disappointment, flickered across his face, but then it was gone and he shrugged as well as he could while carrying her. "Never mind. You're right. It doesn't matter."

It did matter. Lauren could hear it in his voice. She just couldn't figure out *why* it mattered. He had access to his son. What did he want with her?

"Where're the keys?" he asked when they finally reached the car.

"They're in my pocket. I didn't want to worry about watching my purse while we were at the park."

He let her down gently, continuing to bear most of her weight, but her ankle still hurt badly enough to make her want to cry.

"Hang on to me so you don't fall. I'll get them," he said. He slipped a hand into her front pocket, which would have been fine, except her pants were snug and her pocket had worked its way over. Only a thin lining separated his fingers from a very sensitive area.

Lauren drew in a deep breath and thought her ankle had miraculously healed. For a moment, she felt no pain, just the kind of thrill she enjoyed on a good roller-coaster.

Except that a roller-coaster had never made her cheeks grow warm....

"I don't know if I've ever met a woman who blushes as easily as you do," he said, pulling the keys out of her pocket. But he was grinning when he said it, and she wondered if he hadn't been a little overzealous in their extraction.

"I don't blush easily," she protested. "I'm probably getting a fever from my broken ankle."

"Feeling a little warm?"

"Maybe."

His grin widened into a knowing smile. "Well, I've got news for you. That's no fever."

HARLEY COULD TELL the pain medication was starting to kick in and finally relaxed. Lauren was going to be fine. The doctor had said her ankle wasn't broken, just badly sprained, and had advised her to ice it, wrap it and stay off her feet for a few days.

Owing to a car accident, several ambulances had arrived at the same time they did, and it had taken longer to get in and be seen than Harley had thought it would. They'd been at the hospital for more than three hours.

"Who're you calling?" Lauren asked, when he dialed Tank on his cell phone.

"Just checking on Brandon."

"Thanks," she said, "You're a pretty devoted dad."

Harley smiled, liking the compliment almost as much as the response he'd gotten earlier, when he'd had his hand in her pocket, although she'd avoided eye contact with him ever since. Even now she leaned her head against the wall and glanced away as Kimberly answered Tank's cell phone.

"Hello?"

"Hi, Kim. It's Harley."

"Oh, good. We've been worried. How's Lauren?"

"She's doing great. The doctor gave her some Vicadin, so she's a little sleepy, but the pain has eased, and her ankle's not broken."

"I'm glad to hear that. Where are you?"

"We're still at the hospital, waiting for a prescription. We'll be free to go in a minute, but I don't think I should bring Lauren back to the park. She needs some rest."

"We're not at the park anymore. We're over at Tank's, watching a movie."

"Okay. We'll swing by and pick up Brandon on our way to Lauren's."

Kimberly paused. "Actually, we're watching the old *Star Wars* trilogy, and Brandon seems to be enjoying himself. Besides that, he's keeping Lucy occupied. Any chance you'll let him stay a little longer?"

Tank said something in the background, something that made Kimberly laugh as though they were old friends, but then she came back on the line. "How 'bout I drop him by when I leave here? Tank will bring your bike at the same time. That way you can fill Lauren's prescription and take her straight home."

"That sounds fine," Harley said. "Are you sure?"

"Positive. See you later."

"Is Brandon okay?" Lauren asked as soon as he'd hung up.

"Yeah. He's going to stay with Kim and keep Lucy occupied for a few more hours, if that's okay with you. They're watching a movie at the apartment."

She smiled. "Things must be going well with Tank."

"What's that mean?" he asked. "Kim doesn't like Tank, does she?"

"I think so. But she won't admit it."

"She could do worse. Tank's a good guy."

The nurse stuck her head in the room and handed him the promised prescription. "Have her take one of these every four hours as needed for the pain," she said. "And you might want to buy or borrow a pair of crutches to help her get around over the next few days.''

"Right. Thanks," Harley said.

"My pleasure. I'll get you a wheelchair to bring her to the car."

The nurse disappeared and returned only moments later with the wheelchair. Harley helped Lauren inside it, then wheeled her out to the car.

"Why are *you* taking care of me?" she asked suddenly.

"Is there someone else you wish was here instead?" he replied, assisting her into the passenger seat. He'd asked the question flippantly, pretending to tease her, just in case her answer wasn't what he wanted to hear.

At first he thought she wasn't going to respond. She let him buckle her seat belt without saying anything. But before he could go around to get in the driver's side, she caught him by the arm.

"No. There never has been," she said and, judging by her tone and her face, she was serious.

"SO KIMBERLY'S GOING to bring Brandon home?" Lauren asked Harley, who was helping her hobble down the hall to her bedroom on her new crutches.

He turned and cocked an eyebrow at her. "You've asked me that three times already," he told her. "I think the Vicadan's made you a little loopy. Kimberly is bringing Brandon. I'll make sure he has dinner and I'll get him into bed. You don't have to worry about him."

Somehow this didn't comfort her. She *wasn't* worried about Brandon; she knew he was safe with Kim. She was more worried about Harley's constant presence and the way the painkiller seemed to be affecting her mind. It was all craziness, of course, but there were moments when it seemed as if Harley was the man she'd been waiting for, the one who could claim her entire heart.

"So…you're staying overnight?" she asked tentatively.

"I figured I'd crash on the couch, in case you or Brandon need anything during the night."

"We have lots of extra beds."

"That's okay. I'll hang out in the family room. Then we'll see how you're doing tomorrow."

Lauren thought about the dark, still house, Brandon sound asleep in his room, Harley just down the hall, and felt a tingle in the pit of her stomach. Remembering the pocket experience, she couldn't help wondering what he might be able to do with some privacy, a bed and a willing partner, then cursed the painkiller again and shook her head. So much for never having had a fantasy…

"Are you okay?" he asked.

"No. I think I'm losing my mind," she muttered.

"What?"

"Nothing. I'm fine."

Harley turned down her bed and she relinquished her crutches and sat on the edge, planning to undress and change into her nightgown. But first, she had something to do.

"Would you hand me that telephone over there, please?" she asked.

He reached across the bed and got it for her, then watched as she dialed. "Who're you calling?"

"My parents."

He grimaced. "Let's not do that."

"If you're going to stay, I have to," she said.

He didn't respond, but he didn't leave the room, either. Leaning one shoulder against the doorframe, he watched as she waited for the hotel operator to answer.

"The Ritz. How may I direct your call?"

"Quentin Worthington's room, please."

"Just a moment."

When the phone started to ring in her parents' room,

Lauren hung up before anyone could answer. "They're still in London," she breathed. "Thank God."

Harley hooked his thumbs in his jeans and looked at the carpet, a frown on his face.

"What's wrong?" Lauren asked.

He raised his eyes to hers, but the frown remained. "This is beginning to feel familiar," he said.

HARLEY BLINKED into the darkness, wondering what had awakened him. The room was nice and cool, the couch comfortable. Kim had brought Brandon home around suppertime. Harley had fed him, they'd played Nintendo and his son had gone to bed, then Harley had checked on Lauren, who'd been asleep ever since placing the call to her parents. He'd settled in the family room and watched some television before finally nodding off. But according to the clock above the fireplace, it was only two. He'd slept barely three hours.

Throwing off the blanket he'd used to cover himself, Harley pulled his jeans over his boxer briefs, got up and padded barefoot into the kitchen. Maybe he was worried about his business. Weekends were the most profitable, but he'd been too involved with Brandon—and Lauren— to even call Joe today. He could only hope his manager was handling everything reasonably well and there'd still be a business left when he got back.

He opened the fridge and scrounged around, looking for something to eat. He wasn't really hungry, but he was hoping to distract himself from the thoughts hovering at the edges of his mind. Thoughts about taking Brandon to California. Thoughts about Quentin Worthington and the anger and resentment he evoked. Audra and those early years. And Lauren. Lauren was the most difficult subject of all because Damien was right—Harley wanted her. But it was more than that. He cared about her. A lot.

I'll forget about her once Brandon and I hit California,

he promised himself. He had to. Getting involved with Lauren was only asking for more of what he'd suffered ten years ago. It wasn't as though he could expect Lauren to choose him over her father. If Audra couldn't do it, Quentin's favored Lauren certainly wouldn't be able to— and that was assuming she felt something for him in the first place. Remembering the way she'd treated him at karate, Harley knew he couldn't take even that much for granted.

With a sigh, he closed the fridge without raiding it as he'd planned and leaned his forehead against the cool metal surface. He was stupid for putting himself in this position again. He had to keep his mind on Brandon and forget everything else. But the only way Harley could justify taking Brandon with him was to allow Lauren ample visitation, which meant he couldn't cut her out of his life completely. He'd see her and want her and tell himself *no* and stay locked in a never-ending circle.

Dammit, nothing was ever simple with the Worthingtons.

Aggrieved by the whole mess, he headed down the hall that led to Brandon's room, which was on the opposite side from Lauren's, to find his son sleeping peacefully. Moonlight, filtering through a crack in the wooden shutters, cast a silvery glow and made Brandon appear younger, more vulnerable than he seemed during daylight hours. Harley felt his heart yearn as he gazed at the boy's sweet, innocent face. Even at eighteen, the only thing he'd ever wanted where Brandon was concerned was to be the kind of dad he'd never had himself. Was that so much to ask?

He sat carefully on the edge of the bed. The springs squeaked, but Brandon didn't stir. He slept on, with Harley watching in morose silence as the minutes dragged by. This week he'd file papers to gain custody, he decided, as a clock somewhere in the house struck three. But was that really what was best for Brandon? Remembering the concern on his son's face when Lauren hurt herself at the park, Harley wondered if Brandon could ever be happy without her.

Hell, he wondered if *he'd* ever be happy without her. In ten years there hadn't been anyone who affected him the way she did.

Standing, Harley pulled the covers over Brandon, then bent and kissed him on the forehead. "I love you," he whispered.

"Are you leaving?" Brandon asked, waking in a panic.

"Shhh," Harley said, stroking his back to calm him. "I'm not going anywhere. I just couldn't sleep."

His small body immediately relaxed. "Want me to wake up and talk to you?"

Judging by his slurred words and heavy eyes, Harley knew that wouldn't be an easy thing for Brandon to do. But Harley appreciated the offer. Not many kids Brandon's age would be that considerate.

"No need. I'm just checking on you."

"I'm fine." His eyes drooped. "But don't go anywhere, okay?"

"All right, buddy. I'll be here when you wake up."

"Promise?"

"I promise."

Brandon's lips curved into a smile for a split second before he drifted off to sleep, then Harley slipped out of the room and went to peek in on Lauren.

"HARLEY, IS THAT YOU?" Lauren asked when the tread of footsteps stopped outside her door.

"Doesn't anyone in this family sleep at night?" he asked, poking his head into the room.

"Is Brandon awake?" she asked, puzzled.

"Not any more."

"Was something wrong with him?"

"No, he's fine. He just woke up for a minute when I went in to cover him. How are you feeling?"

Lauren tested her ankle and immediately regretted the movement. "I need another pain pill."

"You should eat first."

She was hungry, but she'd been so wrapped up in Harley that she hadn't cooked in the past few days, the way she normally did. "What are my options?"

"Kimberly brought over some of the chicken we barbecued at the park and a few other leftovers," he said.

"That sounds good."

"I'll get you a plate."

He'd carried her to the car after the accident, driven her to the emergency room, waited with her and helped her to bed after bringing her home. Now he was staying here all night in case she needed him. All of this was above and beyond the call of duty. "Harley?"

He turned back.

"You don't have to do this. I'm not your responsibility."

"I don't mind."

"It's three o'clock in the morning."

"Don't worry about it. I can't sleep anyway."

After about ten minutes, the light came on in the hall and spilled into her room, and Harley returned, carrying a plate of food. The aroma reached Lauren before he did: chicken, watermelon, coleslaw, baked beans...

"This looks great," she said. "Did you have some earlier?"

"I had a piece of chicken, but I gave Brandon soup for dinner. He'd already had this stuff, and soup was about the best I could manage."

Somehow his lack of culinary talent came as no surprise to Lauren. She couldn't picture Harley using anything besides a microwave.

"Is the chicken hot enough?" he asked.

She nodded. "Perfect."

He crossed the room and gazed out the window while she ate, leaving Lauren to wonder what held his interest. The moon? The shadowy yard? He seemed different tonight, pensive and remote.

"Why couldn't you sleep?" she asked, setting her plate aside and taking the pill he'd put on her nightstand, along with a glass of water.

He shrugged, leaned against the wall and hooked a thumb in the waistband of his jeans, but kept his focus on the world outside.

Lauren found him incredibly sexy. He wasn't wearing a shirt, the top two buttons on his jeans were undone, and she could see Brandon's tattoo on his shoulder blade. But then, despite her earlier denial, she found him equally appealing in leather. "Were you uncomfortable on the couch?" she asked.

"No."

"Has something upset you?"

"No."

"What are you thinking about?"

He sighed and looked over his shoulder at her. "You."

Her... That could mean a lot of things. She waited, hoping he'd elaborate, but when he added nothing more, she tried to get him to open up. "Have I done something you don't like?"

He didn't answer.

"You're not still mad that I won't get on the back of your bike, are you?" she asked, trying to lighten his mood. But he didn't smile as she expected. If anything, his brows lowered even farther.

"Okay, I'll let you take me for a ride," she said. "Just stop staring out the window like you have the weight of the world on your shoulders."

At last, a smile. "You're such a pushover in some

ways," he said. "You come off tough, like your father, but it's all a bluff. Inside you're soft and sweet."

"Come on, I can be tough," she said, adjusting her pillows.

"You haven't been very tough with me."

Lauren didn't know what to say. She *hadn't* been tough with him. He posed the greatest threat to her happiness she'd ever known, yet she'd opened her house and her heart and let him walk right in.

"How's your ankle?" he asked.

"The painkiller's starting to work."

"Has the swelling gone down?"

"I think so." She pulled her foot out from beneath the blankets to see. She needed something to divert her attention from the brooding male standing at the window. But she regretted giving Harley a reason to draw closer when he sat on the foot of her bed and cradled her injured ankle in his lap. He was only half-dressed. She was wearing nothing but a lightweight nightgown. And they were alone in a semidarkened room.

"You're right. It looks a little better," he said, and then he ran one hand up her leg. She knew the contact was ostensibly designed to lift her nightgown so that he could better see her ankle. But he wasn't looking at her ankle. He was looking at her face. And his hands were gently massaging her calf muscle.

Lauren suddenly found it very difficult to swallow.

"Do you like this?" he asked.

Lauren liked it, all right. She liked it a lot. But she couldn't say so. She didn't seem capable of doing anything except holding her breath.

He inched her nightgown up farther, still massaging her leg, then lowered his head and placed several tentative kisses on the inside of her knee and thigh. "What about this?" he asked.

Her legs were tingling; so were other parts of her body.

And his mood seemed to be improving. No need to bring back the scowl, she thought. She preferred this Harley.... And her ankle wasn't hurting at all. In fact, she scarcely remembered having an injury. "I like it," she admitted breathlessly.

His hands and lips inched their way up her leg until she was sure he could see the silk of her bikini underwear. "Do you want me to keep going?"

Her father and Brandon and Audra... Lauren had so many reasons to say no. But she said yes. And at that moment she knew she could no longer fault Audra for falling in love with Harley. Because she was head over heels in love with him herself.

CHAPTER EIGHTEEN

HARLEY COULDN'T BELIEVE what he was hearing. Regardless of how she'd acted at karate, Lauren seemed happy enough to be with him now. Her soft *yes* made him long to strip her little nightgown off her body and bury his face in her breasts. He imagined her wrapping her legs around him and accepting him completely, imagined easing himself into her for the first time, and thought he might die from the anticipation. But she'd just taken a Vicadin. She was Audra's sister and Brandon's aunt. And he knew there were even greater considerations, although he didn't want to think about them right now.

"Is that the painkiller talking?" he asked, sliding her leg off his lap and kneeling by her bed.

She shook her head.

"Then maybe you've forgotten I'm the bad guy."

"I don't believe you're a bad guy," she said, and raised a hand to trace his lips as he'd once traced hers.

Harley closed his eyes, feeling himself waver, and leaned closer. For ten years, he'd wanted a member of the Worthington family to show some faith in him. Audra had claimed to love him, but she'd clung to her father the way someone who's afraid of water clings to the side of the pool—and Harley supposed he couldn't blame her; they'd been so young. But here was Lauren, apparently offering him the acceptance he craved....

Their mouths met, touching lightly, searchingly at first, then hungrily, and it was as if he'd never kissed a woman before. Desire slammed through him, sweeping him away almost instantly and making him want Lauren so badly his hand shook as he cupped her breast.

She moaned when his fingers found her nipple, and the proof that her arousal matched his own stole his breath. She had to care about him, or she wouldn't be responding this way. She wasn't the type to get physical with just anyone. According to Tank, Damien hadn't gotten anywhere with her.

But there'd been a lot of women who'd wanted him physically, Audra included, and Harley couldn't get past the thought that, in the light of day, he'd suddenly lose his appeal. He couldn't see Lauren introducing him as her boyfriend to her friends and neighbors. He couldn't see her telling her father that he was her man. And if what they did tonight soured things between them, it was entirely possible that she could start fighting him on Brandon's future. No more compromise; no more sharing. For everyone involved, especially Brandon, Harley couldn't let it come to that.

"No," he said, pulling away. "I shouldn't have started this."

He half hoped she'd cling to him, so he'd have an excuse to ignore everything his more logical side was telling him, but she let go of him immediately. "Is it because you're not attracted to me? Is it because I'm not like Audra?" she asked, her eyes wide and uncertain.

Scrubbing his face with one hand, he took a deep breath, trying to gain some control over what he was feeling. How could she question his desire for her? He was rock-hard and aching, and she was so much more than her sister had ever been. Surely she had to know that by now. "No," he said, "It's not you. It's Brandon. I can't do anything to threaten my position where he's concerned. We've lived without each other for the past nine years. I don't want to lose him again, and I won't risk doing anything that could potentially hurt him, even indirectly."

Her gaze dropped to his mouth and then floated over his chest, and he knew she didn't want to worry about such things any more than he did. But how much of her response had to do with the Vicadin—with the here and now—and how much had to do with any kind of feeling that would last?

"I would never use what happens between us to keep you from Brandon," she said. "I'm not like that."

He let himself kiss her, lightly gliding his tongue over her upper lip as he languished in indecision. "So you want this?"

"I've never wanted anything more."

Her words turned Harley's blood to fire. Slipping down the straps of her nightgown, he bared her breasts, which were milky white and perfectly formed. So beautiful... He raised a hand to caress them, watching as Lauren closed her eyes and let her head fall back on the pillow in apparent ecstasy, and thought he'd gladly trade anything to have her.

But some small part of his brain reminded him what it had been like ten years ago when Audra had turned her back on him, and he knew deep down that if push came to shove, Lauren would do the same. Like her sister before her, she'd stand with her father and shut him out. And when she found out he was pressing for custody, she'd hate him, and he wouldn't be able to blame her. That was when Harley realized he'd been wrong. There were two things he wouldn't trade for a night with Lauren—one was her respect, the other his dignity.

"I won't," he said at last. "Not again."

She frowned, a mixture of hurt and confusion on her face, and he forced himself to explain part of the reason he couldn't finish what they'd started. "You should know that I plan to gain custody of Brandon, Lauren. He's my son. I love him and I want him," he said. Then he stood and left before the testosterone coursing through his body made him change his mind about respect and dignity. But he bumped into someone coming down the hall from the other direction, and even before he saw who it was, he recognized the voice.

"You son of a bitch! What the hell are you doing in my house?"

BRANDON AWOKE TO SHOUTING.

At first, he thought he was dreaming, because the loudest voice was that of his Grandpa Worthington, who was supposed to be in Europe. But then he heard Aunt Lauren crying, and his father, whose sentences were short and so low Brandon could barely make out the words.

"Get out of my house and don't ever come back, you hear me?" his grandfather cried. "You're crazy if you think I'm going to welcome you back. I won't—"

"I invited him. He came to see Brandon," Aunt Lauren said, her voice overriding Grandfather's. "You can't pretend he isn't Brandon's father. Please, Dad, if you'll only calm down, I can explain—"

"If you want to explain something, explain what the hell he was doing in your bedroom."

"That's none of your business. I'm twenty-seven years old—"

"I don't care how old you are. I won't have you spreading your legs for this son of a bitch. Not in my house—"

"Don't!" It was his father this time. "That's not fair, and you know it. I'll leave, but don't do this to Lauren. She hasn't done anything. She shouldn't even be up—"

"How dare you tell me how to treat my own daughter! She doesn't need you to protect her. She doesn't need you for anything."

"Then have some consideration for your grandson and

lower your voice," his father replied. "You'll wake Brandon, and he doesn't need to hear this shit."

"He needs to know better than to trust you. Damien Thompson called and told me what you've been doing—"

"And what have I been doing?" his father interrupted. "Visiting my son? That isn't the crime here. The crime was letting you convince me that he was better off without me in the first place."

"Just get out and don't ever come back!"

Footsteps sounded in the living room, moving toward the front door, and Brandon scrambled out of bed. Why was his grandfather home so early? Harley—his *father*—had finally come back, and now his grandfather was going to ruin everything.

"Grandpa, stop!" Brandon cried, running down the hall and hurrying to block the door. "I don't want my dad to leave. I don't want you to be so mad. We only had a picnic, and Lauren twisted her ankle, but everything's okay. It *is* okay, isn't it, Aunt Lauren?"

His aunt was on crutches. She dashed a hand across her face to wipe away her tears. "You're right, honey. Everything's okay," she said, but the sad look on her face made Brandon's stomach hurt.

"Brandon, move away from the door. This man was just leaving," his grandfather said, and he was using that voice Brandon hated, the one that made him feel as though something terrible was going to happen if he didn't obey. But something terrible was going to happen, anyway. If Harley left he might never come back, and Brandon couldn't imagine anything worse than that.

"I won't," he said, clinging to the knob with all his might. "I don't care what you do to me. I won't."

"Hey, buddy, settle down. It's okay," his father said, kneeling next to him. "Your grandfather's a little upset right now, that's all. This is his house, and we need to respect his wishes, so it's best if I go for tonight. But I won't head back to California without calling you. I promise.''

"But you already promised." Brandon couldn't stop the tears that were streaking down his cheeks. He was crying like a little baby. He hated that, but right now, he hated his grandfather more, and Lauren, and his father, too.

His father took him by the shoulders. "I don't have any choice," he said. "Sometimes people have to do things they don't want to do, hard things, and this is one of them. But we'll be together in the future, okay? That's a promise I'll keep if it takes everything I have."

"You won't disappear?"

"I won't disappear."

Brandon glanced at his grandfather, who was huffing and puffing, all red in the face, then at Lauren, who was crying again. Then he turned back to his father. "Take me with you."

"Oh, Bran." Aunt Lauren started hobbling toward him, and it made Brandon cry harder to know that what he'd said had probably hurt her. She loved him. She wouldn't want him to go. But he knew where to find her. She'd be right here, at Hillside Estates. It was his father who might go away and never return, his father he had to keep track of.

"See what you've done!" Aunt Lauren shouted at Grandfather. "You're alienating him and me, too. What's wrong with you? Are you so frightened of Harley that you can't be fair, or even kind, to anyone?"

His grandfather looked as though he didn't know what to do. He smoothed down the sides of his gray hair and took a deep breath, but he didn't say anything. He glared at all of them, then pivoted and marched out of the room.

Brandon threw his arms around his father, who hugged him and rubbed his back and whispered that he'd come for him, and though it sounded like he meant it, Brandon still felt sick inside.

"I'll take care of him," Aunt Lauren said, but she wouldn't look at his father, and it didn't seem as though his father wanted to look at her, either. They didn't seem to be friends anymore, which frightened Brandon more than anything—except the sound of the door closing when his father left.

LAUREN BRUSHED Brandon's hair off his forehead, relieved to see his breathing even out. He was asleep again, thank goodness. But morning would come, and Lauren doubted he was going to feel any better about his father leaving than he'd felt tonight.

It'll all work out, she told herself, which was the same thing she'd murmured to her nephew just a few minutes earlier. Somehow, they'd all get through this. But she didn't know how. She loved her father. She loved Brandon. And, even though he'd just admitted that he intended to take Brandon away from her, she loved Harley. Probably because she couldn't blame him for wanting Brandon. They all wanted Brandon.

Wasn't there some way to compromise? Maybe Harley wouldn't sue for custody if her father would agree to let him have Brandon during the summer break and for certain holidays. And maybe her father wouldn't feel so threatened if Harley would agree to leave Brandon alone at all other times. Then, despite the two men, Lauren might be able to retain some place in her nephew's life. It was a slender thread on which to hang her hope, but she was raising a child to whom she had no legal right, which left her in a very weak position indeed.

"Time to face the dragon," she muttered to the sleeping Brandon. Then she gave him a quick kiss on the brow, struggled to get her crutches beneath her and made her way down the hall, steeling herself for what promised to be the biggest battle of her life.

She found her father in the family room. He was sitting in the dark, facing the couch where Harley's bedding was piled, staring off into space.

"Where's Mom?" she asked.

He barely glanced at her. "I couldn't get two plane tickets on such short notice. She's coming home tomorrow."

If nothing else revealed the degree of her father's passionate response to Harley's return, the fact that he'd left Marilee half a world behind would have served as a pretty good indication. Her father did all the driving, planned every vacation and outing, and oversaw everything of any import. Marilee shopped, bought presents, decorated and basked in her husband's care. And she talked a lot, but most of the time Lauren just smiled and nodded pleasantly because Quentin had the last word, anyway.

"So you left Mom in London?" she said.

"Considering the situation, what else could I do?" His terse words let her know his temper hadn't cooled in the half hour she'd spent with Brandon.

"You could have trusted me to see to things here," Lauren said, stopping at the edge of the carpet and leaning on her crutches. Her ankle was killing her, despite the Vicadin, but it couldn't compare to the pain in her heart.

He finally focused on her. "How can you say that after what I came home to?"

Lauren winced at the loathing in his eyes. She could only see him in the light streaming in from the living room, and the shadows on his face might have made his disgust seem more pronounced, but she doubted it. She remembered that expression too well. It was the one he'd always reserved for Audra when she'd done something he didn't agree with, the one that branded her as unworthy of her heritage and social standing. Until now, Lauren had never realized how belittling that look could be.

"Harley was taking care of me because I sprained my ankle. That's why he was here," she said.

"You're trying to tell me his visit to your bedroom in the middle of the night was completely innocent?"

The accusation in his voice was clear. Lauren took a deep breath, wanting to convince him Harley's visit *was* innocent. Then maybe he'd forgive her. She hadn't seen her father for weeks. Like the child she used to be, she craved the hug he would've given her under different circumstances. But another other part of her insisted that she wasn't a child anymore and demanded she take responsibility for her actions and decisions.

"Maybe not completely," she admitted.

"And you want me to believe he isn't scum to try and take advantage of you that way?"

Lauren shook her head. "You've got it all wrong, Dad. It wasn't him, it was me. I would've slept with him tonight. He was the one who wouldn't."

Her father's jaw dropped and his breath whooshed out. "How can you admit to me that you wanted to…to have sex with that man?" he asked, his voice harsh.

Because I love him, she almost blurted. *Because I'm in love for the first time in my whole life.* But she knew that kind of truth wouldn't justify her behavior in her father's mind. It would only make her betrayal more complete.

"I can't let you go on thinking Harley came back to ruin me, or get revenge on you, or upset our lives," she said, instead. "He's here because he wants a relationship with his son. And Brandon wants the same thing. If you could only see them together, I know you'd—"

He raised a hand. "Stop. I don't want to hear anymore. If you want to sleep with every Tom, Dick and Harry, that's up to you. But don't try and tell me what Nelson

is and what he isn't. For God's sake, your sister's dead
because of him!''

Lauren tightened her grip on the handholds of her
crutches and told herself that her father was acting this
way because he was hurt. She hated knowing she was
adding to his pain. But he was hurting her, too. ''You
know better than to say that,'' she said.

''Why him, of all people?'' he cried, the vein in his
forehead growing more pronounced.

She needed to keep her cool before this whole situation
blew up in her face. She needed to stay focused on what
was really at stake and not let her father's personal insults
distract her. ''My sex life is beside the point. This is about
other issues. I think it's time we quit lying to ourselves
and accepted our share of the responsibility for failing
Audra.''

''*Our* share of the responsibility?''

''That's right. Harley didn't do anything to Audra that
she didn't want him to do. And it was her fault she got
pregnant, not his. She told Harley she was on birth control
pills, then skipped them on purpose.''

''You expect me to believe she tried to trap him?'' he
sneered. ''A boy who couldn't even buy her a pair of
shoes?''

''She didn't do it to trap him.''

''Then why would she do something so foolish?''

Lauren's heart seemed to beat audibly in the dark room.
Did she have the courage to finish what she'd started?
They'd never argued, not like this. Was it truly necessary
to make him see the truth?

For Brandon's sake, Lauren decided it was. She could
only hope her father would love her enough to eventually
overcome his anger and prejudice. ''She did it to punish
you, Dad. She was striking out at you because she didn't
believe you loved her and—''

''What?'' Her father shot out of his chair. ''Now

you've gone too far, Lauren! You're not going to blame me for what happened to Audra. I did everything in my power to save my little girl. I loved her, damn it! I would've cut off my right arm if I thought it would make her happy. I'd do it now if I thought it would bring her back.''

Tears spilled over Lauren's lashes. "I know that, Dad," she said, hobbling a little closer. "I know you loved her and tried your best. But she didn't understand that. Or maybe she did and it just wasn't enough. I don't think she believed any of us loved her. She felt like an outsider.''

"It's Harley Nelson making you talk like this," her father insisted. "He did the same thing to Audra. That son of a bitch poisons everything he touches. He—''

"It isn't him," Lauren snapped, angrily swiping at the tears that were now rolling down her face. "Would you quit blaming him for everything? I know what I know because I've read Audra's journals. You remember, those books we quickly packed away and hid from view so we wouldn't have to know what really happened? Well, I got them out and read them, Dad. I know Harley's as much a victim in this as the rest of us. Yes, he defied you when he was young. Yes, he was a poor boy who partied too much, and he had no business having sex with Audra or any other girl at such a young age. But Audra was definitely a willing partner. At least he tried to keep her away from drugs—''

"He started her on them, you mean.''

"No, he hated it when she got high and they fought about it often. He honestly cared for her. He even tried to stand by her when he learned about the baby.''

"That's not true." Her father shook his head adamantly. "He left her for a measly two thousand dollars.''

"I'm not sure if that was his fault or yours," she whispered.

"Mine?" her father shouted.

"Did he come to you and ask for money?"

No answer.

"Did he?" she pressed.

"He would've ruined her life. I had to get him out of the picture somehow. But the fact that he took the money says enough."

Lauren drew a bolstering breath. "I don't think so."

Her father lifted his chin and narrowed his eyes and, to Lauren, he suddenly seemed like a stranger. "Then you're not thinking straight. All this crap about Audra not knowing how much we cared—you don't know what you're talking about."

Lauren wiped her nose on her robe, now crying so hard she could barely speak. "It's the truth, but even if you refuse to acknowledge it, you have to see that Brandon loves Harley. We can't deny him the chance to know his father. Let's set up a meeting with Harley and see if we can't arrange some kind of visitation. Offer him summers, holidays—"

"No. Brandon will be fine without him."

"Did you see Brandon tonight?"

Her father paused, but only briefly and, when he spoke, he seemed to be talking to himself as much as her. "He'll get over this. We all will."

"No," Lauren said simply.

Whirling on her, he demanded, "What the hell is that supposed to mean?"

"It means it's not going to happen your way this time, Dad."

He stared at her in what looked like utter amazement. "What did you say?"

"I said it's not going to go that way."

"Like hell it's not," he bellowed. "Either you stay out of this thing between me and Harley, or you pack your bags and get out of this house."

Lauren felt as though she was suffocating, as though someone was sitting on her chest and pushing a pillow over her nose and mouth. "Do you realize what you're saying? You're forcing me to take a stand against you."

"I'm not forcing you to do anything. It's your choice," he said. "Either support me, or support him. But if you go with Harley, Lauren, mark my words, you'll learn the hard way. And I won't be there to pick up the pieces. I went through enough because of him the first time."

The worst kind of fear Lauren had ever known crept over her. She'd always had her family, never questioned their love. But now, if she followed her heart, she'd be completely on her own. No more safety net. Once her father made up his mind, he had too much pride to ever back down. Did she believe in Harley that much?

Lauren couldn't answer that question, at least not with any confidence. As much as she thought she loved Harley, chances were good that he didn't care about her in return, at least not in the same way. Maybe he never would. But this wasn't really about Harley; it was about trusting her own conscience and judgement. She believed Brandon had a right to know his father. She had to stand up for that belief and not sell out for a comfortable place to live and a generous monthly allowance as Audra had.

"Please, don't give me an ultimatum," she said softly. "I don't want Harley or anyone else to come between us."

"Then don't let him."

She swallowed hard. "Dad—"

"The choice is easy, Lauren. It's me or him."

"But this has less to do with Harley than you think," she said. "This is about Brandon."

"This has everything to do with Harley. If he hadn't come back and started trouble, I wouldn't be standing here."

Lauren hesitated, waiting, hoping her father would give

her some sign that he might change his mind, but he remained resolute. "Will you at least try to look at things from my perspective?"

"No."

Silence.

"Then I'll pack my things and be gone tomorrow," she said at last. "But I won't leave Brandon behind."

"Oh, yes, you will," he said, but his voice was flat and had lost some of its edge, and he sank into his seat again, as though her answer had deflated him. "Brandon stays with me, or I'll call the police. I'm his legal guardian. And if you leave, you won't be allowed to come back."

For a moment, Lauren wondered if this was all some sort of bad dream. Maybe she'd wake up tomorrow and everything would be the way it always was. But she knew that even nightmares didn't hurt like this. "You can't mean that," she said. "Think about what it'll do to Brandon. He's like my own son. He'll be lost without me."

He was staring off into space again. "Marilee and I will take care of him. He's a good boy, a strong boy. He'll be fine. He survived his mother's folly, didn't he?"

"And you want to add to that?" Again, anger became dominant among Lauren's scrambled emotions, making her firm in her resolve. Her father was wrong. Regardless of his own pain, he had no right to cause Brandon any suffering.

He didn't respond.

"Then, just so you know, Harley's pressing for custody," she said. "And I'm going to support him."

Quentin chuckled humorlessly. "Good luck. That's like the puppy trying to bite the dog. You won't get anywhere. You'll be back on my doorstep in a matter of weeks."

"I wouldn't bet on it," she said, and when she headed to her room, she knew she'd reached the point of no return. She was on her own.

CHAPTER NINETEEN

SURELY HE COULDN'T CARE about Lauren, Harley thought. Not as much as it seemed. He'd only been in Portland a week. What he felt was some trick of his imagination, his worst fear coming true. But he didn't need to worry about it. Last night he'd walked away from her and avoided the emotional entanglement that making love would have caused—not to mention the humiliation of being caught in her bed by her father. Certainly that showed some growth and demonstrated his control.

But if he was in such control, why was he still going over and over that moment and feeling something so close to regret?

"It's only six o'clock. What are you doing up so early?" Tank asked, yawning and scratching his head as he stumbled into the living room.

Harley blinked, returning to the computer screen glowing in front of him. He'd been handling all the panic messages he'd received from Joe yesterday. A customer's down payment had bounced and Joe wondered whether to refer the deal to the collection agency or repossess the bike. A personal friend who'd placed a special order was getting tired of waiting for his bike to come in, and Joe wanted to know if he could sell him another model at a discounted price. And Roger, one of the salesmen, had just given his notice. They were short-handed and needed to hire more help. Joe was asking if he should place an ad in the paper and start interviewing or wait for Harley to get back. It was the kind of stuff Harley normally handled on a daily basis, but he was having a difficult time concentrating on it now, which was probably why it had taken him so long to sort through the messages.

"I've just been getting a few things done," he said. "What are you doing up? It's Sunday. I figured you'd sleep in."

Tank rubbed his stomach. "I was hoping to. But Kimberly and I ate too much ice cream last night. It isn't sitting well."

Harley rocked back in his chair and stretched out his legs. "Did you and Kimberly have a good time yesterday?"

A grin lit Tank's face. "Definitely."

"You seeing her again?"

He rubbed the whiskers on his chin, still smiling. "We're taking Lucy to the lake today. Kimberly's great with Lucy," he added.

"How is she with you?"

The color of Tank's face deepened. "I really like her."

"I thought things had to be going pretty well."

"They're going better than well." He raised a suspicious eyebrow. "But you came in pretty late. What's going on with you?"

Harley swiveled and started to shut down his laptop. He was exhausted and needed to get some sleep. And he wasn't sure he wanted to talk about what had happened last night. "Nothing."

"Come on! You were at Lauren's almost all night."

"I was trying to look after Brandon for Lauren, because of her ankle. But then her father showed up."

"No shit?" Tank said. "Quentin's back?"

"Thanks partially to your brother."

His friend ran a hand through his sleep-tousled hair. "What does Damien have to do with it?"

After zipping up his computer bag, Harley sat down

and settled his elbows on the chair's armrests. "From what Quentin said, Damien was calling him in London, warning him about what I was doing here in his absence."

"Wow, Damien really likes Lauren, doesn't he?" Tank said, shaking his head. "Maybe you should give him a call and tell him you're not interested in her. I've tried to get the message through to him several times, but he won't believe me."

"No," Harley said, remembering the possessive way Tank's brother had behaved around Lauren. He'd sooner break Damien's nose than reassure him about anything.

On the other hand, maybe Tank's idea wasn't a bad one. Claiming a lack of interest in Lauren might not be exactly truthful, but Harley couldn't allow anything romantic to exist between them without asking history to repeat itself, so the reality was the same. Why not make Lauren's life a little easier by getting Damien off her back? Harley hated that everyone close to her, except maybe Kim, seemed to be turning on her, insisting she was making a mistake just because she'd befriended him.

"On second thought, maybe I will do that," he said. "What's your brother's number?"

"You're going to call him this early?" Tank asked.

"Why not? That way I'll be sure to catch him at home."

Tank hesitated, then shrugged. "Okay. Doesn't make any difference to me." He picked up the cordless phone lying on the coffee table, dialed and handed it to Harley, then stood waiting.

When Damien answered, it was obvious he'd been sleeping, but Harley felt no remorse for waking him. *Be civil,* he told himself. But civil wasn't the best way to describe the words that came out of his mouth. "What the hell did you think you were doing calling Quentin Worthington in Europe and trying to make problems for Lauren and me?"

"Harley?"

"Damn right."

"I wasn't trying to make problems for Lauren. I was trying to help her. And her father really appreciated my input."

"I'll bet. And now he can thank you in person. He's back."

"Good. Maybe you'll head home to California or wherever the hell you're from and Lauren will start thinking straight."

"There's nothing wrong with Lauren's thinking," Harley insisted.

"There is if she's willing to associate with you."

Harley's grip on the phone tightened as the nose-breaking image returned. "And you think getting me out of the picture will change things? That she'll suddenly want to get back together with you?"

"Maybe."

Tank waved to attract his attention. "Tell him you don't even think she's cute. Tell him you're only interested in Brandon."

Instead, Harley said, "She's never going to marry you."

"Why not?" Damien demanded.

"Because she's in love with me."

Silence. Even Harley's heart seemed to stop beating. What the hell had he just said and why had he said it?

"That's a lie," Damien shouted. "And if you've touched her or done *anything* to her, I'll...I'll—"

Harley leaned forward, adrenaline pumping through his veins. "You'll what? Tell her *daddy?*"

"Just stay away from her!"

"Sorry. I'll stay away if and when she tells me to, and not until then," he said and hung up.

His friend was staring at him as though he'd just grown two heads. Closing his mouth, which had been gaping open, Tank swallowed visibly. "I think that convinced him," he said.

"LAUREN, WHAT'S GOING ON? When I called your house this morning, your father answered. I've been trying to reach you ever since. Why haven't you been answering your cell?"

Lauren blinked against the light streaming in through a crack in the draperies and blocked the glare with a pillow. It was Kimberly. She was nearly certain. But she wasn't certain of anything else—until she saw the suitcases next to the bed. Last night hadn't been a dream. She'd kissed Harley, her father had surprised them, she'd moved out...

"Yikes, could it have gotten any worse?" she muttered.

"Lauren? Did you hear me? Where are you?"

"I'm at a hotel downtown," she said. "I haven't been answering my cell because I've been sleeping."

"How could you sleep at a time like this?"

"I was up all night."

"Why are you at a hotel?"

"My father kicked me out."

"No! I can't believe that."

Everything had happened so fast, Lauren couldn't believe it, either. She was still hoping the hotel room was some sort of drug-induced hallucination prompted by the painkiller, but those damn suitcases indicated otherwise. "It's true," she said, then winced when pain shot up her shin from her ankle. "And my ankle's killing me, to boot."

"Do you have your pain pills and your crutches?"

"I do. I had some time to pack, thank God." After the argument with her father, Lauren had gone directly to her room, gathered her things and left. She hadn't wanted to treat Brandon to another tearful scene like the one he'd witnessed with Harley.

"Why didn't you come here?" Kimberly asked. "You know we would've taken you in."

Lauren put a hand to her forehead and tried to knead away the last vestiges of sleep. When she'd left home, she'd considered going to Kim's, but she didn't want to be "taken in." She wanted to become independent. She'd decided to bow out of the women's shelter fund-raiser, leave it in Jennifer Pratt's capable hands and, as soon as her ankle healed, she'd find a job. A real job, not the "come in when you want" arrangement she'd always had with her father.

"I didn't want to impose," she said. "Or drag your parents into this disaster. Besides, whether I like it or not, I feel I'm doing what I should've done years ago. I lived at home for Brandon's sake and because I didn't have any real motivation to move. I thought I was happy with my life. But lately I've begun to realize that there are certain things lacking. It's time I grew up for real."

"Come on, Lauren. Don't do anything drastic," Kim said. "This is just a temporary rift. Once Quentin calms down, everything will return to normal, and you and I will be back at the club, drinking lattes."

Lauren sat higher in the bed, careful not to hurt her ankle again. "I won't be able to spend my time at the club drinking lattes—I'll be working," she said. "In any case, my biggest concern is for Brandon. My father wouldn't let me take him, but he won't let me come back and see him, either."

Kimberly made a noise of surprise. "Why would he do something that would hurt Brandon so much?"

"He's a businessman. He was trying to manipulate me into staying put and obeying him like a good girl. Brandon was his bargaining chip."

"But you wouldn't let him get the best of the situation. Good. I'm really proud of you."

"No one got the best of the situation," Lauren said. "We all lost, which is the saddest thing of all."

"Well, you said it yourself. Your father's a businessman. He'll see it's in his best interests to rethink this. I mean, how will he and your mother go to Europe next year with Brandon in school? They're not going to like being so tied down, doing all the stuff you've always done—karate, sewing Brandon's Halloween costumes, dealing with his teachers. You know, everything. Just wait and see."

"I hope you're right," Lauren said, switching the phone to her other ear. "If not, I'm going to help Harley press his claim. I might anyway. He's younger than my parents and eager to be a dad."

"Oh, my gosh! You're not serious."

Lauren hadn't known until that moment that she *was* serious. But thoughts of Audra's journals and the past, and what Lauren had learned about Harley Nelson just by being with him, convinced her. "He's a good man who wants his son," she said. "And I think Brandon deserves the chance to have a real dad."

"Where do you fit into this picture?" Kim asked.

A lump the size of a baseball swelled in Lauren's throat, but she forced her words around it. "I can only hope Harley will be fairer to me than my father has been to him and let me see Brandon whenever I want. I think he will."

"He lives in California!"

"Maybe I'll move to California, too."

"You'd leave here?" Kimberly cried.

"Maybe. It's time to get out on my own, and California's as good a place as any. Regardless, I'm not going to let my father get away with what he's doing. Admittedly, I have no chance of receiving custody of Brandon. Before she died, Audra signed guardianship over to my parents, and because they're not abusive or neglectful, a judge would have no reason to take Brandon out of their home, at least not at my request. But as Brandon's father, Harley has a much stronger case.''

There was a long pause. ''Are you sure you're feeling okay?'' Kim asked, sounding doubtful.

''Not necessarily. Why?''

''You actually seem, I don't know, like you've taken charge of all this...mess.''

Lauren sighed. ''I haven't,'' she said. ''I'm just determined to see it through.''

''I think Quentin's going to be pretty surprised by what he's up against.''

Lauren hated the thought that she was choosing an outsider over her own family. She hoped her decision regarding Brandon had nothing to do with the way she felt about Harley. But she knew it probably had some effect, at least in her willingness to trust him. ''How'd it go with you and Tank last night?'' she asked.

''I don't want to talk about it.''

''Why not?''

''Because I feel guilty about being so happy when things are going so lousy for you.''

Lauren smiled in spite of the pain in her ankle and the fact that her whole life seemed to be crashing down around her ears. ''That means you had a good time.''

''I had a *great* time,'' she said, excitement oozing through her voice. ''And I'm going over to the apartment in an hour to help make lunch, so I'll get to see him again today. We're spending the afternoon at Lake Oswego. But I won't go if you need me,'' she added.

Lauren slid her ankle from beneath the covers and examined the swelling. ''Go have fun. I'll be fine. There's nothing you can do for me, anyway. I'll order room service and eat, take my pain pill and sleep for a few more hours.''

''I'll come over later. Give me your room number.''

"I'm staying at the Renaissance Towers, Room 2323."

"Let me get a pen." There was a pause, then Kimberly repeated the information. "Does Harley know what happened? That you're not living at home anymore?" she asked.

"I doubt it. But he knows Quentin's back. He was there when my father walked in the door."

"Oh, boy. I'll bet that went over well. Did he and your father get into it?"

Lauren winced at the memory of the sick feeling in her stomach when she'd first heard her father's voice and scrambled to right her nightgown, the raised voices that followed, poor little Brandon crying and begging Harley to take him along, and she barely able to get around on her new crutches. It was all pretty pathetic. "Not too bad," she said because she didn't want to describe the details. "Harley handled everything surprisingly well."

Kimberly hesitated. "You're being pretty supportive of Harley."

Lauren didn't answer.

"Is there anything else you want to tell me?"

An image immediately appeared in Lauren's mind— Harley kissing her, touching her—and she felt her cheeks flush hot. "No."

"Right," Kim said, but there wasn't an ounce of belief in her words. "We need to talk."

"Not now," Lauren groaned.

"Then later. But consider it a date."

HARLEY COULD HEAR movement, water turning on and off, a drawer slamming, voices.

"So what time did he get home?" someone asked and, unless he was mistaken, it was Kimberly speaking.

"Had to be after three," Tank replied.

Harley took the pillow off his head and rolled over to check his alarm clock. It was nearly one o'clock in the afternoon. He'd slept for six hours, but somehow that didn't make the day's prospects any brighter.

"Quentin showed up last night," Kimberly said, her voice muffled as though she'd turned in a different direction.

"I heard," Tank responded.

"Did Harley say anything about what happened?"

"Not much. Until he called Damien."

"He called Damien? What for?"

Harley cringed, expecting to hear his blunder repeated. He felt like an idiot for telling Damien that Lauren was in love with him. He'd only done it because he knew it was the last thing Damien wanted to hear. But that was no excuse.

Fortunately, when Tank spoke, there was the sound of a shrug in his voice. "No reason, really. I think he just wanted to piss him off."

Silently thanking Tank for his discretion, Harley started to get out of bed, but froze at Kimberly's next words.

"So, does Harley know Quentin kicked Lauren out of the house last night?"

"He didn't say anything about that."

"I just talked to her. She's at a hotel."

"What happened?"

"She and her father had an argument, and she took Harley's side."

"What about Brandon?"

"Her father wouldn't let her take him. She left during the night, while he was sleeping. And he won't let her come back to see him, either."

Shit. Harley couldn't believe it. Brandon had watched his grandfather throw him out of the house less than twelve hours earlier, and then awakened to find Lauren gone. What had Quentin been thinking? Lauren's father had to be the biggest asshole Harley had ever met.

"That's too bad," Tank was saying, but then Lucy interrupted, asking Kimberly for a drink of juice, and the conversation turned to other things—what they were going to do at the lake, whether or not they needed a life vest for Lucy, what time Lucy had to be home.

Harley sat in his room, deep in his own thoughts, paying little attention to their inconsequential chatter. Finally they trooped out of the house and the door slammed, then silence fell. And he ignored everything his head had been telling him and picked up the phone.

LAUREN'S CELL PHONE would not stop ringing. She fumbled through her covers, searching, but she was so tangled up in the sheets that she couldn't find it. The ringing stopped, and she sighed and sank back into the soft mattress. But then the ringing started all over again.

Surely it wasn't Kimberly. Lauren wasn't expecting to hear from her until later, much later.

Then she sat bolt upright, instantly awake, and began to search in earnest. What if it was Brandon? She hadn't called him after hanging up with Kim because she knew her father would probably be monitoring the phone and she wanted him to relax his guard first, if possible. But if there was a problem and Brandon needed her... Or her father had changed his mind...

Finally coming up successful, she punched the talk button before the caller could be transferred to her voice mail and put the phone to her ear. With the drapes mostly drawn, it was too dark to read her caller ID. She didn't take the time to even try.

"Brandon?" she said, sounding breathless, even to her own ears.

There was a pause. "It's me."

Harley. Lauren would have recognized his voice anywhere, although after last night, she hadn't expected him to call her.

"Hi," she said.

"How's the ankle?"

"It's getting better."

"How's the rest of you?"

"As good as possible under the circumstances, I guess." She thought again of last night and felt fresh embarrassment wash over her. What must Harley think— particularly after rejecting her?

There was a pause. "I heard about what happened," he said. "I'm sorry."

"It's not your fault. My father's just...he's not himself right now."

"Oh, really? I couldn't tell by his behavior."

Lauren tried not to laugh because laughing made her feel too disloyal. But with everything else going to hell in a handbasket, a little laughing didn't seem like such a big deal. Besides, Harley had every right to dislike her father. He'd never seen how loving and caring Quentin could be. He'd only seen him at his worst.

"He's not all bad," she countered. "In most ways, he was a good father to me." She hoped he'd be a good father to her again someday.

"I'll take your word for it. What are you doing right now?"

"Sleeping."

"Any chance you're ready to get up?"

She swung her legs over the side of the bed and ran a hand through her tangled hair. The painkiller made her feel as if she could sleep all day. Or maybe it was the aftereffect of last night's emotional trauma. "What for?"

"You promised to let me take you for a ride on my bike, remember?"

Lauren remembered. She also remembered that she hadn't been completely serious when she made that promise. "I was joking," she said, deciding to play it safe. She needed to talk to Harley about Brandon, but she didn't want to have that discussion on the back of his bike.

"Does that mean you're chickening out?" he asked.

"I'm not chickening out," she protested. "I'm insuring my future health and safety. My ankle's already hurt. I'd rather keep the rest of my body intact."

"We'll wrap your ankle in a brace, and I'll help you get around. You'll be fine."

If he was going to help her around, she'd definitely have an opportunity to talk to him. They'd be together, side by side....

Then again, they could talk right here.

She glanced around the room, remembered the tingle of his kisses last night, and decided maybe it *would* be better to leave the hotel. Imagining Harley's touch, picturing him in her bed—*this* bed—made her feel just as eager and breathless as before.

"Lauren?" he prompted.

"I don't know," she said, forcibly redirecting her thoughts. "Talking me into getting on a bike is a lot like convincing a claustrophobic to shut himself in a closet. What if I freak out?"

"I'll be there with you," he said. "It's time you trusted me."

She already trusted Harley. Or she wouldn't have deemed him worthy of Brandon. But there was one more thing, probably the most important issue of all—would she have time to shower and do her hair?

"When?" she asked.

"Now."

"In an hour."

"Fine. Tell me where you are."

Lauren gave him her hotel and room number, then hung up and hurried to the bathroom as fast as her ankle would permit.

Her life was in complete disarray, but somehow everything seemed all right because Harley was coming to see her. *Go figure.*

CHAPTER TWENTY

LAUREN STOOD BACK and surveyed herself in the mirror. At first glance, her swollen ankle made her appear to have a clubfoot, which wasn't particularly appealing, but barring that, she looked pretty good. Certainly better than she had at the park yesterday when she was sporting Aunt Myrtle's idea of a hip outfit. Today she was wearing the best her hastily packed suitcases could provide—a pair of low-riding jeans, with enough bell at the bottom to allow for wrapping her foot, and a T-shirt top that hugged her breasts and showed an inch or two of bare midriff.

Making an O with her mouth, she quickly smoothed on some pink gloss, then brushed her hair until it gleamed and applied some mascara to make her eyes more noticeable. She definitely wasn't movie-star gorgeous, like Audra had been, but she wasn't half bad since she'd filled out a bit and lost the glasses. After the rejection she'd suffered last night, she needed to feel attractive.

She was just adding a pair of silver hoop earrings when she heard Harley's knock. Crossing her fingers for luck and continued good health, despite the motorcycle, she limped across the room and opened the door.

"Wow," he said, letting his gaze drift over her. "You look—" he cleared his throat "—great."

"Really?" Lauren felt a warm blush rise up her neck. Having Harley look at her so…avidly more than compensated for all the years he'd ignored her.

"You still up for this?" he asked, raising his eyebrows in challenge.

"As long as we don't wrinkle my clothes," she teased.

He scowled in mock warning. "Picking a fight already?"

"Just getting even. Come in. I need to put on my watch and grab my purse."

He stepped inside the room, wearing jeans, a Harley Davidson T-shirt and his jacket, and smelling like soap and leather. Lauren felt her stomach flutter, and experienced a moment of guilt for being so happy to see him.

"Somehow, when I heard your father threw you out of the house, I was picturing you in more…"

She turned in time to see him glance pointedly at the rich furnishings and elegant drapes.

"…desperate circumstances," he finished with a wry grin. "This place doesn't inspire much pity."

"Is that why you're here? Because you feel sorry for me?" she asked.

"No."

She waited for him to explain, but he only frowned and said, "I'm here to give you a ride on my bike, remember?"

"I CAN'T BELIEVE I'm doing this," Lauren said, eyeing Harley's sleek, black bike and its shiny chrome accents as he handed her the helmet he'd fastened with a bungee cord to the back.

"Don't think about it," he said, straddling the seat and raising the kickstand. "Trust me."

Lauren accepted the helmet but she didn't put it on. She continued to stare at the bike. "It looks heavy."

"It is heavy."

"What if it falls over on us while you're trying to start it?"

He gave her a "get real" look. "It's not going to fall over."

"How do you know?"

"Because I won't let it, okay?"

Still Lauren hesitated. "I think maybe you should start the motor before I get on."

"Oh, brother." He rolled his eyes but settled his own helmet on his head and, a moment later, the engine roared to life, making it almost impossible to hear anything else.

Lauren blew air out her cheeks and wiped sweaty palms on her jeans. "One ride," she muttered to herself and fastened her helmet.

"Where are we going?" she called above the noise.

"You'll see," he said, offering her a hand.

Lauren considered his hand, stretched out to help her onto the bike. Once she accepted it, she knew Harley wouldn't let her chicken out. Oddly, she found that knowledge reassuring. Wherever he was going, she was going with him, and it felt right.

"Okay," she said, even though he couldn't hear her, and settled herself behind him.

The vibration of the motor instantly began to resonate through her whole body, but as she slipped her arms around Harley's trim waist, the contact between them seemed to melt something deeper, something in her soul. She loved this man. He was her sister's old boyfriend, Brandon's dad and her father's nemesis, but in this moment, none of that seemed to matter. He belonged to her.

Harley gave the bike some gas and they coasted out of the hotel parking lot, but he stopped at the curb long enough to twist around and look at her. "Your ankle okay?" he hollered.

Tightening her grip, she nodded and closed her eyes.

He turned onto the street, wove through the downtown traffic until they reached the suburbs, then opened up the throttle on the highway.

Lauren felt utterly weightless as they flew over the pavement. Trees, houses, telephone poles, everything blurred before her. There was only the rush of wind, the incredible power of the bike and its deafening noise—and Harley, completely in control, his body firm and warm and pressed against hers.

Sex couldn't be any better than this, Lauren decided, smiling to herself, but long before she was ready to stop, Harley slowed the bike and turned down a dirt road that led to a small pond. Wildflowers in orange and yellow bloomed at the edges of the water amid tall grasses and a copse of aspens that lent dappled shade, making it feel private.

When they came to a stop, Harley put a foot to the ground, turned off the motor and lowered the kickstand.

"This is beautiful," she said, her ears ringing in the sudden silence. Reluctantly, she let go of him and got carefully off the bike to avoid reinjuring her ankle. "How did you know about this place?"

"I used to come here in high school, when I got into a fight with one of my mother's boyfriends."

"Did she have a lot of boyfriends?" she asked, limping to the edge of the pond.

"Loneliness doesn't exactly promote selectivity." He crossed his arms and leaned against his bike, watching her.

"Did her boyfriends ever beat you?" she asked, even though she was almost afraid to hear the answer.

He shrugged. "I took a couple of whippings, but I probably deserved them. I resented the presence of another man in the house, hated the way it changed my mother's focus. All of a sudden, she didn't seem to care about me, so I became determined to make myself noticed—which generally caused a fight that got me kicked out of the house for the night." He shrugged again, a nonchalant expression on his face. "I wasn't an easy kid to raise."

"Did you sleep here when you got kicked out?"

"Sometimes."

Lauren wondered why he'd brought her here, why he'd wanted to take her for a ride in the first place. "Does this little spot hold painful memories for you?"

He grinned. "No, it's just the closest thing to a meadow I know."

Lauren glanced up at him in surprise. Was he referring to the argument they'd had after Brandon's karate class, when he'd accused her of being too uptight? When he'd asked her if anyone had ever tumbled her in a meadow? She couldn't say for sure. He wasn't looking at her. And he certainly wasn't making any attempt to kiss her.

Bending, he found a little rock and skipped it across the water. "What did you think of the bike?"

Lauren tried to rein in her enthusiasm so she wouldn't seem silly for being reluctant before, but he called her on it immediately.

"Judging by the size of the smile that's trying to slip out, I'd say you liked it."

She nodded. What she'd liked was riding so close behind him and having the perfect excuse to hold him. She doubted riding with anyone else would have provided the same experience. But she wasn't about to tell him that.

"So, you're not afraid anymore?"

"I wouldn't want to try driving it myself. But you seem to know what you're doing."

His smile grew crooked. "I'm impressed. Little Lauren Worthington can admit when she's wrong."

"Don't press your luck," she said. "You still can't control the other drivers on the road. You could easily die on that thing."

"We all gotta go sometime."

Lauren sat on the bank and took off her ankle wrap, then slipped her foot in the cool pond, hoping it would ease the swelling. "When are you planning to file for custody of Brandon?" she asked.

He came to sit next to her, clasping his arms around his knees. "I was going to do it this week," he said, gazing into the distance. "But…" He looked at her, then looked away. "I've changed my mind. I don't want to do anything that's going to hurt you. Maybe if you go back to your father and tell him I'll back off, he'll let you move home and everything will return to the way it was before. As far as I'm concerned, maybe we can work out some visitation. Even if Quentin won't agree, you and Brandon could meet me now and then."

Lauren felt a sense of astonishment—of shock. Harley was giving up Brandon, *for her?* "That's the greatest sacrifice anyone's ever made for me," she said, so touched she could hardly speak. "I know how much you love your son."

He said nothing, so she took her foot out of the water and turned to face him, wanting him to see her expression and her sincerity when she added, "But I don't want to move home, Harley."

His brows shot up. "Then, what *do* you want?"

"I want you to get custody of Brandon."

"What?" he said, rocking back.

"My parents are getting older and they aren't prepared to raise another child, at least not without me there to help them. So—" she started wrapping her ankle again so she wouldn't have to see his reaction to this next part "—I was thinking I'd contribute to your attorney's fees and, afterward, maybe you and I can share Brandon. Just like a divorced couple shares their children."

She couldn't help looking at him then, and saw him take a quick breath. "As long as that kind of arrangement is okay with Brandon, of course," she said.

"But I live in California," he told her. "You wouldn't get to see him very often."

"I would if I moved to California. I could rent an apartment or a house not far from where you live."

A gentle breeze stirred her hair, and he raised a hand to smooth it away from her face. "You'd trust me that much?" he asked, and she thought she saw a flicker of strong emotion register in the depths of his eyes.

She smiled and nodded toward his bike. "I'm trusting you with my life, remember?"

BRANDON SAT IN HIS ROOM, reading the same page in his math book over and over because he couldn't seem to understand what it said. He was suspended from school until Wednesday, which meant he had a lot of homework to do so he wouldn't fall behind. But with the way his mind kept wandering and his eyes kept stinging every time he thought of Lauren or his father, he didn't think he'd get anywhere with it.

Propping his chin on one fist, he stared glumly out the window. His grandfather had forbidden him to contact Harley, but Brandon had no plans to obey. Especially now that Lauren was gone. He was just waiting for a chance to slip into the study, to call his father. He'd already tried Lauren's cell once, before Grandfather knew he was up, and received no answer. She'd left a note on his desk telling him not to be upset, that she'd be in touch soon. But Grandfather had been hovering about the house all morning, pacing, growling to himself and snatching up the phone every time it rang. Even if she tried to call, Brandon doubted Grandfather would let him talk.

What if she couldn't *ever* get through to him? What if he never saw her again? The stinging in his eyes grew worse and he pressed his palms against them....

"How's the homework going?"

Brandon dropped his hands and blinked rapidly before turning to see his grandfather in the doorway. "Okay, I guess."

"Do you need any help?"

"No, thanks."

"Well, when you finish, maybe you and I can take in a movie. Would you like that?"

Brandon didn't want to see a movie. He didn't want to go anywhere. He wanted to sit by the phone and wait for Lauren to call, but after the argument he'd seen last night, he didn't dare tell his grandfather that. Grandfather was acting weird. He was talking loud and cheery, although it was pretty easy to tell he didn't feel very happy. It was all so confusing.

"I guess," Brandon said because he was afraid to say no.

"Great. I'll go check the paper for movie listings. After the movie, we'll pick up your grandma at the airport. She'll be excited to see you."

Brandon nodded, wishing he was more excited to see her. He loved his grandmother. She made delicious fresh-squeezed lemonade and bought him lots of new school clothes—but she wasn't Lauren.

"Grandfather?" Brandon said before Quentin could head back down the hall.

"Yes?"

"Do you think we could take Lauren to the movies with us?" he asked hopefully.

His grandfather's smile disappeared. "I don't think so, Brandon. Not today."

"But I *really* want to see her. Pleeease?"

"Not today," he said, more sharply.

Brandon knew better than to push once that tone entered his grandfather's voice. But his eyes were stinging again, and he knew he'd be okay if only he could talk to Lauren.... "Can I call her, then? Will you tell me where she is?"

"I don't know where she is. Now, get your homework done so we can leave." He retreated, his heavy footfalls muffled against the carpet, and Brandon turned back to stare at his math book. He'd only done two problems. He had another fifty to go, and that was just one day's assignment. But when the numbers blurred before him, he shut the book in favor of resting his chin on his hand and gazing out the window again. He was just wishing he'd see Lauren's car come down the street when the telephone rang.

Scrambling out from behind his desk, he ran for the extension in the kitchen, hoping to pick it up before his grandfather did. But the ringing stopped as he reached the end of the hall.

"He got it," he muttered in dejection and started back, but then he heard his grandfather calling him.

"Brandon! Scott's on the phone for you."

It wasn't Lauren. Or his father. Disappointment weighted Brandon's steps as he made his way across the kitchen, but by the time he picked up the phone, he was as eager as always to speak to his best friend.

"Hi, Scott."

"What ya doin'?"

"Homework."

Brandon heard the click that indicated his grandfather had hung up and felt slightly better. At least some things in his life hadn't changed. He could still talk to his best friend without his grandfather breathing down his neck.

"Any chance you can come over to my house?" Scott asked.

"I don't think so. I have to finish my homework, then my grandfather's taking me to a movie." He tried not to sound so dejected, but Scott picked up on it right away.

"Did you get into trouble?"

"No."

"Something else wrong?"

Brandon considered explaining, then decided he didn't

want to talk about it with his grandfather rambling around the house. ''No.''

''That's good. Then maybe you can get out of going to the movies. Your Aunt Lauren called and said if you can come over to my place, she and your father will come by and give us a ride on his bike.''

''She did?'' Brandon said, dropping the pen he'd been using to doodle on Lauren's message pad.

''Yeah.''

''But she won't let me ride,'' he argued. ''She's afraid of motorcycles.''

''She must've changed her mind. My mom said I could have a ride, too. Isn't that cool?''

Brandon smiled, his spirits finally lifting. Harley and Lauren were going to meet him at Scott's, where Grandfather wouldn't be around to bother them. That was beyond cool. Maybe the world wasn't falling apart, after all. Maybe everything was going to work out, just as Lauren had said it would. ''That's awesome,'' he said in relief. ''I'll get out of the movie somehow and be over as soon as I can.''

CHAPTER TWENTY-ONE

LAUREN WONDERED if the sound of a motorcycle engine would bring her father to the door and, for the first time, lamented the fact that Brandon's best friend lived right across the street. She knew she was pushing her luck having her nephew meet her and Harley in the same neighborhood, let alone in full view of the Worthington front windows. But her father was accustomed to Scott and his visits, phone calls and invitations. She couldn't come up with any other way to get Brandon out of the house.

Her nephew and his friend were waiting on the porch when she and Harley cruised into Hillside Estates and parked in the Torrins' front drive. Harley glanced across the street as he got off the bike, obviously checking for trouble, but then turned and smiled easily as his son came running toward them.

"Daddy, Lauren!" Brandon threw his arms around her and then Harley.

"How are you, honey? You okay?" she asked, careful not to put too much weight on her sore ankle.

"I'm better now that you two are here," he said.

"Scott told us you might not be able to come over, that you were supposed to go to the movies with your grandfather," Harley said.

Brandon grimaced. "I just asked him if I could go to Scott's, instead. He was actually kind of glad to let me go, I think. Then he didn't have to pretend to be happy anymore."

Lauren felt responsible for some of her father's unhappiness, but she knew there was nothing she could do about it now. There hadn't been anything she could do about it last night, either. She couldn't help having a different opinion.

"I hope he'll get over what's bothering him," she said. "In any case, your father had better give you your ride before Grandfather sees us. He won't like the fact that we're here."

Brandon waved a hand at the house. "We don't have to worry about Grandfather. He's gone. He went to pick up Grandmother from the airport."

Lauren sent a relieved glance at Harley. She hadn't wanted an angry scene, especially in front of Scott's parents.

Harley winked at her. "Relax," he said. "We're guests of Scott's family. We have permission to be here."

"It's such a cool bike, isn't it?" Brandon said to Scott as they began circling Harley's motorcycle. "It's called a Soft-Tail."

Scott whistled. "I wish my dad had a bike like this."

"So who's first?" Harley asked.

Not surprisingly, Brandon volunteered. Lauren smiled as she watched Harley help his son don the helmet. Then Brandon climbed on and waved at her and Scott, and Harley drove off. She remembered how frightened she'd once been about this exact sight, but it didn't frighten her anymore. If Harley was willing to give Brandon up to avoid hurting her, he wasn't going to drive away with him and never come back.

In the wake of the noise, Scott's mother came to the door. Like her son, she was tall and thin, with red hair, freckles and hazel eyes. Lauren had always thought her an intelligent, striking woman.

"Hi, Lauren," she said. "Is that a wrap on your ankle? What happened?"

"I sprained it."

"Why don't you come sit down? I heard you pull up, but I was on the phone, or I would've come out sooner. Scott told me Brandon's father is in town. I'm looking forward to meeting him."

Lauren hobbled to the porch and lowered herself to the steps. "Harley's a good guy," she said.

Elizabeth Torrin raised her eyebrows, but she was polite enough not to question the statement outright, even though she'd probably heard the story of Brandon's birth through neighborhood gossip. "I was surprised to see your father back from Europe so soon."

"He cut his trip short," Lauren said, her nails instinctively curling into her palms. The fact that she wasn't supposed to see Brandon made her uncomfortable—made her feel as though she was stealing something—which gave her a great deal more empathy for Harley than she'd ever had before. It was miserable to be barred from associating with a child she felt entitled, by right and relationship, to see.

"Your mother didn't come back with him?" Elizabeth asked, joining her on the steps.

"No, he's collecting her at the airport right now."

She lowered her voice. "Well, I should probably tell you that your father asked me not to let you see Brandon, if you called. But this is my house and my property, and I'm the one who decides who's welcome here."

Lauren blinked in surprise. Evidently her father was willing to go to even greater lengths than she'd expected to stop her from visiting Brandon. "Thank you," she said. "I should probably explain that there's been a little family…rift, a difference of opinions, but it should smooth itself out eventually. In the meantime, I really appreciate your letting me see my nephew."

"I know how much you love him," she said. "And I

know how much he loves you. We've raised our boys together these past ten years.''

She said something else, probably in the same vein, but the roar of the motorcycle swallowed it as Harley and Brandon returned.

"Do you mind if Harley gives Scott a ride?" Lauren asked, wanting confirmation even though Scott had already gone charging down the drive, yelling, "It's my turn!"

"If you trust him with Brandon, I trust him with Scott." She got up and walked over to Harley to introduce herself, then gave Lauren's shoulder a reassuring pat as she passed her on the way back into the house. "Now I'll let you and Brandon have some time alone," she said.

"Scott's mother is nice, isn't she?" Brandon said when Elizabeth had closed the door.

"She is," Lauren agreed.

"So, are you coming home tonight?"

Lauren took his hand and pulled him down onto the step next to her. "Brandon—"

"Don't say my name all serious like that," he said, his eyes widening. "It scares me."

"Just listen, honey. I won't be able to come home tonight. I'm not going to be living with Grandma and Grandpa anymore. As you know, we've had a disagreement. I think you should be allowed to see your father, and they think he's a bad influence."

"But he's not! You've seen how great he is."

"Yes, but I can't convince them to trust either of us on that. So what I really need to know is what you want to do. Would you like to live with your father in California?"

"What about you?" he asked, his face clouding with worry.

"I'd move to California, too. I'd rent a house or apartment and find a job, and I'd see you as often as possible. Your father's already agreed to let that happen.''

"So I'd be leaving Grandma and Grandpa?" he said soberly, crossing his arms and supporting them on his knees.

"And Scott," Lauren pointed out. "Which wouldn't be easy. But he could come visit you. And you could visit him.''

"A lot?"

"I don't think your father has much money to spare, and I won't have a lot, either, especially at first. But we'd fly you back as often as we could afford to, as long as you didn't miss school.''

"Could I see Grandpa and Grandma when I visit Scott?"

Lauren stretched her leg out in front of her to ease the throbbing of her ankle. "Of course."

"Then I want to live with you guys in California."

"You're sure?"

"Who else would play Hearts with me?" he asked with a smile. "We can't quit playing till I shoot the moon. At least once.''

Lauren returned his smile. "We'll keep playing long after that," she said. "But you need to be patient. What Harley and I are trying to do might take some time.''

The corners of Brandon's lips turned down almost immediately. "How much time?"

"I can't say right now. We'll just have to do our best. But we'll stay in touch with you through Scott and his mother, okay?"

"Okay," he said. Then Harley pulled up and Brandon helped Lauren take Scott's place behind him.

"I love you," she told him.

"I love you, too. I love you both," he said and waved goodbye as they taxied out of Hillside Estates.

"He said he loves me," Harley yelled, and though Lauren couldn't see his face, she could sense his pleasure.

"He wants to go to California with us," she told him.

"You're coming for sure?" Harley asked, pausing at the gate.

"That's right. We're all going to California," she said and tightened her grip around his middle, wanting to hug him but stopping just short in case he took exception to it.

Then Harley gave the bike some gas and they rocketed down the highway, where the rush of the wind and the roar of the engine took her to that world where only she and Harley existed, and she laughed—out loud.

KIMBERLY WAS AT the apartment with Tank when Harley returned that evening. He'd helped Lauren up to her room at the hotel over an hour earlier, but he hadn't stayed. He'd left as soon as possible and had been driving around the city ever since, thinking. So much had happened in the past few days. Most of it was so far removed from anything he'd ever *thought* would happen that he wasn't sure how to respond.

Brandon's love and wholehearted acceptance had surprised him. But that was the good part, the part that inspired faith and hope in the future. It was Lauren who confused him. She'd gotten on his bike and wrapped her arms around him. She'd smiled up at him and told him she wanted him to have custody of Brandon. She'd stood beside him despite her father.

What did it all mean? He'd never dared hope for such things. Didn't know whether to trust them. Audra had professed to love him so many times, had even promised to run away with him on two separate occasions, but when it came right down to it, she hadn't had the strength to remain true to her word. Which meant she *hadn't* loved him, at least not enough. And as much as he told himself

Lauren was a different person, he couldn't help wondering if she'd change her mind about him eventually. She was still a Worthington. He couldn't expect her to turn her back on her family forever. Quentin would win in the end, and Harley didn't want to be around when he did.

"Hey, where've you been?" Tank asked, muting the television as Harley stepped into the room. "Your mother's been calling. She says you're not answering your cell."

"When I'm on my bike, I can't hear it ring."

"Well, you might want to give her a call. She seems pretty anxious to get hold of you."

"Thanks," he said. "Where's Lucy?"

Sounding disappointed, Kimberly answered him from where she was snuggled up beneath Tank's right arm. "Unfortunately, we had to take her home already."

"How was the lake?" Harley asked.

Tank and Kimberly glanced at each other and smiled. "Great."

Harley was glad life was simple for some people. He headed down the hall to his bedroom, eager for privacy and…he didn't know what. He was frustrated and irritated and couldn't quit thinking of Lauren in that hotel room all alone.

He had to leave, get out of Dodge quick, he decided. He and Lauren were in agreement about Brandon and they had a plan. He should go home, straighten out the dealership and get ready for Brandon—and Lauren, if she really followed through—to join him in California. There wasn't any reason to stay, except for the fact that he was starting to believe in Lauren, to trust her…God, to love her!

With a snort of disgust, he pulled his cell phone out of his pocket and dialed his mother.

"I'm coming home tonight," he said.

"What about the court hearing? I thought you were going to stay until after the court hearing."

"I'll fly back for it."

"What about Brandon?"

"Quentin's home."

"Oh, so you're not allowed to see him anymore. Now I get it."

Actually, she didn't get it at all. Harley wasn't going home because he couldn't see Brandon. He knew Lauren could arrange a visit or two this week. He was leaving because she was making him forget everything he'd sworn to remember about the Worthingtons—like what had happened the last time he'd let himself fall in love.

"It's such a long drive," his mother said. "Why not wait until morning?"

Because by then it might be too late.

LAUREN ATE ANOTHER of the chocolates she'd bought at the hotel gift store and flipped through the Pay Per View menu again, looking for yet another movie to distract her. Harley had dropped her off nearly four hours earlier. She'd watched two movies and eaten almost a pound of chocolate since then, but she couldn't get him off her mind. Why hadn't he wanted to stay with her? She'd swallowed her fear of being rejected a second time and suggested they rent a movie together. But he'd politely declined and hurried off.

Lauren blinked back the rush of tears that filled her eyes—again—and ate another caramel. She couldn't blame Harley, could she? Of course he wouldn't want a twenty-seven-year-old woman who'd spent her whole life trying to please the father she'd just alienated.

Tears rolled down her cheeks, but she didn't bother fighting them. So what if she cried? So what if her nose got all red and her face splotchy? There wasn't anyone to notice. Even Kimberly wasn't coming over tonight.

Lauren nibbled on another chocolate, decided she didn't like the nougat filling and put it back in favor of a vanilla crème. Kimberly wasn't coming because Lauren had told her she was doing fine, that there wasn't any need. She'd insisted Kimberly go ahead and enjoy her evening with Tank. But they were best friends. Kimberly should've *known* she was lying.

Or maybe not. She finished the vanilla crème and shoved the box away before she made herself sick. She'd been pretty convincing on the phone. Kim had sounded so happy, Lauren hadn't wanted to pull her away. It was Harley who'd let her down.

She shut off the television and glanced around the room, wondering what to do now. Her ankle still hurt so she didn't want to go out—it was pretty late, anyway—but she wasn't ready for bed. She'd slept most of the day.

Then she remembered Audra's journals. They'd been under her bed when she packed, and she'd brought them with her because she hadn't read all of them and was afraid her father might throw them away if she left them behind.

Getting up, she opened her largest suitcase, dug through the clothing, shoes, photographs and other things she'd brought, and came up with the whole stack. She piled them on her bed, then settled against the headboard and opened the volume she'd been reading last.

November 16, 1992

My baby was born four days ago—a boy weighing 7 lbs. 8 oz. What an awesome experience. I thought the pain would overshadow everything else, but once I held my baby in my arms and saw his little red face and touched the peach-fuzz on his head, I knew the whole pregnancy was worth it. Even without Harley. I'm going to name him Brandon Matthew Worthington. Dad thinks I got "Matthew" from one of those ''Name Your Baby'' books. But I think Lauren knows it's Harley's real name. Anyway, she hasn't said anything about it, and I'm glad. The name suits Harley's son.

January 3, 1992

Raising a baby isn't easy. Brandon wakes up so many times during the night. If I'm anywhere near him, I can't sleep for more than a couple of hours. Fortunately, Lauren takes him into her room a lot and gives him a bottle when he wakes up. Mom and Dad don't like him getting formula while I'm nursing, but I need the break. Somehow Lauren seems to understand. I should probably tell her I don't know what I'd do without her. But we don't talk like that.

March 1, 1992

Brandon is still waking up in the night, but I'm not nursing anymore. Lauren gets up with him almost all the time now. I don't know how she does it and goes to school, too. But I can't seem to manage any more than what I'm doing. I can't seem to keep anything together.

March 15, 1992

I met someone who reminds me of Harley. He's tall and handsome and rides a motorcycle. Only he's not as self-righteous as Harley about getting high once in a while. He gave me something that dulled the pain and let me float away. When I'm floating I don't hear Brandon crying, and I don't care that I'm letting Lauren do the things I should be doing.

Lauren wasn't sure the journals were helping her frame of mind. She'd done everything she could to share the burden of caring for Brandon, trying to help Audra cope with the demands of motherhood. But maybe she'd been wrong to step in. Maybe she'd actually stolen something from Audra, something she'd had no right to take....

Closing the book, Lauren shook her head. She didn't want to learn any more about her sister's thoughts because of what they reflected about *her*. She'd loved Audra. She'd meant well.

Gathering the journals, she tried to get up to pack them away. But one slipped out of her arms and fell to the floor, and when she bent to pick it up, she saw her name again. The entry was dated less than a year before Audra's death—her sister's last Christmas.

December 25, 2000

Dad and Mom gave me a new car for Christmas. At least it's mine if I can stay clean, Dad said. Lauren gave me a pair of pearl earrings, and she gave Brandon exactly what he wanted. I don't even know what it was. Some kind of Nintendo game or something. I can't seem to get through the day, yet Lauren hears everything Brandon says and remembers. And she makes him happy. That's the real gift, isn't it? I could never thank her enough for loving my son and for being the mother to him I should have been. But then, she's never been like me. She's always been special.

"Oh, Audra." Burying her face in her hands, Lauren cried like she hadn't cried since she was a child. "I'm so sorry," she whispered. "How I wish things could have been different. But I'll keep taking care of Brandon for you. I'll keep trying to make him happy. I promise." Then she thought about Harley, and the fight she had on her hands to ensure that Brandon could have a relationship with his father and knew, regardless of how Harley or her father felt about her, she'd stay the course.

She'd do it for Audra.

CHAPTER TWENTY-TWO

HE HAD TO BE an idiot. He'd already made the decision not to come, yet here he was, standing in the hall outside Lauren's room less than eight hours after he'd dropped her off. Worse, it was the middle of the night. He'd driven nearly to Mount Shasta before turning around.

Harley glanced up and down the long, empty corridor, trying to talk himself out of knocking. The thought of Brandon had brought him back to Portland. He'd promised his son he'd give him some warning before heading back to California, which he hadn't done. But it was the thought of Lauren that had brought him here, to her hotel room at two o'clock in the morning.

"She's asleep," he muttered, and began to retrace his steps. But his feet dragged as he neared the elevators, and he turned back. "What the hell. Life is a series of risks."

He rapped lightly on her door and waited. No answer. He knocked more loudly, and this time he heard her say, "Coming." But her voice sounded muffled. She had been asleep. He shouldn't have disturbed her. He was starting to feel pretty foolish for appearing out of nowhere in the middle of the night when he heard her again.

"Who is it?"

Silently cursing himself, he cleared his throat. "It's me. Harley."

The click of a retracting dead bolt broke the silence, the door opened and he no longer felt foolish. He felt hopelessly in love.

"Harley," she breathed, but it wasn't a question. It was a statement. And somehow that seemed to say it all because a moment later, she was in his arms, and he was kissing her as though he'd die if he couldn't.

"I'm sorry I woke you," he murmured against her lips.

"I'm not," she said.

The door across the hall opened and a man with a Bart Simpson haircut peered out at them. Harley ignored the intrusion but swept Lauren into his arms and carried her inside, away from the man's prying eyes, pausing only long enough to close the door with his foot.

IT WAS MORNING. Reluctant to let the night end, Lauren snuggled closer to Harley, who was sleeping with his legs tucked up under her bottom and one arm curled possessively around her. She didn't want to move for fear of waking him, but she had a cramp in her leg and she wanted to be able to see his face. Easing herself out of his arms, she turned—and found him staring at her.

"Good morning," he said.

Lauren tried not to blush, but she felt warmth rise from her neck all the same. She knew he'd noticed when he chuckled and said, "You're so innocent and vulnerable and sweet."

She waited, hoping he'd add that he loved her. He'd said it during the night. More than once. Each time he made love to her, in fact. But the first time had been the most meaningful. He'd whispered it when he'd entered her as slowly and gently as possible, and Lauren knew she'd go to her grave treasuring that moment, along with the ones that came just after, when they were fully joined. But she wanted to hear him say it again, wanted to see his face more clearly this time, wanted to be sure he loved her forever and not just for one night.

"You were so…" She paused. *Good* sounded tacky, and gave what she was trying to communicate the wrong

slant. She didn't want to say "good," but she wanted to let him know that she appreciated the consideration he'd given her. He'd been so careful of her ankle, so…
"…perfect," she finished.

He grinned. "You weren't bad yourself, for something of a novice," he added teasingly. "How'd your ankle survive?"

"It's fine. It's starting to get better, I think," Lauren said, but she couldn't help wondering if her heart was going to be hurting next.

"What are you thinking about?" he asked.

Lauren raised her brows in surprise. "Nothing, really. Why?"

"I thought I saw a flicker of a frown cross your face."

She shook her head. "No frown."

"Good, because I like your smile. It's a seductress's smile, and you don't even know it."

Leaning forward, she kissed him softly on the lips. His hands trailed up her bare back and he pulled her tightly against him, and she felt her breath shorten as he deepened the kiss and—

Her cell phone rang. She wanted to ignore it, but she was afraid it was Brandon or Kimberly. If it was Brandon, she wanted to be available to him. If it was Kimberly, she had to answer or her best friend would probably stop over. Which was worse than being interrupted by a quick phone call.

"Hold that thought," she said and reached over to the nightstand to retrieve her phone. The light in the room was too dim to read the caller ID, so she simply pushed the talk button.

"Hello?"

"There you are. Don't you ever check your messages anymore? I've left you at least five."

Damien. "*This* is a frown," she muttered to Harley, covering the phone as she demonstrated.

"What did you say?" Damien asked.

"Nothing," she replied, drawing the sheet to her chest, "but I'm pretty busy right now. Is there something I can do for you?"

"I just heard you moved out. I've been worried about you, wanted to make sure you're okay."

"That's really nice of you, but I'm okay." She grinned at Harley. "Better than okay."

"Who is it?" Harley asked.

"Damien," she mouthed.

"You could always stay at my condo," Damien was saying. "You know I've got plenty of room."

"No, thanks. I'm fine right here."

"In a hotel? There's no need to spend the—"

"Tell him you have to go," Harley said, kissing her arm all the way up to her neck.

"Who's that?" Damien asked.

"Umm…" Lauren stifled a giggle despite the fact that Harley's lips were sending goose bumps down her spine. "Umm…it's Harley," she finally admitted.

"Harley!" Damien cried. "So it's true what he told me?"

"I don't know. What did he tell you?"

Suddenly Harley rolled onto his elbows. "Hang up," he whispered, trying to take the phone away from her.

"No, wait." She held the phone higher. "What did Harley tell you, Damien?"

"That bastard said you were in love with him."

Lauren blinked in surprise and Harley finally stopped trying to take the phone. With a groan, he buried his face in the pillow.

"Is it true?" Damien demanded.

She hadn't told Harley she loved him during the night because she'd assumed her actions had already revealed as much—and she was afraid she wouldn't measure up to Audra. As far as guys went, she'd never measured up to

Audra, and Harley would know that better than anyone. But Damien had put the question to her, and she wanted to answer.

She took a deep breath, gathering her nerve, and Harley finally lifted his head to look at her.

"Do you?" he whispered. "Do you love me?"

She put her palm against his whisker-roughened cheek. "I do," she said, and for Damien's benefit, "I love him."

"Does that mean you'll marry me?" Harley asked.

"Lauren, no! Don't do this," Damien shouted in the background. "Your father'll never talk to you again. How can you turn your back on everything you've ever known? On your family? How can you give yourself to a man like him?"

"I'm sorry, Damien," she said, "but he's the only man I've ever wanted." Then Harley hung up the phone and kissed her lips, her cheeks, her forehead before tucking her head beneath his chin and pulling her close.

"You won't change your mind when you have to tell your father, will you?" he asked.

"I THINK MAYBE we should talk about my finances before we visit your parents today," Harley said, leaning against the bathroom door while Lauren was getting ready. Except for the time they'd taken to attend his hearing, they'd spent two full days together at the hotel.

Lauren had realized this was coming. At some point she and Harley had to figure out how they were going to survive and provide for Brandon. She understood that motorcycle salesmen didn't make a lot of money. She wasn't expecting the kind of life she'd lived in the past. And she was perfectly willing to go to work. But now was not the time to discuss any of this. She could make her feelings clear to Harley later, when she was relaxed and could concentrate on protecting the infamous male ego. "Can we talk about it tomorrow?" she asked.

"Why?"

She shrugged. "I just don't want to deal with it right now. Money doesn't really matter. The only thing that matters is the fact that I'd marry you if you had millions—" she turned away from the mirror for a quick kiss "—and I'd marry you if you were penniless."

He rested a hand on his hip. "But things might not be as bad as you think."

"I'm sure they're not. We'll manage somehow," she said. "But right now, my cell phone's ringing. Any chance you'd be willing to grab it off the nightstand for me?"

He grinned. "Just don't get mad at me later."

"For what?" she said, but he was already gone, and after a moment, she heard him on her phone.

"She just got out of the shower. Hang on a minute."

"It's Kimberly," he said, reappearing in the doorway. "And because I doubt your parents will have the same forgiving views of my finances, I've got to go out for a little while."

"For what?" she asked.

"You don't want to talk about it, remember? I'll pick you up in an hour or so, okay?"

She nodded and he dropped a kiss on her forehead on his way out.

"Hi, Kim," she said, returning to the application of her mascara.

"You didn't call me yesterday. How did Harley's hearing go?"

"You're spending so much time with Tank, I thought *he'd* tell you."

"I'm spending time with Tank, but Harley isn't. Not since he started staying with you."

Lauren smiled to herself. The past two days had been the best of her life. "The hearing went well," she said. "No jail time, just an eight-hundred-dollar fine."

"Ouch, but I guess it could've been worse."

"Harley's just glad it's over, I think."

"How's your ankle?"

"Almost as good as new. I can walk on it now."

"Great. Want to go to lunch later?"

Finished with her mascara, Lauren dropped the tube in her cosmetics bag and rummaged for her blush. "You're not seeing Tank?"

"He can't get away from the job site today, so he's coming over after work instead."

"I'd love to do lunch," Lauren said. "Only I'm seeing my parents this morning. I don't know where things will go from there. I might not feel up to socializing, you know?"

"Uh-oh. Is Harley going with you?"

"After all the things my father did to him, I'd actually prefer to go alone. But Harley insists that he's going with me. He says he wants to be there, just in case."

"In case of what?"

"In case I need protecting, I guess."

"That's so sweet," Kimberly said. "I know we were worried about Harley at first, but I think you've got a good guy."

Lauren imagined her upcoming marriage. *Lauren Marie Nelson...Mrs. Matthew Nelson...* She'd wake up in bed with Harley every morning for the rest of her life. "I know I do," she said.

"Good luck with your parents."

"Thanks. I'm afraid I'm going to need it."

HERE WE GO, Lauren thought as she knocked at the door of her parents' house. She'd postponed delivering the news of her upcoming marriage until Brandon was back in school, so he wouldn't be around to hear what her parents might say. But the idea of facing Quentin and Marilee hadn't gotten any easier with the passing of time.

Harley stood silently at her side, more withdrawn than she'd ever seen him.

"Are you okay?" she asked.

"Are you?" he replied, but there was no opportunity to answer because her mother opened the door.

"Lauren!" Marilee moved toward Lauren, apparently intending to hug her, but then her eyes darted to Harley, and she stepped back, pressing a hand to her chest instead. "What are you doing here?" she said. "Your father's home, you know," she added to Lauren.

"We were hoping he would be," Lauren said. "We want to talk to you both. May we come in?"

Her mother hesitated and glanced over her shoulder as though she couldn't make the decision on her own. But then she nodded. "Okay."

Harley held the door for Lauren before following her into the living room, where her mother motioned them to the tapestry-covered chairs near the window. "Please, have a seat," she said, as formally as if they were new acquaintances.

Lauren tried not to let it bother her. She told herself she could withstand the pain even if her parents disowned her, but deep down, she wasn't so sure. *Please, let this go smoothly, help them understand...*

"I'll get Quentin," Marilee said, but Lauren's father was already coming down the hall.

"Who was at the door?" he asked. Then he saw Lauren and Harley, and stopped, his eyes narrowing.

"I thought I told you never to come back here," he said to Lauren.

Lauren stood, as did Harley, and swallowed to ease the sudden dryness of her throat. "I know you're unhappy with me," she began. "But—"

"*Unhappy* with you? Do you think you're going to make me any happier by bringing this man into my house again?"

"I just came to tell you something. I...I—"

"You're not pregnant," her mother said.

"No." Lauren looked over at Harley for strength. "I'm not pregnant. At least not yet. We'd like to have a baby fairly soon, though."

Marilee swayed and grasped the back of a chair for support, but her father showed no outward sign of surprise. "You want a baby with *him?*" he said in obvious disgust.

Lauren nodded. "Harley and I are getting married this weekend. In Vegas. And we want Brandon to live with us in California."

"Have you lost your mind?" her father yelled. "What does Harley have to offer you? Or Brandon? He's a motorcycle salesman, for Pete's sake. Do you want to spend the rest of your life working to support him?"

"Lauren won't have to work unless she wants to," Harley said.

"And you're going to keep her in comfort, is that right?" her father shot back. "You're going to maintain her standard of living? With *your* background? With *your* income?"

Harley drew an envelope out of his jacket pocket and handed it to her father. "There's nothing wrong with my income," he said. "You can see for yourself."

"What's this?" her father asked.

"Just a little something I had my manager fax me this morning."

Her father opened the envelope, withdrew the documents inside, and smoothed them out so he could read them. Then he looked up at Harley, an expression of stunned surprise on his face. "This is a Profit and Loss Statement."

"It's *my* Profit and Loss Statement."

"But...this says you own the Harley Davidson dealership in Burlingame, California."

"I do. It also says I'm worth about five million dollars. Is that enough?"

Lauren felt her jaw drop. Harley was rich? He *owned* the dealership in California? "But you told me you were a salesman," she said, confused.

"I never told you I was a salesman," he said.

"But you let me think you didn't have any money. Why?"

Harley scowled and ran a hand through his hair. "You said it earlier. Money doesn't matter. I'm still the man I was ten years ago. And—"

"And what?" she prompted.

"And I think I wanted you from the moment you opened that door. If I was finally going to be good enough, I didn't want it to be because of the money."

Her father shoved the Profit and Loss Statement back at Harley. "You *are* still the man you were ten years ago. If Lauren's willing to let you use her to get to Brandon, that's up to her, but I'm not going to make the same mistake."

"God, you always look for the worst in people," Harley said. "I'm not marrying Lauren to get to Brandon. I'm his *father*. I'll press my suit in either case. I'm marrying Lauren because…" He glanced at her. "I'm in love with her," he finished, lowering his voice. "And I plan to do everything I can to make her happy."

"As if you *could*—" Quentin began, but Marilee, who'd been standing silent and wringing her hands, stopped him by putting a restraining hand on his arm.

"Didn't you hear that, Quentin?" she said. "Aren't you listening? He loves Lauren. He loves our little girl."

"I don't care if he loves the man in the moon! We lost Audra because of him!"

"We lost Audra because of Audra," Marilee said. "Will you let what happened ten years ago cost us another daughter?"

Quentin opened his mouth, then closed it again. "Looks like it already has," he muttered. "But I won't let it cost us our grandson, too."

"Then stop shoving them all away," she said. "Brandon's talked about nothing but Harley since we returned. It's obvious where his heart is. As soon as he's old enough, he'll leave us and go to them. We're just his grandparents and we don't hold the same appeal. That's only natural. But Harley *is* Brandon's father, and Lauren—" she paused "—well, Lauren's his mother in every sense of the word. You should know that better than anyone."

Lauren felt her knees go weak. She'd never seen her mother contradict her father before and doubted Quentin would tolerate it…but he did. He stood silent, his chest rising and falling as he stared at his wife. Suddenly all the fight seemed to drain out of him.

"You're right," he said at last. "I don't know what's wrong with me. You're right." And then he left the room.

Her mother frowned as she watched him go. Turning back to Lauren, she said, "I'll have Brandon's bags packed." Her voice was resolute. "When will you be coming for him?"

"Is Friday after school okay?"

She nodded.

"Will you and Dad come to Vegas with us for the wedding?" Lauren asked.

Her mother cast another glance in the direction her father had disappeared. "Probably not," she said. "Your father's going to need some time to adjust to this, and I'm going to be here with him until he's ready—provided he doesn't take too long. You," she said to Harley, "promise me you'll take good care of my daughter and grandson, and that the three of you will come back and stay with us for Thanksgiving."

"I promise," Harley said.

Lauren smiled despite the tears streaming down her face. "Thanks, Mom."

"I love you, honey," she said. "Be happy."

"Do you think you can come over tonight?" Scott asked Brandon just after the afternoon bell rang.

Brandon started gathering his books from his desk. "I hope so. I don't like being home without Lauren. My grandma doesn't know what to do with me. She keeps baking cookies and bringing them to my room and asking me if I want this or that, but I don't want anything, except for Lauren to come back."

"I thought you wanted to move to California with your father."

Brandon shrugged. "I think my dad's really cool. But I've never lived with him before. I don't know what it's going to be like. And I'll miss Lauren even if she lives in the same city." He slung his backpack over his shoulder and followed Scott out of the classroom, then grimaced when he nearly bumped into Travis and Theo hurrying down the hall.

"Thanks for getting me suspended, Worthington," Theo said as they pushed toward the front steps, along with everyone else.

"I got put on restriction because of you," Travis added, glowering. "Just because you're so touchy about being a *bastard.*"

"Shut up," Brandon said, "or I'll land you on restriction again."

"The fight was your fault, anyway," Scott told them. "That guy by the fence last week *was* Brandon's dad. I've met him. I've even ridden on his motorcycle."

"And you think I'm stupid enough to believe that?" Travis rolled his eyes. "You'd say anything, Torrin. You're his best friend."

"Scott isn't lying," Brandon insisted, cutting the other

two boys off just as they exited the school. The rest of the children continued to flow around them, rushing off to catch their rides home, but Brandon wasn't in any hurry to meet up with his grandfather. He was tired of Theo and Travis's taunts and the snickering they'd done earlier in class, when they kept whispering the ''b'' word at him. He wanted to shut them up once and for all. After everything that had happened at home, getting suspended a second time seemed like the least of his problems.

''You'd better quit bothering me,'' he said.

''Or what?'' Travis said. ''You'll fall and get a bloody nose again?''

Theo started laughing and Brandon shucked off his backpack.

''Don't,'' Scott warned him, grabbing his arm. ''Come on, school's out. Let's go home and see if my mom'll take us miniature golfing.''

''I don't want to go miniature golfing,'' Brandon said, jerking away. ''I want to make these guys mind their own business.''

''Ooh, I'm scared,'' Theo said.

''You think you can do that, Worthington?'' Travis asked.

''I'm ready to try,'' he replied and drew back to give Theo a bloody nose this time, but a large male hand cupped his fist and stopped its forward motion.

''What's going on here?''

It was his father. Brandon immediately recognized the voice and blinked up at Harley in surprise, then dropped his fist to his side. ''Dad, what are you doing here?''

''I came to give you a ride home on the bike.''

''But Grandpa—''

''Gave his permission. So did Lauren. Only I don't like what I'm seeing. This looks like another fight about to happen.''

"It wasn't Brandon's fault," Scott volunteered. "They were calling him a bastard again, just like before."

Eyes widening, Theo and Travis took a step backward. "We didn't mean it," they said. "We were just having fun."

"Fun?" his father echoed, disgust apparent on his face. "So, you think it would be fun if Brandon called *you* names?"

They shook their heads. "No, sir."

"And they said you weren't Brandon's father, that a guy like you wouldn't want Brandon for a son," Scott piped up.

Brandon stared down and scuffed his tennis shoe against the cement. Some of the last stragglers leaving the school were hanging around, hoping to find out what was going on; Melissa Hayes was one of them. He didn't want her to see him getting in trouble again, didn't want her to hear what Travis and Theo had been calling him. But he was penned in on all sides and couldn't think of a quick escape.

"Well, now we know these guys don't have a clue about anything," his father was saying as he put a hand on Brandon's shoulder. "Because Brandon's about the best son a guy like me could have."

"Sorry," Travis mumbled.

"We didn't mean anything by it," Theo added.

And when Brandon said goodbye to Scott and climbed onto the back of his father's bike a few minutes later, Melissa waved at him.

BRANDON FELT BETTER than he had in a long time. He'd known he would, if only he could be with Lauren. It felt pretty great that his dad was there, too. And the fact that Lauren wasn't making him do his homework right away didn't hurt, either.

"It's your turn," his aunt said as she tossed a nine of

spades onto the middle of the bed they were sitting on in her hotel room. "Don't forget that the queen isn't out yet."

Brandon checked his cards. The queen wasn't out because he was holding it, on purpose. They'd played three hands already, and he'd lost all three, but he was only losing by twenty points. If he could shoot the moon he'd win the game. He frowned, wondering if his hand was good enough. He didn't have a lot of high cards, but he did have the ace and the king of hearts. The rest was mostly one suit, which improved his chances...

"Brandon?" his father prompted. Fortunately, Harley was just learning the game. Because he didn't really know all the rules, there was a possibility he might not realize what Brandon was trying to do until it was too late.

What the heck, he thought. He'd go for it. He threw one of his lowest spades on the pile to get rid of it before any of the point cards came out, and his father took the trick and led with a five of clubs. Then it was Lauren's turn, but she was looking at him in a funny way, as though she wasn't really paying attention to the game, and Brandon wasn't sure he liked that. It made him nervous to see her preoccupied. Come to think of it, she'd been acting strange all afternoon....

"Is something wrong?" he asked.

"No, why?" she said.

"Because you keep looking at my dad, and he keeps looking at you, and you sort of smile when he does, and...I don't know. Something's different."

His aunt glanced at Harley *again,* who nodded for her to continue, and she put her cards facedown in front of her. "Brandon, your father and I have something we want to tell you."

Oh, no. He'd asked for it. What now? "What is it? Is it time to go home already?" he asked, knowing by the tone of her voice that it wouldn't be so simple. He just didn't want to hear anything upsetting.

"No."

"Then what? Is Grandpa mad at us? Did he and Grandma really give us permission to be together?"

"That's not it, either," she said. "They gave us permission. As a matter of fact, they've given their permission for us to be together from now on."

This came as a surprise. Finally Brandon folded his own cards and forgot all about the strategy he'd been planning to use later in the game. "So they're going to let us move to California?"

Lauren nodded.

"That was quick. I thought you said it would take a while."

"It would have, if Grandpa and Grandma hadn't agreed. Fortunately for all of us, they did. But there's been one…small change to what we talked about."

Brandon felt his stomach tense. What kind of change? Most of the changes lately hadn't been good ones. "What's that?" he asked hesitantly.

"Your father and I are going to get married."

"Married?" he echoed, looking from one to the other.

"Is that okay with you?" Lauren asked.

He swallowed, feeling a flutter of excitement he was afraid to trust. "When?"

"Soon. This weekend in Vegas. We want you to be there. And we want you to come and live with us." She searched his face before continuing, "And if you'd like this as much as I would, I want to adopt you, to be your mom instead of just your aunt."

"Really?" he said.

"Really."

"We'd still go to California?"

"Yes. Your father owns a Harley Davidson dealership out there, so he'll be pretty busy, but I'll be taking care of you during the days, just like always. And he'll be with us whenever he's not at work...."

"And I'll work from home a lot," his father said, "or take you and Lauren with me. When you get older, you can work at the dealership if you want. And we'd like to have other children so you'll have some brothers and sisters."

"Wow, a real family," Brandon breathed. He'd have a mom *and* a dad. And brothers and sisters. Just like the kids at school. Life couldn't get any better than that.

A smile stretched across his face, a smile that felt wider than any he remembered, and he shoved the cards aside in favor of giving Lauren and his father a big hug. "I'd like that," he said. "I'd really like that."

His father ruffled his hair and kissed Lauren's temple, and they made plans together for the next hour. They were going to live in a big house not far from San Francisco. Brandon would go to a school that was just as good as Mt. Marley, his father said, and he was going to fly back and see Scott over the summer. And they'd spend Thanksgiving with Grandma and Grandpa Worthington. He even got to call and talk to Harley's mom, his new grandmother.

"Are you ready to finish the game?" Lauren asked, when he'd hung up and they'd finally stopped dreaming about what it was going to be like.

Brandon glanced at his cards. "No," he said, "not tonight."

"But I thought you wanted to shoot the moon," she said.

He smiled. "Somehow if feels like I just did."

EPILOGUE

HARLEY BRACED HIMSELF as he pulled into the Worthingtons' front drive and parked. Autumn was already turning to hard winter in Portland—there were patches of snow on the ground and the sky was gray and overcast—but it wasn't the cold that made him reluctant to get out of the car. It was the past. After six months of heaven, he had to come back and face this place, face Quentin.

Brandon obviously felt none of the same hesitation. He hopped out of the Suburban as soon as it came to a complete stop, along with Duke, the dog Harley and Lauren had bought for him when they moved to California, and dashed to the house.

"Wait till Grandma sees you," Brandon told his dog.

Harley watched the pair ruefully. He sincerely doubted Grandfather Worthington was going to be very pleased about having a canine guest. Her father wasn't an animal-lover, Lauren had explained, telling Brandon to make sure the dog didn't lick Grandpa or jump up on him. But as unhappy as he might be to have a dog in the house, Harley knew Quentin would prefer the dog to him. After all, he was the man who'd taken both of Quentin's daughters away from him. He was the son of a bitch who wasn't good enough to—

"You nervous?"

Harley glanced away from the Worthington house to focus on Lauren, who was sitting with her door open, waiting for him. "No," he lied.

"You don't have to come with us, if you don't want to," she said. "I'll understand. You can get a motel, and we'll meet up with you after a short visit."

"No, I want to come. I promised your mother I'd bring the whole family, and here we are. I'm sure your father will deal with it." *He'd better deal with it,* he thought, *because if he hurts you again...*

The old anger flared up, flashing through Harley as hot and bright as lightning, but Harley consciously forced it down. Today was Thanksgiving. He and his little family had flown from California and rented a car in anticipation of spending the holiday with Lauren's parents. Harley was going to assume the best and do all he could to make it pleasant for Lauren and Brandon, even though he hadn't heard anything in the past six months to give him much hope that Quentin had softened. Lauren and her mother frequently spoke on the telephone, but every time Harley questioned Lauren about her father, she shook her head. "He still won't talk to me," she always said. "Whenever I call, he immediately passes the phone to my mother." Then she always finished with a smile and a "he'll come around."

Harley hoped he would, for Lauren's sake. He hated the sad expression that flitted across her face when her father was mentioned and she thought Harley wasn't looking, hated the fact that she wanted something he couldn't give her.

"What do you think he's going to say about the baby?" he asked.

Lauren patted her round belly and shrugged nonchalantly, but Harley had spent too much time memorizing her every expression to miss the uncertainty in her eyes. "What can he say?" she said. "I'm thrilled. And our baby is part of us now."

That was what worried Harley. The baby was part of *him,* which meant Quentin wouldn't want anything to do with it, and the rejection would probably devastate Lauren....

"Let's go," he said, before his mind could present him with any more possibilities.

Rounding the car, he helped Lauren out, then walked beside her to the front door, which stood open. Inside, Harley could hear Marilee gushing over Brandon—how tall he was getting, how handsome—but there was no sign of Quentin.

"Hi, Mom," Lauren said.

When Marilee looked up, her face brightened even more. "I'm so glad you're here," she said. "I've missed you so much." She embraced her daughter and they talked briefly and excitedly about the pregnancy, then Marilee turned to Harley.

"You brought them back to me," she said. "Just like you promised."

Harley nodded. "It's good to see you, Mrs. Worthington. You're looking fit as ever."

"Oh, don't give me that flattery stuff," she said with a chuckle. "You're the one who looks good. Still handsome as the devil, I see. Lauren must be feeding you well."

He smiled at Lauren and felt suddenly glad that he was standing in Quentin Worthington's living room. It was where his wife had been raised, where she belonged this Thanksgiving, and whether it was a pleasant stay for him or not, he knew, in that moment, he'd walk through fire for her. "I certainly can't complain," he said. "You taught her well."

"I can't take the credit for her, but I will ask you for one more thing."

"What's that?"

"Don't call me Mrs. Worthington."

Harley hesitated. "Would you like me to call you by your first name?"

Marilee took Lauren's hand as though they stood together on this issue. "I'd like you to call me Mom, if you can get used to it. I realize we've had our differences in the past, but—" she made a nervous gesture with her free hand "—well, I'm hoping we can put it behind us and be a real family."

Harley knew the "mom" part would feel strange on his tongue, especially at first, but he was all for putting the past behind them. "Sure," he said. "No problem," and was rewarded with a dazzling smile from his wife that made him want to pull her into his arms and kiss her breathless. How he loved her. He was so happy to have her and Brandon and their baby....

"Where's Grandpa?" Brandon asked, and the kissing fantasy instantly dissipated.

"He must not have heard the doorbell," Marilee said, but she seemed as tense as Lauren. They exchanged a look, then Marilee headed out of the room. "I'll get him."

"It'll be okay," Lauren said in her absence.

Brandon didn't seem to be paying much attention. He was too distracted by his Golden Retriever, which was still only a puppy, but Harley put a hand on Lauren's lower back to reassure her.

"Sure it will," he said, and then Quentin was standing at the end of the hall, staring at him, and he wondered if he'd been wrong.

"Hi, Daddy," Lauren said, her voice full of hope and longing.

Answer her, Harley thought. *Give some welcoming sign....*

But Quentin didn't speak. He stood rooted to the spot, and shoved his hands into his pockets. Just when Harley was about to take Lauren's hand and insist they leave rather than let Lauren be hurt any more, he noticed tears pooling in the older man's eyes.

"I'm sorry, Lauren," Quentin managed after several

seconds. "I'm sorry." The words sounded as though they'd been wrung from him, but they were there, soft and sweet and best of all, sincere. And they were enough for Lauren.

She immediately launched herself into his arms. "Oh, Daddy, it's okay. I love you," she said, but he held her off and directed his gaze at Harley.

"I'm not finished yet," he said. He cleared his throat and his chest expanded as though he'd just taken a big gulp of air. "I owe Harley an apology, too. If he'll accept it."

Harley couldn't believe his ears. Quentin Worthington was apologizing *to him?* "Of course I'll accept it," he said.

"You've done right by my daughter," Quentin went on. "Marilee's told me how happy she is about the baby. And I've seen the wedding photos she sent. That one with both of you on the motorcycle, driving away, and her in her wedding dress..." He smiled vaguely and shook his head. "Anyway, Brandon's happy, too. I'm grateful for that."

"Thank you," Harley said and suddenly, all the anger he'd ever felt, all the resentment, drained out of him, and the seeds of something else took its place, something a lot like love, or respect, or both. He watched Quentin hug Lauren and Brandon, then felt Marilee at his side, nudging him toward Quentin. Closing the gap between them, he stuck out his hand and smiled when Quentin clasped it.

"To forgetting the past," Quentin said as their hands met.

"To a bright future as friends," Harley replied.

"As family," Quentin corrected, giving his hand a solid shake. Then Lauren was hugging Harley and he could feel the swell of his baby as she pressed close. Bran-

don was hugging him, too, and Lauren's parents were
holding each other and smiling and crying, and Harley
thought coming for Thanksgiving was the best promise
he'd ever kept.

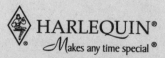

These New York Times *bestselling authors*
have created stories to capture the hearts and minds
of women everywhere.
Here are three classic tales about the power of love—
and the wonder of discovering the place
where you belong....

FINDING HOME

DUNCAN'S BRIDE
by
LINDA HOWARD

CHAIN LIGHTNING
by
ELIZABETH LOWELL

POPCORN AND KISSES
by
KASEY MICHAELS

Available only from Silhouette
at your favorite retail outlet.

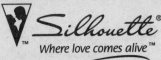

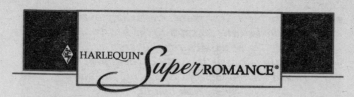

HARLEQUIN *Super* ROMANCE®

They'd grown up at Serenity House—a group home
for teenage girls in trouble. Now Paige, Darcy and
Annabelle are coming back for a special reunion,
and each has her own story to tell.

SERENITY HOUSE

An exciting new trilogy
by
Kathryn Shay

Practice Makes Perfect—June 2002
A Place to Belong—Winter 2003
Against All Odds—Spring 2003

Available wherever Harlequin books are sold.

HARLEQUIN®
Makes any time special ®

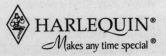

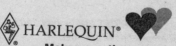